HONEYMOON BLUES

HONEYMOON BLUES

HONEYMOON SERIES, BOOK 3

LILY ZANTE

Copyright © 2014 Lily Zante

Lily Zante

Honeymoon Blues

AUTHOR'S NOTE

'*Honeymoon Blues*' is the third book in the '*Honeymoon Series*'.

I have also started writing a spin-off series called the '*Italian Summer Series*' which tells the stories of some of the minor characters who first appeared in the '*Honeymoon Series*'.

The timelines of both series are connected and you can find a recommended reading order here

Honeymoon Series:

Honeymoon for One
Honeymoon for Three
Honeymoon Blues
Honeymoon Bliss
Baby Steps
Honeymoon Series (Books 1-3)

Italian Summer Series:
(A spin-off from the Honeymoon Series)

It Takes Two
All That Glitters
Fool's Gold
Roman Encounter
November Sun
New Beginnings
Italian Summer Series (Books 1-4)

CHAPTER ONE

In Denver...

"Yes," replied Ava. She held her cell in one hand, a damp cloth in the other, and her eyes were glued to her laptop screen, now littered with images of Nico Cazale.

Multi-tasking, she was in the middle of wiping down her mom's kitchen and looking through her online store stats and emails.

But in between these two tasks, she'd ended up doing what she had been doing every time she powered up her laptop, ever since her arrival back home: she Googled 'Nico Cazale' and devoured every piece of information on him.

Kim, her virtual assistant, was on the line.

"Yes, you want *me* to go ahead and deal with all the queries or yes, *you'll look* into them?" Kim's voice was laced with irritation.

"Yes, I mean, *no*. I mean *you* deal with them, for now." Ava paused to examine a photo of Nico with yet another beautiful young thing. "I'm still busy uploading the ... images ... for the new products." It was an old picture, judging by Nico's boyish grin.

She threw down her damp cloth and sniffled into a Kleenex. The first few days of discovering all about Nico's love life had her in tears. Now the floodgates were under control, sort of.

"Have you got a cold?" Kim asked.

"No. I'm fine."

"It's just that you sound unwell."

"I'm fine."

"Okay, well, let me know if you need a hand with anything for the new products."

She knew what Kim was thinking but was too polite to say. *What the hell have you been doing for the past week?*

"I will. Thanks, Kim. Bye." Glad to have ended the call, Ava knew she could never afford to lose Kim. This woman was a super VA. She was indispensable. She'd been running Ava's online store just fine while Ava had been in Italy and now that she was back she really did need to get on with things. She'd sunk a ton of money into buying products from Italy and now she needed to make sure she sold them.

Or else there would be trouble.

Wiping her nose again, she clicked on the pictures on her screen. This man was so annoyingly handsome, and women were always draped around him. She knew these pictures well. Had stared at them for days.

She hated looking at them and yet she couldn't tear herself away from them either.

It had been seven days since she'd left Nico high and dry. Seven days she had spent moping around her apartment, except for the few times she had gone out to stock up on groceries.

Seven days where she had wondered whether she had been hasty in jumping to mile high conclusions and rushing back home.

Only the imminent arrival of her mom and sister tomorrow had propelled her into getting out today. She had hoped that cleaning up her mom's apartment, having a change of scenery, might motivate her into getting some actual work done, instead of endlessly and obsessively reading about the man who was out of her league.

The man who was also the father of the child she now carried. Something he had no knowledge of.

She touched her belly again, something she been doing a lot ever since she'd found out. She still had a few months to think things through; she was only around six weeks pregnant and the baby wasn't due until mid-November. Time was on her side.

Time to figure out what she was going to do.

In the cold light of day in Denver, away from the headiness of Verona, Venice, and Nico, she was aware of her haste in rushing back. Staring at the countless gossip column inches and photos of Nico and various beauties from his past, she had to wonder: what had he ever seen in her?

Finding him with that woman in his office had tipped her over the edge. She'd left Verona and flown back to Denver, leaving her mother and sister wondering what on earth had happened.

Now she was left wondering if she'd done the right thing.

Shouldn't she at least have given Nico the chance to explain himself? Could a man really be different things to different women?

The shock of her pregnancy and the sudden panic of being with a man she couldn't trust, who might hurt her again, had panicked her into fleeing. Nico had never even told her he loved her.

Maybe he didn't love her.

Maybe a man like Nico was incapable of loving anyone. And the only way he operated was by having many women at his beck and call.

Something about the air in Verona had made her throw caution to the wind, and the beauty of Venice had made her drunk on life and love. Her guard had come down, and she'd let Nico in. Somewhere, somehow, she had started to think that this jaw-droppingly handsome man would want her. She had made the mistake of allowing herself to believe it.

But even though she had tried to overlook his past and his reputation, believing he had changed, *her* doubts about herself never really disappeared. It wasn't just the woman in his office, or the women everywhere that he seemed to have dated at one time or another.

It was *her*.

Why would a man like Nico Cazale ever be interested in her?

The jeering voices from her past, from high-school, when she'd been labeled a freak, for being so tall and so thin, still screamed out at her at times when she felt vulnerable.

She got up, just to get away from the images on her screen and started wiping down the kitchen cabinets again. It was therapeutic. Being busy with housework kept her mind free from drifting.

Maybe she wasn't good enough. It wasn't just Nico who'd had a roving eye. In the end, even Connor had cheated on her.

She'd left Verona, knowing that she had only a short window of time to tell her mother of her last-minute decision to get the next flight out. It had been a freaky stroke of luck to get a seat the next morning. She'd flown back on the same flight as Connor, and he'd managed to get their seats so that they ended up sitting together. It was a small price to pay for escaping from her summer romance.

Surprisingly, Connor had left her alone during the flight. He hadn't asked any questions, but she knew he had them, especially after she'd asked him to hand back the Flamentagostini bracelet.

Ava wondered what Nico would have made of that. She hadn't thought it through when she'd given it to Connor. But now, according to her mom, Nico believed she'd gone back to Connor and *that* was her reason for absconding to Denver so quickly.

Finally finished with the cleaning, she collapsed into a chair and looked around the kitchen. She ran her hands over her flat belly. Hard to imagine that in eight months' time she would have another little person to take care of. It was something she had never considered, and it was so far off her radar that even now she had problems trying to get used to the fact that she was pregnant.

In the space of a year she'd gone from being almost married, to going on honeymoon alone, to now dealing with being pregnant.

Alone.

She moved her hand away from her belly; she would need to be extra careful around other people, especially her family, since she planned on keeping them in the dark for as long as possible, until she was used to this life-changing event herself.

She also planned on keeping Nico in the dark, until she figured out when she would tell him. Or whether she ever would.

If he ever found out that he was the father of her baby and that she had kept it from him, there would be hell to pay.

It would be another three months before anyone noticed

the weight gain. She wished she had paid more attention to her sister when she'd been pregnant, because Ava knew next to nothing about pregnancy.

Like most things in her life, she would have to learn as she went along. Her sickness wasn't too bad, just early morning for now. But come late summer, the news would no longer remain hidden.

And she had to make sure she worked hard during the next few months to ensure the success of her online store so that she would at least have some sort of income for them both; the baby and her.

She got her things together and got ready to leave. She had filled up her mom's refrigerator with milk, bread and a few other essentials, and had baked a small lasagna.

Carlos, her sister's husband, said he'd pick them up from the airport when they arrived later tomorrow night. Ava would visit her mother in a couple of days. She was in no hurry to confront her so soon. Not with her mother still looking for answers from her.

She would call Andrea tomorrow, feeling guilty because deep down inside, she was avoiding it.

Anything to do with Italy instantly reminded her of Nico, and she intended to forget that she had ever set eyes on him. Right or wrong, that was her plan, and she was sticking to it, for now.

CHAPTER TWO

In Verona...

Were it not for the fact that her youngest daughter had fled this idyllic place a week ago, Elsa would have enjoyed sitting out in the wooden pergola on a warm sun-kissed afternoon. And she would have stayed a little longer, had Ava been here.

She sat, gently swinging on the swing chair, while Edmondo sat next to her on the wicker chair.

A pitcher of lemonade was on the table in front of them.

"You worry too much, Elsa," cautioned Edmondo. He poured the homemade lemonade into two glasses. "Whatever it is, I am sure the two of them will be able to work it out."

Edmondo was right. Her twenty-eight-year-old daughter was old enough to take care of herself but with Ava and Nico being so far apart—and in another country altogether—didn't bode well and she worried about that. She picked up the cold glass and put it to her lips. "They're in two different continents, Edmondo. It won't be easy."

"My son isn't one to reveal his innermost feelings, but I can tell you this much; Nico has been swept off his feet by your daughter. I don't think he's ever met anyone like her. I certainly have never seen him so happy, and he seems more driven, as though he wants to race ahead and fulfill all of these ideas he has in his head. I put it down to the effect Ava has had on him."

The cold, sweet lemonade left an icy trail as it seeped down her throat. Elsa put down her glass carefully. "That's what worries me. What could have happened for Ava to react in such a way rush back to Denver?"

Edmondo looked at her and shrugged. "I'll speak to Nico when he gets back. He's been busy in Rome and he's not so easy to get hold of at the moment."

"Rest assured I will try to get it out of my daughter, once I'm back, too." Elsa knew she'd be in for a battle. Ava was quiet and introspective, unlike her older sister Rona, and Elsa naturally worried about her more. "We've been over this again and again, but I refuse to believe that she's gone back to Connor. That's absurd."

"It's what Nico tells me," Edmondo remarked. "Why else would she hurry to catch the same flight back?" He looked at her, a question in his eyes. "I don't believe it either, but Nico seems to. Why else would he let her go so easily?"

They sat quietly for a few moments.

"I do hope we will see Ava again," started Edmondo, "and you, too."

Elsa's cheeks heated. This was her last day with Edmondo and tomorrow she was due to fly back with Rona and Tori, Rona's baby.

During the past few weeks she'd seen most of Verona, and

not just the popular tourist sights, either. Edmondo had shown her the lesser-known parts, too. He had filled her days up with visits to beautiful monuments, memorable meals at different places, and above all, injected her days with humor and kindness.

She had come to look forward eagerly to each new day. Lately, she hadn't spent much time with Rona, and tried to make up for it by babysitting in the evenings. Even if that did come at a price.

Most evenings, Rona would take up her mother's offer and disappear, returning home around midnight. Any attempt on Elsa's part to find out exactly *where* she went and with *who* was met with a cold dismissal.

And because Elsa was out during the day with Edmondo, she didn't feel she had any right to question what her daughter got up to in the evenings. But as a mother, and because Rona was married and with a young baby, Elsa worried about it.

Spending her days with Edmondo had given her a spirited sense of adventure, making her realize she didn't have to concern herself solely with worrying about her two grown up daughters.

Her friendship with Edmondo had blossomed quickly. It had happened naturally when their one-day sightseeing trip around Verona had turned into a daily occurrence. Elsa found herself eagerly anticipating their daily jaunts together. After a while it got to the point where it wasn't so much about where they went; she simply looked forward to spending the day with him.

Now the time had almost come for them both to go their separate ways and they were spending another day in the gardens of the Casa Adriana.

An unknown part of her felt guilty for hoping it wouldn't

be the last time she would ever see this man. Rediscovering feelings that had lain dormant so deep inside that she barely knew they existed was a revelation in itself. It was like polishing a stone and discovering a gem underneath. Shiny, new, and breathtaking. These new feelings had begun to stir inside her because of Edmondo Cazale.

While she felt a little relieved that nothing *had* happened, there were times when she sometimes wondered about the possibilities of a romantic dalliance.

Edmondo coughed and his gaze rested on her face, fleetingly. When she looked up, he turned his gaze away, picking up the glass of lemonade again. Sitting here was more like sitting in a living room that had been placed in the middle of Eden. A few comfortable wicker armchairs were protected from the rain by a thick lattice, covered by creepers. Wherever she looked, an abundance of green rewarded her, and the scent of lemon trees and jasmine swam around in the air. It was paradise, these beautifully kept lush gardens of the Casa Adriana. She could see why it was one of Edmondo's favorite places and it had quickly become one of hers.

"Elsa," he began and moved his gaze to her face once more. He blinked a few times, and she instinctively turned and gave him her full attention, but he appeared to hesitate. When he didn't speak, she took a bigger sip of lemonade, hoping that the bittersweet taste of cold crushed lemons would soothe her.

"Elsa," he began again. "I want to say something, but I don't want to jeopardize our friendship. I would say nothing, but in my wiser, older years, I know it is important to say what is in your heart, because you might not get another chance."

She rubbed her fingers together—they were wet with cold moisture from the glass—and raised her eyes to his face, almost feeling his unease. "Go on, Edmondo." She smiled to reassure him, even though her heart was beating furiously.

"I..." He shook his head and smiled at himself. "I feel like an awkward young man again; I had forgotten how hard this was." He stared at his glass, and she felt for his shyness. He was going to say something and it would be nothing to do with the sightseeing. She waited, not daring to look away, treasuring the moment already.

"I have had the most wonderful time with you." He lifted his head up and looked at her with gentle eyes. "And it makes me sad to know that you are leaving tomorrow, and that you will be so far away."

Sensing his unease, Elsa moved forward, and the act of doing so caused the swing chair to move back a little. "Edmondo, I've had the most wonderful time here. I can't begin to thank you enough for all that you've done. I feel I've come to know this place so well because of you."

He still sat with his head bowed, and her words brought a smile to his face. He looked up when she had finished, and then he got up and sat beside her, making the chair swing backwards. He turned to face her.

"Showing you around Verona has been such a pleasure. It will be one of *my* precious memories that I will remember forever. The time we spent together, in getting to know one another, was an unexpected joy and for that I thank you."

She bathed in the warmth of his words and found it hard to express just how sad she felt about leaving all of this behind.

"This doesn't have to be goodbye forever, you know, Elsa." His face turned serious. Her heart missed a beat.

"I'm not asking for anything"—his gaze never left her face —"but to let our friendship grow. Once Ava and Nico sort out their differences, who knows what the future might bring?"

Elsa smiled, a little hesitantly. "You could always come to Denver, and I'd be most happy to show you around there."

"If Nico takes over the business completely, I will have more time," he agreed. "I could come, but you could come back, too."

Her heart flip-flopped. "Someday, I would like that very much."

"I would like to see you again, Elsa. I know we're both in our later years. I'm just thankful I got to meet you. I'm not expecting anything, and I apologize if I'm being too forward."

"No," she rushed to reassure him, lest he stop; she could see the unease he felt, saying these things. "You're not being too forward, Edmondo."

"We could start by emailing. Do you have an email address?" he asked.

"Yes, I just don't use it very much. But I can see now that I might need to."

"It's a start." He looked hopeful.

She felt relieved, because this wasn't goodbye. She could feel it in her bones.

"I feel happier, because I have known you, Elsa. I didn't know it could be possible to feel this sense of connection again after all these years. I don't know if that makes any sense." His face, soft and lined, and the way he looked at her with his eyes warm and shiny, melted her heart.

She was momentarily overcome with a complete sense of contentment. "It makes perfect sense." She looked dreamily ahead into the distance and felt happier than ever.

Edmondo leaned back into the chair and made himself more comfortable. For a brief second, his hand brushed hers as it rested on the soft cushioned seat. Elsa didn't move hers away, either.

She felt content.

CHAPTER THREE

In Rome...

Nico slammed down the pen and rubbed his eyes. It was late. Three o'clock in the morning late. It had been almost midnight last time he'd looked at his watch. His body ached; it felt stuck, as though his bones were glued together. It shouldn't be like this, not for a healthy thirty-two-year-old. A heartbroken thirty-two-year-old.

It didn't matter how late it was. He got through the days by being busy and focusing his mind elsewhere. If he worked until his body was so tired that it turned stiff just by sitting here, unmoving for hours, then he wouldn't have time to think about *her*. He wouldn't have to fight away the images that were etched in his mind of *her* with *that man*.

Because for the life of him he couldn't figure out what it was he had done to drive Ava away.

Even if he closed his eyes and tried to get some shut eye, sleep still eluded him. Images of Ava tormented him as he tossed around ceaselessly. He'd lie in bed, restless and weary, missing her. He missed her lying beside him, nestled up in the crook of his arm.

But she was gone now, back to Connor, and he had to accept that.

Only he couldn't let it rest. Because just when he'd found the perfect woman, something had driven her back into the arms of her ex-fiancé. Maybe if he just knew *why* she had gone back to him, he could let it rest.

He had arrived in Rome more than a week ago, and it was only the next day that he'd found out Ava had taken the first flight out that morning. She had calmly walked away from him, forgetting about their days in Venice and Verona, and returned to Denver—*with her ex.*

The idea was crazy; it made no sense. He hadn't seen it coming. He'd drawn up his own conclusions about Connor long before he had met the man—he disliked him. Here was a man who had, casually and cruelly, dumped Ava on New Year's Eve, weeks before their wedding, while he was at a party and Ava, who was ill, was home alone.

He as sure as hell didn't deserve a second chance to be with her. Nico had never seen Connor as a rival or considered him a threat. The man was such a worthless loser that Ava hadn't wanted any more to do with him. At least that was what she had told him.

So *why* she had returned to Connor was the question that kept Nico awake during his nights in Rome.

For now, he was relieved to be madly busy working and far away from Verona and from his father, who would no doubt hound him with questions on his return.

His father who had spent his days showing Ava's mother around Verona.

His father who had demanded to know what had

happened between him and Ava. It had only been through his father that Nico had heard the news in the first place.

He'd been ready to rush to the Rome airport to see her, but everything changed the moment Gina told him Connor was also on the same flight out. There was only one possible explanation as to why Ava would ask Connor to return the Flamentagostini bracelet which he'd given her: she didn't have the nerve to tell him herself. And so she'd sent her ex-fiancé to do it. If Nico himself hadn't gotten the hint earlier, *that* was a sure sign that their brief holiday romance was over.

There was no way he would ever go running after her.

Not when he was staying up until way past midnight with his head buried deep in the hotel's books analyzing the figures. He'd stayed on a little longer so that he would be around while the new chef started. He wanted to ensure there would be a smooth settling in period. No further chances of dissent among the staff.

In a week or so, he would know how things were progressing at the Cazale Riccione, the first hotel, outside of the Casa Adriana, where he had implemented his systems processes. Getting all the other hotels to the same level was going to involve time and effort and he was feeling stretched as it was, but he had to do it. His father's approval was everything.

Thinking about the Cazale Riccione brought back memories of the short trip barely a week ago. Once again the image of Ava—tall, beautiful, happy and smiling—fell before him.

He scrubbed his face with his hands, needing to physically wipe the picture away. Somewhere in the far recesses of his brain, he had a decision to make about the new hotel in Ravenna. The one he had shown to Ava.

Ava. Ava. Ava. She lingered in front of him, and try as he would, he couldn't go long without remembering her.

As impossible as it seemed to erase all traces of her from his mind and heart, he had to do it. Otherwise he would lead a life of emptiness and heartache.

The dull ache in his back, from sitting so stationary at his desk, gave him hope that tonight he might fall asleep. If he took a few pills, he might be able to quiet his mind down enough to avoid thinking about the woman who had captured his heart before trampling on it.

CHAPTER FOUR

Ava stood up straight, hoping it would make her appear slimmer, as she leaned against her mother's work counter.

She wore a big baggy sweatshirt over her jeans. It wasn't that she was any bigger now than she had been a few days ago. It wasn't even that she *looked* big. She was paranoid about looking pregnant, or at least giving cause for suspicion in an area that would give away her secret.

Her mother was already on the hunt for clues and Ava wasn't ready for her secret to be out just yet. Once it was, she wouldn't hear the end of it.

Elsa had just finished washing up and Ava had cleared away the table after lunch. The time had come when all the pleasantries had been done away with and the only thing that remained for discussion now was the one thing, the very absence of which stared at them both so fully.

She wanted nothing more than to escape back to the safe haven of her own apartment, but she had to get this over and done with. Doing anything else would only throw more suspicion towards her.

"Come on," said Elsa, drying her hands on the kitchen towel. "Let's sit for a while; you can rush off later. At least let your food digest."

The interrogation begins, thought Ava, swallowing.

Her mother made herself comfortable in her reading chair and Ava sat on the sofa nearest to her. Up until now they had talked only of general issues, such as the flight, Rona, Tori and the weather in Denver. All mention of Italy, Verona, Nico and Edmondo had been off the cards.

Ava prepared herself. *Might as well get the topic started.* "Was Mr. Cazale sad to see you go, Mom? I wonder how he'll spend his days now that you're gone." She watched her mother's face color with happiness.

"I'm sure he'll keep busy in those gardens of his. We were both sad—we had such a wonderful time together, sightseeing and all."

"You could have stayed on, Mom."

"I could have; I had planned to. But I couldn't really stay on now, knowing you'd come rushing back. Edmondo said you were the best thing to happen to his son. I don't understand how things suddenly turned sour between you both."

"He really said that?" Ava felt pangs of excitement at the thought. *I was the best thing to happen to Nico?*

"He really did. So ... what happened?"

She could feel her mother's eyes on her, knew she was waiting for an answer and expected an explanation that Ava wasn't yet ready to give. She ran the words in her head once more. If Edmondo drew that conclusion, why would Nico ruin everything by one indiscreet fling? It didn't make sense, and the more she thought about it the more she became puzzled.

Was it possible that she had read the situation so completely wrong?

"Ava?" Her mother gently prodded her attention away.

"Nothing, Mom. We just kind of...drifted apart. A long-distance relationship would never have worked. What made you think we'd end up together?"

"Because one moment you came back happy from your little trip, and the next moment, you're on the next flight back home."

Ava made one final attempt to cover up. "Mom, I've been away more than a month. I've got a business to run, and ... and ... things to take care of. I've bought all this expensive stock and I need to start selling it. I couldn't stay in Verona forever."

This was a total lie because there had been times when she'd wondered about the possibilities of this very thing.

"And you came back with Connor?"

Ava blinked. Her mother believed this too? Signs were good that Nico was telling Edmondo and Elsa the same.

"Nico seems to think you've gone back to Connor."

Ava squirmed in her seat at her mother's words. Whatever she said now might implicate her. Keeping quiet would be better.

"You don't seriously expect me to believe that, do you?" Her mother would make a good FBI agent.

"It's complicated, Mom." That was the best she could come up with, for now. She didn't for one minute want to put lies about, but if this was the way Nico seemed to have taken the news, then so be it until she figured out how she was going to deal with things.

Elsa remained quiet and Ava sensed that she hadn't convinced her. She was having problems convincing herself. Better to leave things unsaid, rather than give anything away.

"What does Rona make of all this?" Ava asked carefully.

"Rona?" Elsa rolled her eyes. "Who knows what Rona thinks? I didn't see her much towards the end. I babysat for her on a few evenings because she went out; she never told me where. I don't think your sister spent too much time worrying about you."

Ava hadn't spoken to her sister for a while and the two of them hadn't contacted one another since Rona had arrived back yesterday.

She and Rona hadn't exactly seen eye to eye from the beginning, when Ava had first told of her intentions to travel to Italy alone. Things hadn't gotten any better once Rona arrived in Verona. She had seemed to take an instant dislike to Nico.

Already doubting herself when it came to men, anyway, it bothered Ava that her entire family had decided to set off for Verona just because she'd let slip to her mother that she had met someone. When they had appeared en masse at the Casa Adriana, she couldn't bring herself to tell them that her love interest had become a *disinterest*. And also, it was important to her to keep up the pretense of their relationship, only because she didn't want to prove her sister right. Rona had warned her that Italian men were hot-blooded lotharios who would use her and throw her away.

"Look, honey," Elsa sat forward and clasped Ava's hand. You've gone through a bad time in your life this year. In Verona you seemed so happy and content. I assumed it was because of Nico. When you came back from your little break with him, you looked joyful. If you don't want to talk about this now, fine. But, when you're ready, I'm always here for you."

Ava turned the attention back to her mom, in case she was tempted to disclose everything to her in a moment of madness. "Thanks, Mom. I'm sorry you felt you needed to cut your trip short."

Elsa shook her head. "We still ended up having an extra

week. With Edmondo, I got to see so much more—we spent nearly every day together." Her mother blushed, and looked at Ava, whose heart tripped.

Elsa glowed, and this made Ava happy. It was at that moment that she realized just how much Mr. Cazale had come to mean to her mother. He was more than just a sightseeing companion.

"Mom?" Ava whispered. "Did anything happen?" She leaned in closer, taking her mom's hand in hers.

"No," Elsa replied calmly. Then, indignantly, "It was nothing like that!"

Ava didn't let go of her mom's hand. "The way you're looking right now, doesn't seem to me as if it was nothing."

For a second there she felt like an intruder into her mother's secret world. There was an uncomfortable silence. "Do you miss him?" It was so quiet in the room.

"Very much. He was wonderful to me. We ... connected. I never expected that to happen ever again, not after your father." Her mother looked sad, and Ava's heart broke hearing these words. She didn't know whether to hug her mother or stay where she was. The magnitude of her mother's admission slammed into her.

Then the boulder fell down on Ava: Edmondo Cazale had no idea that she was carrying his grandchild.

"Oh, Mom," Ava struggled with the idea of concealing something so big from not one, but two people whose lives would be greatly affected by the news. She placed her hand over her stomach, trying to reconcile the image of Edmondo with the idea of the baby inside her.

Keeping the baby a secret from Nico and his father was going to take greater strength than she had at first envisaged. She would need to steel herself to make sure she kept to her resolve.

Otherwise what was the alternative? A life with Nico in which she always wondered where he'd been if he came home late? A life where she fretted about him going away on business, wondering where it would take him, and with whom? Would she put up with this for the sake of her child? Is that what women did? Would that be fair, to the child, to her?

She moved her hand away, paranoid about drawing attention to her stomach but Elsa had a faraway look about her, and was lost in her own little world.

Looking straight ahead, Elsa spoke softly. "Edmondo thought you were a great influence on Nico. He told me not to worry about you and that the two of you would sort things out soon enough." She braved a smile, but Ava saw right through it, saw the sadness that laced it.

While she didn't for a minute think that anything physical had taken place between her mother and Nico's father, she understood all too well how strong an emotional attachment could be. The wistful look on her mother's face gave it all away.

"Mom?"

"Not now." Elsa shook her head, obviously not wanting to discuss the matter further. Ava could see she was sad, and yet she couldn't let the matter rest either. She felt even guiltier now of her disapproving attitude in Verona when she had been none too eager about the idea of her mother going around with Edmondo.

All her life her mother had been there for them—widowed before her fifties, too. It couldn't have been easy. Her parents had had children late, after years of trying, and then she and Rona had come along one after the other. Elsa had felt blessed, only to have her husband taken away suddenly in a car accident when Ava and Rona were not even ten.

Ava couldn't let it go. "Mom, I'm sor—"

"He was good company for me. He made me laugh. We talked about all sorts of things and he was so easy to get along with. I felt as though we had known each other for many years, not just for the short time we had together."

Her mother got up and started reorganizing the books on her shelf even though they were already neat and tidy. "I'll need to give this a good dusting."

"I thought Rona might have come over," ventured Ava.

"Tori has a cold, so Rona stayed back. I had asked her to come for lunch. Why don't you visit them and see how they're doing?"

Ava had been secretly relieved to see that Rona hadn't come along. She hadn't seen her sister before she'd left Verona either. The two of them had pretty well kept out of each other's way after their disagreements over Nico.

"I wish you and your sister would stop fighting. I've told you before, you don't get to choose your family, and so you must always get on." Her mother stopped rearranging the bookshelves and eyed Ava.

Family. And to think she was now connected to a family who didn't yet know anything about that connection. "I'll go see her. Poor Tori." The words tumbled out, because Ava didn't want to think too much about the idea of Nico being part of her family.

But before long their child would bind them together, in some way. And she wasn't sure if she'd ever be ready for that.

CHAPTER FIVE

The good thing about her mother being distracted with thoughts of Edmondo meant that Ava had had an easier time of avoiding talk about her own situation.

She walked up the driveway to Rona's place and thought about the lunch she had just escaped. Her mother was onto her and sensed there was more to Ava's hasty return than just needing to deal with her online business, but she wasn't about to tell her mother that she would soon be a grandmother.

She didn't like lying, least of all to her family, but she wasn't ready for the truth to be out just yet either.

She rang the doorbell and braced herself. Turning up unannounced and with Tori being unwell, there was no chance that Rona would be out. She was going to have to face her.

The door opened. "Hi." Rona flashed her brightest smile. It suddenly melted Ava's hardness. "Mom said you were on the way." So much for being unannounced.

They hugged each other, stiffly at first. "I haven't seen you in a while," said Ava, realizing the truth of her statement. She walked in briskly.

"'Shhhhhh." Rona put her finger to her lips, signaling that Tori was asleep.

"Can I see her?" whispered Ava. She suddenly had a longing to pick up the little girl but knew it was out of the question; now that Tori was down, Rona would make the most of this quiet time. Her sister led the way to Tori's nursery, bright yellow with a blue trim of animals along the middle of the wall.

"Aaaawww," Ava gushed. "She's *so* cute, I want to pick her up." She gazed at the sleeping baby.

She would have her own baby soon.

"She's had Calpol. Got a bit of a cold. Hopefully she'll sleep a while. Come on, let's grab a coffee." Rona was obviously anxious not to disturb her.

For a guilty moment, Ava wondered if she had interrupted her sister's quiet afternoon by turning up. "I won't stay long," she offered, sitting down at the kitchen table. "You can get some rest yourself; you look tired."

Rona pulled a face and handed her a cup of coffee. "Wait until you have kids, then you can tell me all about tired." She sat down wearily opposite Ava. For a few seconds, the two sisters sipped their coffee slowly, watching each other warily.

"How come you came back so early?" Rona's words dangled in the air.

Ava shrugged. "I had stuff I needed to take care of, website issues, customers getting irate. Kim started to struggle towards the end."

Rona didn't look convinced. "So you had to jump on the next available flight out which just happened to be the one Connor was on?"

"I didn't take it because Connor was on it," Ava replied defensively. But if Rona also had the same idea about her and Connor, maybe it would be better to let it ride for now?

"Have you and lover boy had a tiff?" Rona alluded to Nico, and Ava wondered exactly what Elsa had told her.

"Why can't you call him by his name?" Ava had hoped that she and Rona would be able to put some of their differences behind them, now that they were back. But with their conversation going this way, it didn't look as though that was going to happen.

Ava took off Rona's ring, surprised that she hadn't done it sooner. "Here." She handed it back. "I don't need this. It would have been a lot simpler if I'd never taken your misguided advice."

Rona, always the protective older sister, had offered Ava words of wisdom about keeping herself out of what she believed to be harm's way, warning her against hot-blooded Italian men who would only want one thing. She had been so adamant about her prophecy that she'd given Ava one of her rings to wear as a wedding ring in hopes that it would help ward off eager suitors.

"I see it didn't exactly keep the men from you. I mean, come off it, Ava, you go there to clear your mind and end up with a lover instead? Is that taking time out for yourself?"

The malice of her sister's words struck her.

"What is it, Rona? What's the thing that's making you so unhappy about all of this?"

Rona didn't like Nico, but just hearing about their romance made Ava's heart zing. Because now that time had passed and there was distance between them, she was having doubts about her reaction. There were moments, like now, where she had golden memories of their time together. She remembered how good he had been to her. How good they had been together.

He *must* have cared for her. Surely she had meant something more to him than a short term fling?

For the few precious days they'd shared together, in Riccione and Ravenna, and their time in Verona and Venice, she'd seen a tender, sensual, caring side to the man she had fallen for.

"I didn't *not* like him. I'm just saying, you need to think more with your head than your heart. I don't want you to hurt yourself again. A long distance relationship like that, how was that ever going to work?"

Ava wondered exactly what Rona knew as her sister carried on. "So it's true then? The two of you aren't together anymore? I did wonder. Mainly because we never saw you go out with him much. Mom says you went away for a few days somewhere."

"You make it sound as though you weren't there in the pensione next to me. Come to think of it, where were you?" Ava took her opportunity to attack.

"Out. You were unavailable, Mom was busy with Edmondo"—Rona rolled her eyes—"and Carlos had already flown home. What was I supposed to do?"

"What *did* you do?"

Temporarily stunned, Rona was speechless. Ava stared at her. Rona couldn't have been that silly could she? Would she go a step further and do something really stupid?

Would she?

Rona got up, taking both their coffee cups which were empty by now. She moved over to the sink with her back turned to Ava. When several seconds had passed and still no reply from her sister, Ava got up, now more than a little worried, and walked over to her sister's side.

"Did something happen?" asked Ava gently. She had tried to think who her sister knew in Verona, or where she would go. Ava was certain she didn't know anyone there. Except for Gioberti.

Rona washed the cups slowly.

"Did you go out for dinner? Meet friends?"

"Friends? Which friends? I didn't know anyone there." Her sister turned to her hotly and wiped her hands dry. "If you're trying to make me feel guilty—"

"No, no." Ava was feeling guilty for neglecting her sister. But she'd had enough to deal with. Nico, arguments, good days, passionate nights. For chrissakes, it had been *her* vacation. She had never expected her family to turn up and join her uninvited. "I'm sorry I didn't make more time for—"

"This isn't always about you, Ava." Rona cut in, still with her back to the sink, and Ava turned to her side to face her.

"I know," she said in a gentler voice. "I'm not making this about me. I was just worried. Mom was worried. Where were you?"

"Gioberti was the only one who ever showed me kindness."

Ava's blood boiled. Gioberti, the restaurant owner with a blindingly brilliant white smile for all women, a perpetual womanizer, and a notorious flirt. Nico hadn't spoken of him in a good light.

Of all the people in the whole of Verona, trust her sister to hang out with him.

"And you tell me to steer clear of hot-blooded Italian men!" Ava hissed. "Gioberti is the king of hot-blooded!"

Rona crossed her arms defensively.

"And you're *married*. How could you?"

"We didn't do anything," Rona protested. She glowered at Ava. "I didn't do a thing."

Ava looked into her sister's eyes, not sure she could believe her. Her sister wouldn't go that far, would she? "Does Carlos know?"

Rona flung her arms wide open and stepped away. "Of course not; there's nothing to know." She stood in the middle of the kitchen and gripped the cuffs of her cardigan between her fingers and the palms of her hands. It only made her look more like a guilty child.

"Then why go to see him at all? He didn't just give *you* attention, Rona. He did that with *all* the women who walked into his restaurant." With the roles reversed, it was now her turn to scold Rona.

"It wasn't like that. I'd go there to eat. He'd sit and chat for a while. I admit—I liked the attention. I know he did that with any woman who came in." Rona looked down at her cuffs.

I bet he did, thought Ava. She remembered what a flirt the man was. He'd latched onto her the very first time she'd gone out in Verona. Then Nico had joined her for lunch; he'd been so worried about her leaving the Casa di Giulietta in tears that he'd followed her the whole way, wanting to make sure she was all right.

Memories of that day mired her and she suddenly longed to see him again.

"Okay," said Ava, dragging her focus back to her sister. She pulled out a chair and sat down, and Rona did the same. "Do you want to talk about it?"

"You don't know what it's like," Rona began. And Ava saw the puffy eyes with dark circles. Rona looked exhausted. Would this be her in a year's time once the baby came?

"Since Tori was born, our lives have been all wrapped up around her. We hardly have time for each other. I thought we might have some quality time in Verona, but Carlos had to rush back. You know how his family is so demanding when it comes to their restaurants."

Ava knew all too well. Carlos's father ran a few

restaurants and the poor man worked long hours most evenings, and a lot of weekends. Rona looked beat most of the time looking after Tori and she and Carlos didn't get to spend much time together as a couple any more. No wonder her sister had leapt at a little attention, even from a character as unsavory as Gioberti.

Ava felt sorry for her. "How about you go and get some sleep? I'll stay here a while and look after Tori if she gets up."

Rona didn't need to be asked twice. She got up. "You sure?"

"I'm sure. I'd like to spend some time with my little niece, too. I hardly saw her in Verona." Ava decided that she would offer to help babysit Tori once a week. This would give Rona and Carlos time to have a date night on one of the few nights he was free and it was obviously something they both needed.

"Thanks," said Rona, with a trace of a smile. She walked over to Ava and kissed her on the head. As she stepped away, she turned back, "It's true then? You and Nico really have split up? That's what Mom was worried about."

Ava winced, not quite sure what to say.

"Are you really thinking of getting back with Connor?"

"He's come to be a better friend," said Ava carefully, thinking back to their flight from Verona to Denver.

"Really?" It was obvious that Rona was having a hard time believing this.

"Who knows what the future might bring." Ava added, needing to add a layer of suspense to the equation. She didn't want to outright lie about her and Connor getting back together again, for clearly that rumor had already started to make the rounds, but if she could say something, anything that would deflect the attention from her and her baby, then it could only help her situation.

"That's a real shame." Rona made it to the door and

stopped. "I know I dissed him most of the time, but I actually thought Nico was a decent guy, and so goddamn hot. For a moment there, I was almost jealous of you." She disappeared out of the kitchen.

Damn hot, thought Ava, miserably. Damn. Hot.

CHAPTER SIX

Nico waited patiently as his father took the call. He had arrived back from Rome late last night.

The problems had taken nearly a week to resolve, but at least the hotel now had a reliable chef and one who was not going to cause further problems with the rest of the staff. Dealing with people was infinitely more challenging than dealing with systems and processes. People were a pain. Matteo, the hotel manager at the Cazale Roma, could not thank him enough by the time he had left.

Nico had good reason to be suitably satisfied with himself and had met with his father this morning to update him.

Of course, he could have finished up a couple of days sooner. Only he had been in no hurry to return to Verona. There were too many memories here that he wasn't ready to face. Too many ugly truths that he wanted to avoid. The biggest one being that Ava and Connor were back together again.

On his arrival back at work he'd been grateful that Gina had not been on duty at the reception desk. She would have probed him for details and she would have extricated the necessary details from him, too. He was in no mood to talk about Ava or speculate on why she had gone back to Connor.

His father put down the phone. "Why the bank manager can't come and discuss these matters with me in person instead of on the phone, I don't know. We never did business over the phone like this, not in my day. It was face-to-face. And that's how it should be even now." He shook his head, then pushed his glasses up.

Nico agreed, letting his father finish his rant.

"Your trip went very well, by all accounts. Matteo can't say enough good things about you."

Nico shrugged. "We'll still need to keep an eye on the Cazale Roma. We neglect it because it's the farthest away, but we can't afford to neglect any of our hotels."

The older Cazale nodded in agreement. "I didn't expect you to stay there so long."

"These things take time, especially when the problems are related to people."

Edmondo gazed pensively. "People problems are the hardest to solve."

Nico sat forward, anticipating having to explain the specifics of the issues he had been dealing with. "The new chef seems good, very good. I have high hopes—"

"What happened between you and Ava?" His father caught him off guard and before Nico could answer, Edmondo added, "You seemed so taken by her, Nico. How can you just throw that away?"

Ah. So his father believed the fault lay with Nico. He battled to say something, anything, to get the topic away from his personal hell. He had thought of nothing but Ava, even when he kidded himself that he was working so hard he almost fell asleep at his desk most nights. In his waking moments, his first thoughts were of her. He craved her, wanted her with an intensity that bordered on addiction, until he reminded himself that she was with Connor. And at that point, he slowly relinquished all memories of her.

He sensed that his father wasn't going to let him easily forget her. Perhaps he'd seen how much she'd come to mean to him.

"That woman had an effect on you; it was plain to see." Was that a hint of disappointment he heard in his father's voice?

"Do you think so, Papa?" Nico asked in mock surprise. "I hadn't realized you scrutinized the effect my girlfriends had on me. In fact, I didn't realize you paid any attention to them at all." He was warming up for his next question, but Edmondo interjected sharply.

"There's never been much cause to before, but with Ava, you were different. I've never seen you happier, or more focused. It was obvious to most."

It was true. He had dared to consider a future with her, dared to think bigger, and act bigger. It had been the reason he'd visited the hotel in Ravenna. The reason he had made a start on rolling out his hotel blueprint to the hotel in Riccione. He had taken Ava with him, not only because he wanted and needed time alone with her, but because he dared to imagine a future in which she belonged. He had wanted her to see that. He had always dreamed big, it was just that with Ava he'd actually been moved to act on his dreams.

He fell silent, thinking of these things. His father's words were the not wanted he wanted to hear. He'd managed to successfully dodge Gina this morning, but he had never expected his father to be more interested in his love life than the business. This was new, indeed.

Connecting the dots, Nico made a sudden leap in realization. "Elsa Ramirez has had an effect on you, Papa."

Edmondo cleared his throat but held his gaze steady. "She is a wonderful, warm woman. I am honored to have met her and spent time with her." Even behind his reading glasses his father's eyes twinkled but his lips stayed pursed. "She is worried about Ava, and you, and whatever it was that forced her daughter to return to Denver so quickly."

Nico sighed. "I didn't know Ava was going back, Papa, not until you told me." He remembered that phone call out of the blue when Edmondo had asked him why Ava was returning so quickly. That had been the first that Nico had heard of Ava's sudden return to Denver. Gina's call a while later confirmed that Connor had taken the same flight out. That, coupled with the fact that Connor returned the bracelet, proved without a doubt, her intentions.

And yet Nico struggled to accept the idea of Ava returning to Connor. Especially after they'd spent those three intimate and blissful days away and the things they'd said to one another. He *knew* she loved him. It didn't make sense then, for her to leave without saying anything.

There *had* to be more to it.

But he'd be damned if he knew what. She'd returned the bracelet and gone back on the same flight as Connor. The facts spoke for themselves. He didn't need it to be spelled out any clearer than that.

"There's nothing I can do about it now. She's gone back to that idiot and that's the end of it." He could never bring himself to refer to Connor by name. Good luck to Ava and the new future she had with him.

"You believe that, do you?" his father asked. "Because Elsa refuses to see any truth in that."

Nico wondered if a word with Andrea might help shed some light on what had gone wrong. Ava had spent a lot of time with her and the two women had become friends. He suddenly remembered he also needed to take care of Ava's shipments. She'd asked him to look into it a while back, and aside from making a few queries, he'd never gotten around to doing anything about it. He'd been so absorbed in Rome, he had completely forgotten.

She would need her products shipped over as a matter of urgency. Yet she hadn't called him regarding the shipments at all. Did she hate him that much that she would risk her business? The shipments had been a priority for her, but if she hadn't even contacted him to see how things were progressing on that front, she clearly wanted nothing further to do with him.

His father watched him silently, waiting for his answer.

"We didn't really argue about anything in particular. One moment she was here, the next, she left." This wasn't entirely true but Nico didn't think his father needed to know every minute detail. Nico had an inkling that the journalist had been a factor in Ava's decision to leave but it still didn't explain why she'd asked Connor to return the bracelet.

"Son, sometimes life tests us to see whether we really do deserve the very things we claim to want." Nico stared at his father blankly. "Don't let her go so easily, Nico."

Nico shifted in his seat, "But—"

"Some things are worth fighting for."

Trying to forget Ava had been near impossible but if his father was going to be on his case at every opportunity, he was already fighting a losing battle. He put his hands up. "Enough, Papa. Don't you want to know more about the Cazale Roma?" His father usually had a long list of questions.

His father shook his head. "If you say you've dealt with it, then that's good enough for me." His father seemed calmer, more laid back, less on his case. Was it that Nico had changed, or had his father changed, too?

Nico persisted. "It seems to me that Elsa has most definitely had an effect on you."

"We'll be keeping in touch," his father replied calmly, twiddling his thumbs.

"You will?" The news took Nico by surprise.

"Of course. Sometimes you meet people for a reason, a season, or a lifetime. Perhaps Elsa is all three. Who knows? For the few years I have left, I am determined not to let special moments and memories pass me by."

Nico blinked. For as long as he could remember, his father talked business, all the time. These philosophic moments that he now shared with him gave Nico a completely different perspective on the man.

If Edmondo was going to be in touch with Ava's mother, then Nico's plan to get Ava out of his mind forever was going to be difficult.

He couldn't sit here a moment longer and listen to his father go on about Ava or her mother. He strove to get his father back into business mode. "I've done some projections and costings for the Ravenna hotel, and I'd like to go through them with you."

"Maybe we should drive out to see it."

Nico looked at his father in surprise; he had clearly gotten used to not being locked up in his office all day. "Of course," Nico promised. He got up, ready to take on a full day's work. "I've got lots of things to deal with and all of them are urgent, supposedly. Maybe in a few days' time we can drive to Ravenna."

"I'd like that. I'm most interested in seeing this hotel that you're so passionate about." His father gazed at him proudly.

CHAPTER SEVEN

Elsa finally understood what all the excitement was about. She could now see why so many people around her, the younger ones as she called them, were forever plugged into their devices wherever she went.

She found herself experiencing the very same thrill now that she and Edmondo had started emailing one another.

Each morning she would wake up to one of Edmondo's emails and when she turned on her laptop, her heart fluttered with rising excitement. Her day didn't start until she'd read what he'd sent her. The last thing she did before she went to bed was to reply to Edmondo and his reply would be waiting for her, when she awoke. They kept it at one email each a day and whenever she read his emails, it left her smiling and her heart singing with joy.

It had started slowly. She emailed him first to let him know that she had arrived back safely in Denver. He had replied within the hour that first time. The immediacy of hearing from him had thrilled her. She'd felt a little sad on the return journey and missed her daily dose of Edmondo and

Verona. So, when she received his first email, she was over the moon.

It felt as though Edmondo was still beside her, and it instantly brightened her day.

Slowly, what started out as nice polite emails, talking about niceties, became longer, lingering over their days together. They wrote about the places they had been to, the things they had talked about, what they missed...all interspersed with nuggets about their current daily lives.

It made Elsa feel that Edmondo was a small part of her life and it helped lessen the vacation blues.

And there was that other little matter to discuss, dear to both their hearts. But now that each of them had been able to talk to their respective children, she and Edmondo were still no nearer to the truth of what had gone wrong between Nico and Ava.

Dear Elsa,

I have spoken to Nico at length and have tried to get to the bottom of the problem, but I have not been successful in getting the information out of him. He avoids the subject about him and Ava and I find this most annoying. He is adamant that Ava is back with Connor and that they are 'over.'

I am no nearer to getting anything out of him and I'm sorry to say that I have nothing concrete to give you.

I have tried to impress upon him that love is fleeting, transient, ephemeral, and that when you find 'it' you should hold on to it, fight for it and never let it go.

We realize the significance of these things in our later years. You and I both know the meaning of this, since we have both experienced such losses. I know your loss has been for longer and that your girls were very young then. I can't imagine how hard it must have been for you.

April is here and the gardens at the Casa Adriana are as beautiful as ever. My daily walk each morning brings me some quiet time and I often think of the last days we spent here.

The pergola is where I spend most of my afternoons, and I sit on the swing chair, looking at the lemon trees you so loved. And I am reminded how it is all the emptier because of your absence. I wish we had spent more time here in the garden. Perhaps next time you are over.

Fondest,
Edmondo

Elsa read his emails over a number of times, poring over his words, savoring them. For the time she read them, she felt an instant closeness to him and it immediately filled her with lightness.

The connection that had begun in Verona stayed and got stronger each day. It was a new and giddy feeling; unlike any she had experienced before.

Her friends complained that they didn't see her as much. It was true. She'd had a very busy social life, helping at the voluntary shelter every week, and then there was the book club, and some painting classes too. But since her return she had gone out maybe twice in the two weeks she had been back. Both times it had been to the mall and only because her good friend and neighbor, Faith, had insisted on it.

These days, Elsa preferred to sit at home reading, thinking and reminiscing. And, of course, there were Edmondo's emails to read and reply to. Her mind and heart were still in Verona.

The only other things that occupied her were her daughters and granddaughter. Ava had put Elsa's mind at rest by informing her that Rona's late-night jaunts in Verona had been harmless, although she hadn't elaborated on what her sister had done or where she'd gone.

But Elsa wasn't worried about Rona. It was Ava who worried her more.

Just as Edmondo was finding it difficult to extract from Nico what had gone, she was having difficulty eliciting details from Ava. It wouldn't matter so much if Nico and Ava had naturally drifted apart. But Edmondo was saying otherwise, and Elsa had only to look at Ava to know the girl was miserable. *What* was making her so miserable?

Everything her daughter told her was vague. She was vague about her relationship to Connor, and as vague about the circumstances that had made her leave Verona. Vague, in Elsa's books, meant she was hiding the truth, and Elsa was determined to get to the bottom of it. She had the feeling it was something big.

This morning Faith had insisted on Elsa attending the weekly drop-in art class they'd both started a few months ago. The hobby had allowed her to indulge her lifetime interest in art for Elsa had loved painting and drawing in her younger years.

She knew Faith wouldn't take no for an answer today, and Elsa was fast running out of excuses. She quickly wrote Edmondo a reply, knowing that he would be waiting for it.

Dear Edmondo,

You are so right, of course. Love is fleeting. Lucky are those who get to spend a lifetime with their loved ones. But we all move on and get by, don't we? After all, we have the children to think of. They might be all grown up now, but to us they still remain children forever.

I cannot get any more information out of Ava either, and goodness knows I have tried. She refuses to give up anything. She also does not, I have noticed, confirm that she and Connor are back together.

I find the whole 'story' around Connor to be completely confusing, I must confess. My daughter doesn't lie, that I am aware of. So I know that by refusing to wholly admit to her and Connor getting back together, she is withholding the truth. That I have to resort to detective-like clues to find out what's going on in her love life is beyond me!

Safe to say that I am worried. It doesn't add up. That morning after she and Nico arrived back from their trip, she looked so happy. You and I were heading off somewhere—do you remember? It was the day we had lunch at the Piazza delle Erbe. Just as we were leaving the Casa Adriana, Ava was on her way to see Nico.

The next time I saw her was at the pensione later in the evening where she told me she had booked the first flight back.

Something happened that day that neither one of us is a party to.

I suppose we will have to wait it out a little and hope that the two of them can work things out, although being continents apart does not bode well for solving such arguments.

I loved the gardens at the Casa Adriana, Edmondo. I wish we had spent more time there, too. Though I will forever be grateful to you for showing me so much of your beloved Verona.

I would love to come back. There I said it. I would. Maybe time will tell.

I must go now. I am going to an art class with my neighbor

and good friend whom I have known for years. She must replace my good friend Edmondo for now!

Best wishes,
Elsa

CHAPTER EIGHT

Ava glanced at her website stats and a smile crept out across her lips. She had almost doubled her daily visitor numbers ever since she had sent out a newsletter last week. Putting an advertisement on a few high traffic mommy blogs had also paid off.

She'd been busy in adding in lots of new products and changing the product descriptions so that the products sounded much more appealing than the bland manufacturer descriptions. She'd also touched up the images and uploaded them to her site.

She and Andrea had been swapping emails, since phone calls were a little trickier with the eight-hour time difference between them. Her friend had been wonderful in dealing with the shipping side of things and the first of Ava's shipments had arrived a few days ago. Just in time.

She'd received a couple of emails from customers who asked her about some of the new products. This was a good sign. Most of these speculative emails came from interested parties, and she hoped they would end up buying the very products they enquired about.

She still sold her existing products through the drop shipping company, and while they were easier to handle in that she never got involved with sending them out, her profits were less because she competed with most of the other baby and children's sites that all sold similar products.

However, her Italian inventory was full of products that were new. Nobody else, as far as she could tell, sold them here in the US and that was a major win right there. The profits she would make would be hers; she didn't have to give a cut to the middleman and she could dictate how much she charged per item. Though she had to factor in costs for shipping; from what she remembered these were going to be high.

Now that she had some products in her hands, she could take her own photos of them, from different angles and maybe even create some videos as well. Most of her customers preferred watching videos of products to reading the product description. It excited her, that she could provide these little extras merely by stocking inventory. Of course, it was a little more work, especially when it came to processing the orders and dispatching them, but she stood to make more profit.

She got up from her desk and walked around her small apartment. It was already starting to look a little like Andrea's warehouse, with all the baby products stacked up wherever she could find an empty space. The lighter things were now being placed on the couches. Luckily she'd managed to carve out room for her to sit on one of them.

Things were coming together and she spent less time thinking about Nico when she was immersed in her products. It had been hard resisting the temptation to call him—something she had felt like doing lately—but she always managed to talk herself out of it. She was worried that one of these days she would give in and call him, just to hear his voice.

She ran her hand over her stomach. It was still as smooth and as flat as ever; at times she wondered if there really was a baby growing inside her. But her tiredness was a sign that her body was changing even if her pregnancy wasn't obvious to others yet. She chewed her lip, wondering if she was going about it all the right way. Denying Nico the right to know about something that was rightfully his was wrong, wasn't it?

She was too tired to think about it.

Yesterday, she had finally gone through all the items in her shipment and had been exhausted by the end. She had opened up all the boxes to check the contents were intact, then checked off each item, examined each carefully before finding a place for it somewhere in her apartment and then made a list of the few products that had become actual orders and would need to be shipped out to her customers. It was a lot of work and she now knew what to expect when the other two shipments arrived.

She walked around, mentally rearranging her apartment so that she could accommodate the rest of the products. Her living room was out of the question, packed to the full as it was. She had space in her bedroom, and there was the hallway, too.

The baby cribs hadn't arrived yet. She knew they would take longer, being bulkier and bigger in size. Ava scratched her head and looked around, wondering where on earth she was going to store them. With any luck, she'd sell them as fast as they arrived.

Was she ever glad that she'd held on to her apartment and not moved in with Connor last year. Otherwise, where would she be now?

She looked at the space on the side of her dresser; she could store a few boxes here. Her cell rang, distracting her from her reorganization and she fished it out of her loose tracksuit bottoms. Her face dropped as she saw the caller ID.

"Hey, Connor." She held her breath, unsure of his feelings toward her, now that they were back. He'd given her the space she had needed on the flight home, but recently, he'd taken to calling her at least every other day. With no Silvia around, Ava felt slightly hesitant in taking the call.

Despite everyone else thinking she and Connor were back together, Ava knew this was something that was never going to happen. Hell would freeze over before she'd ever go back to Connor Beachcroft.

"Ava. Hard to get hold of you these days. Are you really that busy all of a sudden?"

She grimaced, knowing he had called her a dozen times since they had arrived back and she hadn't called him back. It wasn't the case that she was purposely trying to avoid him, she really had been busy. "Sorry for not returning your calls but the shipments started arriving this week. Mom and Rona got back last week, so I've been over to see them, too."

And I'm tired and exhausted from this pregnancy.

"No worries, that's cool." *Cool?* Since when had Connor ever used the word 'cool'? "I wanted to make sure you were okay, that's all," he said. "I haven't had a chance to speak to you since we flew back."

She rearranged a few boxes in the corner of her room, her cell held in place by her jaw at an awkward angle as she listened to him talking. If she moved her chest of drawers from the foot of her bed to the corner beside her, it would be a tight squeeze but she'd be able to get out of bed the other side. It would free up a nice sized space opposite her bed. She might be able to store a few of the cribs there. Her mind drifted to her crib order and the size of the boxes they would arrive in. Andrea said they'd be flat-packed. She'd ordered ten, so she should be able to store these in her apartment comfortably enough, she imagined.

"How about it?"

"Er..." What had Connor asked her?

"You weren't listening, were you?"

Uh. Nope. Guilt washed over her at the lull in his tone. "I'm sorry, Connor." She genuinely was. She sat on her bed, giving him all her attention. "I'm up to my eyes in boxes. You should see my place, it's overflowing."

"I was only wondering if you'd like to go out to dinner one evening, say sometime next week." His voice rose up at the end.

Now he had her. She felt mean for turning him down but she didn't want to go out to dinner. Sitting in a restaurant with Connor would herald acceptance, in his eyes, of some sort of shift. She hadn't said anything to him about her and Nico splitting up, but the fact that she had left so suddenly, and the fact that she had asked him to return a bracelet would have raised questions. Connor wasn't stupid. He was a smart lawyer and he'd figure it all out. It sounded as though he already had, which was why he was asking her out to dinner.

He obviously thought the coast was clear once more. She had been lulled into a false sense of security, since he had been so good as to leave her to wallow in her misery on the flight back. He had given her the distance she had needed, but then again, maybe he was only trying to be her friend.

Was she reading too much into it?

"Connor, I—"

"It's only dinner, Ava. I'm not asking for anything more. I still care about you and I'm worried about you."

"Uh ..." She needed a friend right now. Someone unconnected to Nico, but she wasn't in the mood for going out, not now, while she was taking care of her business. She didn't have an evening to spend with Connor. Heck, any free evening she would probably just flake out in front of the TV. "I'm so busy, Connor. I just handled a shipment and I'm expecting another two in the next few weeks. I didn't realize working for yourself meant working twenty-four seven." She laughed, hoping to diffuse the awkwardness of the conversation. When Connor didn't reply, she felt compelled to add, "Maybe you could come over one evening and we'll get takeout or something."

"That sounds pretty cool. Next week, then? Friday night? I know how you liked takeouts on Friday night."

Ava groaned inwardly. He sounded excited. She wished she hadn't been so hasty in her offer. Now she seriously hoped he wouldn't be thinking there was any chance of them getting back together again.

"Sure. Next Friday sounds good." She hung up, coming off the phone with a sinking feeling in the pit of her stomach.

She pushed herself further up the bed then lay down on it fully. Just like that, a wave of tiredness washed over her and she was ready to fall asleep. The conversation with Connor had done exactly that and she soon found her eyelids becoming heavy.

The next thing she heard was the sound of her cell phone ringing again. She tried to ignore it but, purely by automatic instinct, she picked it up and answered it. "Connor, can I call you later?"

"Hello, Ava. It's Nico."

Even before he said his name, his voice pulled her out of the half sleep she had sunk into and jerked her wide awake. She had missed his voice. She had missed him.

Her eyelids fluttered open just as her heart whooshed into overdrive. It was only a few seconds, but it felt like minutes before she gained a clear enough mind to speak.

"Nico." She said it as if it were a statement.

"You were expecting Connor?"

"No. Yes. Uh..." Brain freeze.

"How are you?" he asked, his silky voice making her heart thud to a stop. She knew the cadence of his voice and she knew instinctively—could feel it deep in her soul—that he still cared. His voice became suddenly softer whenever he spoke to her.

"I'm fine, Nico." *I miss you.* She gulped, forcing back words that she was scared would fall out, now that she was under his spell once more. She pictured him in her mind's eye and her resolve melted like cooking chocolate.

"I rang you by mistake, actually. I was after Andrea."

His words smacked her hard. "Oh...okay." She couldn't string together any words that made sense.

"It's to do with you. I need to check with Andrea first, but since I already have you on the line..."

All her soft, mushy, fuzzy feelings that had been wrapped up in her head with Nico sitting comfortably in the middle of them, hardened into shards of glass. "What's the matter?" Animosity in her voice was tempered with curiosity. What could Nico want to speak to her *and* Andrea about?

"I needed to check the order quantity on your cribs. Did you order one hundred? The shipping costs are going to be expensive."

She was picking herself up from the disappointment of him telling her he had called her by mistake.

"Ava? Did you order one hundred cribs?"

Her mind zeroed in on the problem. "A hundred?" she asked, confused. "No. I ordered ten."

"Obviously there's been a mistake made somewhere. You should check your invoices, Ava. That's going to cost you a lot of money."

"The order says one hundred?" She swallowed slowly, anxiety clawing at her as she considered the extra cost.

"Yes, but don't worry. Leave it to me, I'll speak to Andrea about it."

She didn't like the thought of Nico talking to Andrea. Why was she jealous when she needed him out of her life? She became so wrapped up in these thoughts that when Nico mumbled his goodbyes and quickly hung up, she was too shocked to realize.

Until the line went dead.

She clutched the cell tightly in her hand. In the silence that followed she scrambled to replay their conversation in her mind—just so she could hold onto the sound of his voice, so sexy, so low. She lay back on the bed, still clasping the cell, wondering if he would call again, knowing that he would not.

With her hands resting lightly across her stomach, she marveled at the idea of the precious life they had created together and wondered why it was that things had come to this.

She was so lost in a sea of sadness that it never occurred to her at all to query why Nico was dealing with her shipments.

CHAPTER NINE

He sat in his chair brooding for almost half an hour, mulling over the conversation with Ava.

That it had come to this was devastating. He'd been a fool to think he'd found his soul mate.

Ava had left him and she had returned to *that* man—of all people.

Why?

He thought he could forget her by working harder, but the more he tried to forget her, the more she tormented his thoughts.

He knew every inch of her body intimately. He knew what she was thinking just by looking at her and he could often second-guess her words before she spoke them.

That he had come to know her, and she him, so well in such a short space of time together—surely that meant something?

He had never lied to her before, but he had told her a little white lie just now when he told her he'd called her by mistake.

He had been looking for an opportunity and this order

size had him perplexed. All of her orders were in quantities of ten, so an order size of one hundred had naturally raised his suspicion. It had given him the perfect opportunity to call her. And he was grateful that Andrea had asked for his help with Ava's shipping. It had been his responsibility in the first place, only he'd become distracted. Ava had distracted him, and then they hadn't actually gotten to the point of talking about her return to Denver.

Until she had just upped and left him.

The shipping quotes Andrea was getting were coming in at exorbitant prices so, when she had turned to Nico, he had been only too happy to help out. He had contacts and he'd make sure Ava's products got to her at a reasonable cost.

But the large crib order would have been hard to drive down and he'd needed to confirm it first. He could have as easily spoken to Andrea about it, for the products were in her warehouse but with a solid reason to speak to Ava, he'd called her on the spur of the moment before he could talk himself out of it.

Despite his valiant efforts to forget her, he still missed her and he needed to hear her voice. And yet when she had answered his call and had so clearly expected Connor, he knew instantly that it had been a mistake to call her at all.

But in hearing her voice, he sensed her somber mood. He could hear it, could tell in an instant. Maybe things between her and Connor weren't going so well? The idea pleased him.

In the meantime, he'd promised her he would take care of her shipments, and he wasn't a man who went back on his word.

Even if she'd broken his heart.

He needed to speak to Andrea. In fact, Nico looked at his watch, he would pay her a visit this afternoon; he was starting to feel hemmed in, sitting in his office all day. He needed to get some fresh air.

***

Driving alone to Montova brought back bittersweet memories for Nico.

Hearing Ava's voice for the first time in weeks had recalled her vividly to the forefront of his thoughts again. Her absence in his car served to remind him of her even more, and he missed their conversations, her laughter, the shared silences.

As he walked into Andrea's warehouse, it felt as though he'd taken a step back in time. Memories dragged him back to the time he had first brought Ava here and introduced her to Andrea, his one-time lover but now a good friend.

Andrea's warehouse, in the industrial town of Montova, was thriving. Ava had been drawn to the place and it was one of the reasons she'd ended up staying longer in Verona. She'd wanted to source new items to sell on her website. While this was true, Nico also liked to think that she'd stayed on because of *him*.

The two women had become good friends over the course of Ava's stay here and she'd come to Montova most days, looking for more products to sell.

All of that seemed a long time ago because of everything that had happened inbetween and he felt strange to be returning.

"Nico!" Andrea rushed toward him with a smile. Her exuberance threw him off guard and for a moment he forgot about the sad memories that silently accompanied him here.

"How are you?" His hands lightly brushed her arms as she

moved away from their hug. Their relationship had taken place many years ago and he liked to think that they now had an easy friendship, unbound by awkward moments. Now when they met it was to discuss business matters. Andrea often came to him for advice and he was more than happy to help her.

"Good. It's great to see you again." She beckoned him to follow her into her office at the back.

"I'm sorry, I should have called before turning up. I decided on the spur of the moment. I needed to see the paperwork, all these phone calls and emails back and forth between us and the shipping company are confusing the issue."

Andrea sat down in front of her computer, and looked up sharply at his last words. "Is it something I've done?"

Nico shook his head as he sat down in front of her. "I don't mean *you're* confusing the issue. There seems to have been a discrepancy with one of the orders."

"Oh?" asked Andrea, brushing her curls away from her face. "I feel bad for putting this on you, Nico."

"You shouldn't. I was supposed to take care of her shipment in the first place."

"I know, but Ava insisted I take over and she specifically asked me to take care of things."

"When was this?" Nico raised an eyebrow; this was news to him.

"The last time she was here, just before she flew back."

"Why did she want you to handle the shipments?"

"I don't know." Andrea looked at him, with a face full of questions. He clenched his jaw. Had she really started to hate him from that day on? If Ava had reacted the way she had because of the journalist, then she had interpreted events wrongly. He couldn't believe his single act would have led to their splitting up but then he was reminded of the bracelet she returned. And Connor. And *that* said it all.

He fell silent and he wasn't sure whether Andrea even knew that he and Ava had started a relationship. In any case, it didn't seem appropriate to discuss such matters with his former lover.

"See, here, ten units." She pulled out the sheet of paper and pushed it toward him. "I ordered ten units so the mix-up must be at the manufacturer's end."

Nico glanced at it briefly. "Could you scan and email me a copy?"

"You'll have it by the time you get back." Andrea slipped the piece of paper into her scanner and waited for the image to process. "Her ex was with her," she said. "I don't know if she was upset because he was here."

Nico raised his eyebrow at the mention of Ava's ex. "Apparently she's back with him."

Andrea tapped away on her keyboard. "I find that hard to believe. She broke down in tears the last time."

"In tears?" Nico lifted his head in surprise. What had she been so upset about? The journalist? Connor? But then why bring Connor to Montova?

"She seemed upset about something." Andrea gave him an apologetic look. "There. I've just emailed the order to you."

"Thanks." He wished she would tell him more. "You said she was in tears?"

"She seemed upset. I don't know. I thought at one point that maybe you and Ava had a..." She gave an uneasy laugh.

Nico braced himself. Andrea was fishing for more information. "Ava is a very special woman and a good friend. She was looking to expand her business and I wanted to get her off to a good start."

"Maybe Connor annoyed her that day."

"What makes you say that?" Nico pressed.

"A feeling, that's all. The way they were. She seemed irritated by him, more than anything. Here." She picked up a pencil and ringed some figures on the sheets of paper. "You'll need these for the rest of the shipments. I'll talk to the manufacturer about the ninety extra cribs they've ordered." She pushed a pile of paper toward him.

"She was irritated?" Nico was trying to be patient. He took the papers and slipped them into his leather folder.

Andrea shook her head slowly. "He was constantly criticizing the products she'd bought, and I got the feeling she was irritated by him. She tried to avoid listening to him. But I spoke to her a few days ago and she mentioned that he was coming over in the evening for dinner. She's mentioned him a couple of times and I guess they managed to work things out in the end."

"She actually said they were a couple?" Nico asked, needing to know for certain. Ava had more or less implied as much but he needed definite confirmation.

Andrea flicked her hands, as if to say that she knew nothing. "Who knows? I love her dearly as a friend, and I don't want to see her get hurt again. I hope it works out for her sake." Her eyes met Nico's straight on and she held his gaze. It was Nico who looked away first.

He slipped his fingers into his pocket. "I'll take care of the shipments. If you could follow up with that incorrect order, otherwise it's going to cost a lot more to ship and buy. I told her that myself." Nico got ready to leave.

"You spoke to her?"

"Yes. About the shipments."

Andrea's face fell. "I was hoping she wouldn't find out that I'd enlisted your help, Nico. She really didn't want you involved."

He rushed to reassure her. "Don't worry about it. I don't think she realized. The order quantity shocked her. Besides, you asked me to help because your shipping agent was charging too much. I've got a much better deal, and it will cost Ava less money. Between the two of us we're doing the best we can for our friend."

Andrea's face brightened up at this. She walked around the desk as if to see him out of the office but when he hugged her, she held on a little bit longer than seemed right.

"I'll be in touch, Andrea."

"I hope so."

CHAPTER TEN

"There's no need to worry about a thing. You're down for ten cribs now and they should arrive in either of the last two shipments." Andrea's cool voice tried to calm her down but from where Ava stood, far away in Denver and drowning in a cardboard sea of boxes full of infant bathers, baby backpacks and storage baskets, she was still worried about the imminent arrival of more products.

It was getting to the point where she was no longer able to see much of her floor. Products were stacked high everywhere.

Andrea's warehouse had been huge, maybe at least twenty times the size of Ava's apartment. What had she been thinking when she had placed her orders? Storage problems had been the least of her concerns, obviously.

She walked around in her tiny kitchen; it was the only area in her apartment where she could comfortably walk. There was no walking room anywhere else except for the bathroom and pretty soon Ava knew she'd probably have to start stacking some of her shipments in here.

"Thanks for sorting this out for me, Andrea. I'm feeling a little overwhelmed. I don't mean to sound so grouchy."

But I feel God awful, too.

"How's it going anyway?" Andrea asked, sounding full of life and her usual chirpy self, but it was late afternoon in Verona, and first thing in the morning for Ava.

"It's going really well." Ava tried to sound enthusiastic. She was overjoyed with the progress she was making with the new products, but mornings were not a good time for her. She envied Andrea's exuberant outlook and she imagined her in her huge warehouse, nestled out in Montova.

She missed Italy.

"I'm so happy for you, exclaimed Andrea. "I told you we had good products!"

The stock was moving; and it was moving consistently. There had been trickles of orders at first, with little spikes every few days, but over time these turned into higher order numbers on a more consistent basis.

"It helps that no one sells products like that over here," said Ava.

"Nico noticed the order quantity was wrong on the cribs."

Ava frowned. The question had been eating away at her since Nico had called to query the order size. "Nico? Now that I'm thinking about it, I did wonder why he'd queried it in the first place. I specifically asked you to do it."

"I'm sorry. It's just that the shipping agent I found was coming in at way too high a price. I should have checked with you first, but honestly, the only person I usually go to when I have business problems is Nico. I needed his help to get your products shipped on time and at a good price. Nico got a much better deal."

It might have been her mind playing games, and her oversensitivity regarding all things connected to Nico, but she was left with the distinct impression that Andrea's voice grew chirpier whenever she spoke of him.

Lately, it seemed that every email and phone conversation Ava had with Andrea, the conversation always seemed to come around to Nico. This was Andrea's doing, not hers. "It's all right. I'm sorry to land this on you. You're going out of your way to help me and you're already so busy with your own business."

"It's not a problem, Ava. Nico has been very helpful. We both want to make sure you get a good deal on this and that you get your products fast. We know how much it meant to you, to have everything available so quickly."

Quickly, being the operative word, thought Ava. *You have no idea how quickly I need to get this to work.*

She looked down at her clothes. She now lived in tracksuit bottoms and T-shirts, a far cry from her usual trendy casual wear of jeans and slim tops. Working from home was a lifesaver in this respect. She could look like a slob all day long and it didn't matter one bit. Her clothing was comfortable, with the elasticated waists. Perfect for her rapidly expanding waistline.

The more Andrea talked about her and Nico, the more it grated on Ava. The way she heard it, there was something more than just a business relationship going on.

"How has he been?" Ava asked, coming to a standstill against the kitchen sink. Despite her best efforts to remove the man from her thoughts, it wasn't working. She wanted to hear more about Nico. How could she ever forget him when she was carrying his child?

"He's been a great help."

That's not what I wanted to know.

"How are things with you and Connor?" Andrea asked.

"He's coming over on Friday." There wasn't much more to

add than that. "He's fine." The idea of casually implying, if only vaguely, that she was with Connor was starting to wear thin. She'd been trying to build up the courage to call Nico ever since he'd called her.

She hadn't been able to stop thinking about him. Even though she had walked out on him, he was still going out of his way to help her out and he was always there when she needed him. Unlike Connor.

It was obvious: Nico still cared about her.

Each day, her resolve softened and when she relived the passionate moments they had shared together, especially in Venice, she sometimes felt like jumping on a plane and returning to Verona. Maybe because of her hormones, or the knowledge that she carried his child inside her, she no longer tormented herself by sifting through his former conquests. These things had ceased to upset her.

Sometimes she dared to believe—maybe because of the baby—that she was more than a match for him.

"Things are good between you two, then?" Andrea asked.

"Who?" Ava's mind was in Verona, with Nico.

"Connor. I wasn't sure last time I saw you both. I was surprised to learn that you'd gone back to him."

I haven't.

Ava sank back further against the sink. "News travels fast."

"Nico told me," Andrea offered. Ava should have felt victorious that the news she'd intended to put about had gotten through to the person for whom it had been intended. Except that it felt more like a hollow victory than anything else.

"I mean," Andrea continued. "It was so unexpected. I really thought that you and Nico..."

Maybe it was better to continue with the rumor mill.

After all, Nico hadn't exactly come after her, or offered to explain the situation she'd found him in with that woman.

"You thought wrong. Listen, Andrea, I've got to go, I've got emails to reply to. You know how it is."

"Sure. It's been great talking to you but I miss seeing you. When are you coming back? It sounds to me as though you'll need to make another trip to Italy since your stock is moving so fast."

Ava tried to laugh the matter off. "It is moving fast. I haven't thought that far ahead. I'm too up to my eyeballs in packaging and dispatching right now."

Andrea said her goodbyes and hung up, and all Ava could think about was the fact that she now didn't want to hear any more about Andrea and Nico.

She quickly forgot all about Andrea and thought about Connor. Should she call him over tonight just to get it over and done with? The poor man was going to think she really was avoiding him when she wasn't.

Not much.

She was, as she'd told Andrea, up to her eyeballs in her work and maybe it would be better to have him over now, before the rest of her products made her home a no-entry zone.

She sighed and wandered into her hallway. She needed to work first and worry about Connor later.

She'd settled into a routine and her mornings were spent reading emails and checking orders before beginning the bigger task of fulfilling them. She would check each order carefully, write out a handwritten note to the customer, package the box back up again, and get it ready to take to the post office. Around late afternoon she would deal with more emails and queries and make any changes to her website. She was always looking to improve her copy. Later in the evening she would look at marketing opportunities, and try to see where to place an advertisement, and how to make her small marketing budget go a long way.

After this, it would be around nine or ten at night and there wasn't any time left for anything else.

She often felt the need to be in bed by nine most evenings. Her once slim and toned body had begun to feel a little softer and curvier; her breasts felt a little fuller, her waist a little thicker and her hips became more rounded. She was starting to fill out. At first she thought she imagined these things but as the weeks went by, there came a point when she could no longer fit into her bootleg jeans. She'd given up the skinny jeans a while back, fearful that she'd be harming the baby in jeans so tight they looked as though they'd been spray painted on.

Comfortable elasticated clothing was the answer. She wondered what Nico would make of that.

CHAPTER ELEVEN

Nico pulled up right at the front of the battered-looking hotel. He cast an uneasy glance toward his father, trying to determine his reaction because he knew the first impressions of the hotel were not going to sell it to his father.

Inside was even worse.

Even Ava had been surprised when he'd told her he was considering buying it. But once he'd begun to describe his visions for the place, for the spa retreat he wanted to transform it into, even she had seen his dream coming to life and she'd loved the idea.

Edmondo looked at it carefully once more.

"Shall we go in, Papa?"

His father paused and swept his gaze carefully around the white and black painted facade. Without a word, and displaying no emotion, he followed Nico inside.

There were two realtors this time: the one whom Nico had met on his last visit and an older man accompanying him. The way he carried himself, he looked to be the more senior of the two and Nico instantly gravitated towards him. This time he was armed with a longer list of specific questions. Since his initial visit he'd put together a list of problem areas that would give cause for concern if he went ahead with the purchase. He needed to get the asking price down by a substantial amount, and the huge list of problem areas would be his weapon.

There was a huge amount of work needed just to get the hotel to a proper enough standard fit for living. Turning it into the luxury spa retreat would require a lot more. But what this hotel lacked it more than made up for with its location near the sea and the available land that it came with. It had a lot of potential and Nico had a lot of grand ideas.

The younger man showed Edmondo around, and Nico knew that his father had his own list of questions. From time to time, whenever Nico looked over, he saw his father examining everything carefully: the walls, the doors, the windows, the paint, the woodwork, the brickwork. He skimmed his hands across surfaces, knocked on walls, stamped on floorboards.

The hotel visit lasted for well over an hour at the end of which the realtors slipped away and left Nico and his father alone. Nico was anxious to discover his father's opinion but he knew better than to probe for it; his father would tell him in due time.

"Well?" he asked, clenching his fists in his pockets.

They stood in the hotel lobby by the large reception area which was much larger than the one at the Casa Adriana. Edmondo walked about, scrunching his face as he carefully scrutinized the shabby interior decor. The lobby was not a great showing off point with its dirty walls and ready-to-collapse curtains on the windows.

Edmondo revealed nothing. "You were right, it needs a lot of work."

Nico nodded. He couldn't dispute that.

"And from the outside, very costly. The roof is falling, the brickwork is shabby, paper and plaster everywhere will need to be redone."

Nico braced himself. It was always this way with his father but this trait of examining everything with a critical eye had made him the successful businessman he was. He waited for the blow—knowing that he couldn't buy the hotel without his father's financing.

"But, it has potential. It has a lot of potential and even though I don't own any spa hotels, I find myself very interested in seeing how this venture turns out for us. I assume you've done your due diligence properly?"

"Of course I have," Nico replied, relieved. He'd pored over reports and researched the market and he knew that hotels were evolving. This would work—his idea of a spa hotel. It would work or he'd die trying.

"It's about time we increased our portfolio, son."

"Really?" Nico tempered down his rising excitement. It seemed that his father had given him the green light a little too easily. Edmondo took a few strides around the lobby. "It has a lot of land outside and that's always a good thing to have."

"It's a lot of money, Papa."

"That it is. We'll have to get our lawyers to look into the finer details and then we had better get started on the financing of it."

"It will need more money on top just to get it up to living standards, then we need to build the spa center itself, with the treatment rooms ..."

"You've done the costings? The analysis? The projected cash flow? Are the plans drawn up? Do you have estimates for each of the intended works?"

He had. "Of course." What else did his father think he'd been doing working long hours and well into the night? His father's face melted into a smile. "Then we had better go through them together and work out the financing."

A surge of relief flowed through him. It wasn't until his father had given him his seal of approval that he realized just how much of his hopes and dreams had been tied up in his father's final words.

"How soon could we do that?" he asked. He wanted to get started straightaway. By his estimations, and from what the architect had told him, they could have this up and running by November. It was April now. They had seven months.

"As soon as you set up the meetings with our bank manager."

Nico nodded. "I'll get onto it."

Edmondo placed his hands lovingly on his son's shoulders, taking Nico by surprise. "I like your vision, Nico. You're bringing fresh ideas to the Cazale business. That's the thing we need—your ideas."

Nico barely had a chance to soak in his father's praise when Edmondo's cell rang and his father wandered off towards the hotel entrance to take the call. Nico was left alone, looking around at the building they would soon own. This would be a part of the Cazale empire.

He walked around, thinking back to his last trip with Ava. He'd been eager to share his new dream with her and he had purposely wanted to see it with her.

That had been part of the reason he'd wanted her along. As well as to spend time with her away from the Casa Adriana, away from her family and his father. Alone, just the two of them. But he had made sure that a visit to Ravenna, and therefore to this hotel, was part of their short trip.

That had been back when he'd started to think of a future with Ava, when he'd envisioned her being by his side for, hopefully forever.

While he had known ways of securing the hotel, he hadn't been so sure about how to convince Ava that he was worth betting on. As things had turned out, he hadn't needed to after all.

She'd left him without even saying goodbye.

CHAPTER TWELVE

"What if you need to get to the toilet quickly?" Connor navigated his way carefully around boxes of nursery closet organizers as he followed Ava into her tiny kitchen.

It was small, and she didn't have a table in here for precisely that reason but at the moment it had more standing up space than any other room in her apartment. Not to mention that she felt more comfortable being in here than sitting squashed up on the couch next to Connor.

Her living room was chockablock full with packages, which had now spread out everywhere. There was only space for one on the sofa and there was no way she was sitting bunched up in there with Connor beside her.

She berated herself for not clearing up more space before he had arrived but she'd spent the entire day packaging up her orders. Judging by the emails she had received from happy customers, they loved her new line of stock.

"We haven't had a chance to get together since we got back," remarked Connor.

So you keep saying. Ava poured him a glass of Coke and

handed it to him and he stood awkwardly at the side of her worktop. "This is amazing." He gestured towards the hallway that was filled with boxes. "Things have taken off for you, haven't they?"

She poured herself a glass of milk and shrugged. Now nearly two months pregnant, she had started to suffer a little heartburn. She had never experienced this burning sensation in her chest before and it was another irritating symptom she could do without.

Connor looked at her oddly. "Milk?"

It helped relieve the heartburn a little. "It's quite refreshing." She leaned against her sink and automatically pulled her spine straight so that she stood tall.

Connor shifted toward the hallway and looked out at the packages piled up. "Are you expecting any more of these packages to arrive?"

"I'm always going to get regular shipments," she explained, worrying about the next one.

Connor scratched his head. "It looks unsafe. What if these boxes fell on top of you?"

She laughed, dismissing his comment even though he was right. The pile of boxes in the hallway was high and heavy and if it fell on her, she didn't want to think about the consequences. Especially in her condition.

"I'm extra careful when I walk around and they're selling quite quickly, luckily. It looks like a lot, but within the week, this pile will reduce. I'm going to have to order more but that's not really a problem because it means my turnover is fast. It's a good problem to have."

At least half of the boxes were already accounted for by orders that had been placed but she would need to order more stock from Andrea—maybe even make a quick trip to Verona soon. She'd need to do it before the baby came.

Connor gulped down his Coke. "That's excellent. I'm so pleased for you, Ava. You've achieved exactly what you set out to do."

Have I?

Far from it. The business side was working out but she had lost everything else she had ever wanted along the way: love, her soul-mate, and a contented, happier life. Now, with the baby coming, things were more complicated than ever.

No, she hadn't achieved everything she had wanted.

She drank her milk and felt the coldness of it take away the burn. "These new products are flying off the shelves and it's great they're selling fast but at this rate I won't have anything left to sell!"

Connor laughed. "But you don't have anywhere to put new stock." He placed down his glass and shifted toward her. "What will you do when your business explodes? What then?"

She hadn't thought about '*what then.*' She was too busy dealing with '*what now.*' The pregnancy books she read each night were her pointers of what to expect during each month of her pregnancy. It was only because of this that she had an idea of what lay before her.

A part of her hated that she was keeping her news from her mother. Elsa would have been thrilled about the baby, and worried about everything else. But her mother would have advised and guided her. By keeping her mother—and everyone else—out of the picture, she'd lost the excitement that came from the announcement of a pregnancy.

As far as her business went, she was so busy getting through each day, that she'd lost the long-term focus. It was all now, now, now.

She had started using Kim, her virtual assistant more often. Instead of just getting her to work through a monthly list of things that needed taking care of, Ava now needed Kim's help on a weekly basis. There were many emails coming through, newsletters to send out, statistics to sift through, product details to rewrite and images to touch up, as well as incoming deliveries to tend to and orders to process.

She couldn't do it all by herself anymore.

No wonder she hadn't thought about replenishing stock.

"I haven't thought of that." She hadn't spent much time considering the ramifications of sustained exponential growth. "It's too much to think about and sometimes I feel as if my brain will go into meltdown at this rate." She raised her eyebrows, but she was secretly worried. Thank goodness she was too busy to worry about it yet. As usual, she would deal with it when she was forced to.

"If I can help in any way…" Connor began. He stared at her intensely and she recoiled under the weight of his stare. She suddenly felt claustrophobic.

"Thank you but I can manage." Yet it was so glaringly obvious that she couldn't.

"You can use my garage if you run out of space."

Ava began to pooh-paah his suggestion, but it actually made sense and Connor didn't live too far away, either. Ten minutes tops in a car. She could use his garage for storing the cribs that were yet to arrive, as well as other heavy items. It would be safer to store them there than to try and make these packages stack up neatly and safely inside her apartment.

"That's very generous of you but—" She needed to know why he was offering this. Why, after the way he'd treated her in the past, was he being so nice?

"But? Go on, let's hear it." He sounded weary.

She sighed and pulled on her ponytail, making it go higher, since it was starting to slide down again. The only 'but' was her fear about the motivations behind Connor's offer. Saying it out aloud would be rude. She was fine with him helping her, with him being around, despite how their relationship had ended, but she needed it to be crystal clear that nothing else would ever take place between them.

There were times, like the way Connor was staring at her now, when she wasn't so sure that he completely understood this.

Connor hooked his thumbs into his jeans. "No strings attached, I promise. I'm saying this to you because I can see that's the thing you're worried about. It's written all over your face."

She could only nod, because he was right. She couldn't bring herself to utter a word.

"I still care for you, Ava, and I know we'll never get back together again but I'd rather have you in my life, as a friend, than out of it. I hope you'll at least let me have that." He stood where he was, not edging any closer to her.

She felt guilty. Even when they had traveled back on the flight together, he'd given Ava her space and he'd left her alone. Back then, she was sure he'd had a lot more questions to ask but he hadn't asked her a thing.

Maybe she could let him in, just a little. After all, she'd need to draw on the help of family and friends once the baby was born.

She couldn't stay a hermit forever. "Okay." She let out a smile of relief.

"Okay you'll let me help you?"

She nodded.

"I'll make sure the garage is clear and when your shipments arrive, you let me know and I'll move them over to the garage and give you a key so that you have access. We can set it up with a table and chair in there for you to do your paperwork, if you want."

Ava was overwhelmed. "Thanks, Connor." She clasped her hands together, only realizing now what a huge help this was going to be. Huge. She stepped toward him and gave him an awkward hug. Good to his word, he didn't hug her back, though he seemed a little taken aback by her sudden gesture.

"Don't you run anymore?" he asked, as the color rose on his cheeks.

She looked up at him. "Not much. Why?"

He shook his head. "Nothing. I just wondered."

"I don't have the time to do much else these days." She stepped away.

"It's just that you look a little ... healthier," he said with hesitation. She crossed her arms lower down, over her stomach.

This conversation couldn't continue. "Let's order. What do you feel like? Pizza or Chinese?"

<hr>

When the Chinese takeout finally arrived half an hour later, they plowed straight into it.

Having cleared a little room on the second couch and the table, Ava and Connor were able to eat in the living room. She was so hungry that she dove right in, causing Connor to look at her in amazement when she refilled her plate.

"I haven't had much lunch," she offered. It wasn't a lie—she had eaten lunch, a huge one with half a quiche and some salad but could happily have eaten a whole one. She'd always had a good appetite; it was only that her portion size was changing and she needed to eat more often. And if it weren't for the heartburn, she'd be eating a lot more.

"This was always our favorite," said Connor, filling his plate up high.

"It was," Ava agreed, overdosing on her Chinese cabbage and mushrooms.

The evening with Connor hadn't become the ordeal she had been expecting. They talked, and none of it had been about the past or their relationship. It had been relaxed and he had been easy to be with.

She told him about her business and her routine and he told her about his workload at the law firm. He, too, appeared to be a lot more relaxed than she remembered.

"I need some more Coke," he said, getting up. "Can I get you anything?"

Ava shook her head. "There are more cans in the fridge."

Connor made his way back to the kitchen and she heard the distant sound of her cell phone going off. "It's in here," he yelled, then carried the still ringing cell phone back with him; with a glass of Coke in one hand and the phone in the other.

Ava grabbed it from him before it stopped ringing and didn't have time to see who it was.

"Hello?" She heard a muffled cry at the other end. "Hello?" she repeated, sensing alarm immediately when she couldn't make out any words, only sobs.

"Yeeooow!" Connor tripped over a box, the corner of which had peeked out from the side of the couch. He went flying onto the table, sending his glass of Coke crashing to the floor. Coke spilled everywhere but luckily the glass didn't break.

"Damn it! I'm sorry, Ava. I'll clean it up." He got up and wiped down the spillage with the takeout napkins.

Ava had turned away from the commotion enough to hear Nico's words for the first time.

And that was when her plate of food crashed to the floor.

She felt faint, as if she'd been physically struck a blow.

"No, Nico. No! No!" She placed her hand loosely over her mouth. "I'm so sorry." The color drained from her face.

Connor immediately moved toward her. "What is it?"

But Ava turned away, clutching the cell closer to her ear. "Nico? Nico?" But the line went dead. He had hung up.

"What is it?" urged Connor. But his question fell on deaf ears. She called Nico back, but the line went to voicemail. The cell dropped from her hand and she let out a mangled cry as huge tears washed down her face.

A concerned Connor waited, unable to elicit a response from her. After a few moments she wiped her red, blotchy face with the palms of her hands.

"Edmondo—he's gone, he ... he ... he's dead. He had a heart attack."

CHAPTER THIRTEEN

Nico hung up on Ava and hugged his head.

Time had slowed down and he'd lost track of the hours since his father had died. Since then many people had come and gone but it was all a haze to him. People who heard the news, the priest, medics, his father's most trusted friends... all of them shocked to the core.

He sat in his office in the early hours of the morning, feeling helpless and very much alone.

The news was impossible to accept. His beloved father, the man who had guided him, supported him, chastised him, and done his very level best for him, had died.

This wasn't supposed to happen. Not yet. They had so many things left to do. His father had been looking forward to winding down. Not going suddenly like that, without notice, without warning.

Without preparing Nico.

It had only been a few days since he'd taken his father to see the hotel in Ravenna.

Edmondo was supposed to come home this evening; they were supposed to have dinner together. They were supposed to see the bank manager tomorrow. Life was supposed to carry on as normal, every day a guarantee. Every event in his father's diary was supposed to take place, in time, with his father there.

Life was not supposed to stop this suddenly.

Slowly, as the news got out, it shocked everyone who heard. His father had been fit and healthy enough. He went for walks every day in the gardens of the Casa Adriana. He loved his food and only drank moderately, but he seemed to be healthy in his choices.

He looked after himself.

And yet he had died from a heart attack.

The first that Nico had known anything was wrong was when the hotel driver had come running into his office screaming at him to follow him. Nico had leapt out and run into the gardens to find Gina bent over the figure of his father as he lay on the ground. Nico rushed to him and pulled his father's just warm body into his arms. He'd held him tightly, and cried out in anguish, knowing then that he was already too late.

It had been too late long before anyone got there.

But Nico still refused to let go of his father. Gina had stayed by his side, crying uncontrollably.

The heart attack had been too big, and his father had died alone, drawing his final breaths in his favorite place. But he had been alone. It was this very thing that saddened Nico as much as knowing that his father was no more.

Now, as he sat in his office, the world seemed surreal. That he now lived in a world his father no longer inhabited was hard to believe.

Red-eyed and trying to hold it together, Nico pushed away the thought that he could walk into Edmondo's office and never see his father look at him with his puffy brown eyes again. Or push his glasses up to give him that all knowing stare or ask a question or demand a report.

The emptiness in his chest hurt more than a sharp knife slicing through it would have. He'd give anything to have his father back and it tore him to shreds, the thought that he would never hear his father's voice or see his face ever again.

Once the mayhem of the initial shock had died down, he just sat, thinking about things. And he felt he needed to let Ava know. It didn't matter how things had ended between them; he forgot it all and called her. He *needed* to tell her, but telling her, telling *anyone*, that his father had died was so strange to him that it took him a while to say the words.

Hearing Connor's voice in the background smacked him into the harshness of his reality. He could no more go to Ava in his darkest hour. She had taken the news badly, and it was only now, a while after he had hung up, that he pondered the extremity of it. He had no idea that she had grown so fond of Edmondo. She had sounded distraught. Much more than he had expected. He'd sought her for comfort but she had taken the news badly and it sounded as though she needed comforting herself.

Maybe she was feeling bad for Elsa? Nico had come to learn how taken his father had been with Elsa, and the feeling seemed to be mutual. He knew Ava would need to pass on this sad news to her mother.

He was thankful that the last month of his father's life had been made happier by the arrival of Ava's mother. He'd not seen his father so happy for a long time and he would forever be thankful that Elsa Ramirez had brightened some of his last weeks. Elsa would find this news hard to bear.

He closed his eyes, his chest heaving as he fought to contain the sobs that broke free. For years he'd worked hard to prove he was capable of handling the Cazale empire. But this hadn't been the way he had wanted to have it. He'd wanted to run it with his father by his side.

Now he had to pull himself together for there was much to do. He had to make the announcement, he needed to make business arrangements, he needed to tell the staff, he needed to consult with the family lawyers.

And above all, he needed to deal with the funeral arrangements.

CHAPTER FOURTEEN

"Do you want me to pull over?" Connor's hand gripped the steering wheel firmly, but he kept looking over at Ava who sat holding a plastic bag on her lap.

"No." She wanted to throw up. The food didn't sit too well anymore and she felt it hovering around in her stomach, the threat of it spewing out ever present.

How could Edmondo be gone?

She still remembered his kind face and his warm eyes. He was such a thoughtful and friendly man, and he had made her and her family feel at home while they had been guests at his hotel.

He had pined for grandchildren and he had no idea that his wish would soon be granted.

Guilt ate away at her conscience and she felt more than a deep sense of loss; she was bathed in regret. Her heart strained at the thought of breaking the news to her mother. Life could be so bitterly cruel. First, it had taken her father from them instantly, in a freak accident. Now, just when her mother had formed a warm friendship with a man who seemed so ideal for her, life had snatched him away, too.

The pain of Edmondo's death weighed Ava down but the guilt of the secret she'd kept from him weighed much more.

Concern for her mother kept her, for now, from wallowing in the ocean of misery that she knew she would sink into once the truth of this news sank in.

"We're nearly there," Connor told her. Once again he had been around at a time when she had needed someone. Nico's news had broken her and she couldn't begin to imagine his pain. She thought of him, sitting by himself in the early hours of the morning and it crushed her even more. She'd called him a few times but he'd been unreachable. She had wanted to leave him a message but she was too raw with emotion to find the right words to say to him. She needed to speak to him, not leave a string of words for him to play back. She was desperate to comfort him and she longed to be with him again.

Her mind, when not wrapped up in the final images of Edmondo from their time in Verona, was filled to breaking point with thoughts of Nico alone. He had nobody to turn to, as far as she knew. As soon as he had given her the news, she had been ready to jump on the next plane to be with him. She needed to be with him. The fact that he'd called and told her meant that he still had feelings for her. Perhaps they still had a chance to salvage their relationship? To salvage something—at least for the sake of their unborn child.

The mistake she had made in keeping news of his grandchild from Edmondo was something she would regret for the rest of her life. She would take this guilt with her to the grave and she resolved not to make the same mistake with Nico. Her mind had already been made up—she was going to Verona and she would tell him about his baby.

Somehow they would sort out their problems.

Somehow.

She had no idea exactly how just yet, but this wasn't the most important thing to think about right now.

"We're here." Connor stopped the car and they sat outside Elsa's apartment block. Ava felt suddenly nauseous and stuck her face into the plastic bag. She inhaled and exhaled slowly. Nothing came out, but her insides lurched. Her heart began to pound and the cry she wanted to let out stuck in her throat. Unable to contain her grief, she started to cry again. Breaking this news to her mother would be one of the hardest things she would ever have to do.

"Hey." Connor leaned over and touched her hand. "Ava, come on. Do you want me to tell your mom?"

She dabbed at the corners of her eyes and blew her nose. "No, I have to." She wasn't good at hiding her emotions and knew that her expression would give something away, preparing them all for the worst kind of news.

They got out and slowly walked up the driveway. Carlos answered the door, all smartly dressed up. Rona's scream over his shoulder confirmed that they were likely dropping Tori off for babysitting; a rare evening out for them both.

But Carlos's surprise at seeing Ava and Connor together soon turned grim when he saw Ava's cry weary face. She said nothing but walked in to find her mother folding up the laundry.

"Hi, honey. This is a nice surprise." Elsa's easygoing welcome soon petered away as she stared at her daughter. She stopped folding the towel she held in her hands. She looked from Connor to Ava and then back to Connor again. "Honey, what's up?" But Ava moved to her mom and took her arm, gently making her sit down. The subtle hint of apprehension on Elsa's face turned to full-blown worry when Ava struggled to compose herself. "Honey, what is it?" Elsa's voice was tetchy and she clung to the towel.

"Mom," Ava couldn't hold back and through racked sobs forced out the words that choked her. "It's Edmondo, Mom. He's gone. He died earlier today. I'm so sorry." She burst into a fresh round of tears.

Elsa's face turned pale and she clutched the towel tighter in her hands. "Edmondo?" she asked, her eyes darkening.

Ava gently tugged the towel away and clasped her mother's hand, rubbing it gently. "Yes, Mom. Edmondo." She wasn't sure she was getting through, but the empty look in her mother's eyes told her that Elsa had understood.

"Can you keep the noise down?" Rona hissed, walking into the room. She shut the door behind her. "I've finally managed to get Tori—what's going on?" She stopped and stared at the downcast faces that met her.

Carlos shook his head, his face solemn. Connor spoke up. "Edmondo, Nico's father, died from a heart attack. Nico just called."

Rona put her hand to her mouth. She rushed to her mother who sat still, white as a sheet, with one arm rigidly around Ava, and the other clenched into a fist in her lap. She didn't cry or make a sound.

"I can't believe it. He seemed like such a nice man, too," Carlos said in a quiet voice, looking somber.

Connor let out a loud breath. "He seemed pretty nice though I didn't really know him."

Rona put her arm around her mother's shoulder. "Mom?" But Elsa seemed to be in a faraway place. Ava blew into her tissue again. Her face wet, her eyes veiny red. Her sister stared at her helplessly.

"Mom, say something," urged Ava but Elsa seemed distant. Ava knew how much Edmondo had come to mean to her. Elsa removed her arm from around Ava's shoulder, folded the towel and placed it by her side.

"Can you pass me some more, honey?" She motioned towards the laundry basket. Rona sat immobile and looked at Ava for guidance, until Ava nodded. Then she did as her mother bid. Finally, Elsa asked, "How did he die?"

"Nico said he had a heart attack. That's all I know, Mom. I can't get hold of him."

Elsa shook her head slowly, and her lips wavered. She clutched her hand to her chest as her eyes filled with tears. "He was such a dear friend." Her voice was so quiet that only the girls heard.

"We won't go out tonight." Rona shook her head at Carlos who still stood there transfixed. He nodded his agreement.

"You must go to the funeral," Elsa said, turning to Ava.

"I am going," Ava replied. It felt strange to her that she could sit here so quietly and be composed enough to think about and make plans for the funeral, when inside, she felt battered and bruised. "Why don't you come with me, Mom?"

Elsa shook her head. "It would be hard. I can't imagine Verona without Edmondo."

Ava disagreed. Wouldn't it be better for her mother and enable her to handle Edmondo's passing if she had some closure? Ava felt closure would come from going to the funeral.

"He seemed so well," mumbled Rona. "Didn't you walk about a lot when you went sightseeing, Mom? He was fine then, wasn't he?" Rona nudged her mother gently. Though it seemed to Ava as though Rona was trying to make up for the blatant show of disapproval she had exhibited whenever her mom went out with Edmondo.

Not that Ava had been any less to blame for the same behavior herself at that time.

"He was fine, full of energy. He was full of life and I

cannot accept that he has gone." Elsa sat with a pillowcase in her hands. She was composed, her face calm yet hardened.

"That's the thing about life," said Connor, finally taking a seat on the couch opposite. "You never know what's around the corner, or how much time you have left." It was the most profound thing he had ever said and it had never rung truer.

If Ava had known that this would happen, she would have told Edmondo her secret in a heartbeat. She would have let him know that the grandchild he yearned for, the one he had dreamt of playing with in his garden, was on its way. But she had robbed him of that news and she was determined not to make the same mistake with Nico. If anything, she had to forget the past and hope for the best for the future.

A sudden and sharp cry from the other room made Carlos rush out.

"I'll stay here tonight, Mom," offered Ava.

"No, honey, you don't need to." Elsa patted Ava's hand. "You go home and get some rest, you look tired."

I need to stay here for me, Mom. "No, Mom. It's OK. You shouldn't be alone." *I shouldn't be alone.*

Carlos walked back into the room with Tori snuggled up against his chest. "She's drowsy. She might have had a bad dream. Maybe we should go." Rona got up and gave her mom a hug. "I'll come by and see you tomorrow, Mom. We'll see ourselves out."

Elsa barely nodded and remained on the couch, as Carlos and Rona with Tori saw themselves out.

"If you don't mind, I'm going to lie down. I'll turn in for the night." Elsa got up and left.

Ava was desperate to go after her, but a shake of his head from Connor changed her mind. When Elsa had gone, he said, "You have to let her be, Ava. This has been a huge shock to your Mom."

"I'm sorry the takeout didn't work out." Ava looked at Connor apologetically.

"Don't worry about it. I'd better go." He got up and made his way to the door. He turned and asked her, "Are you all right?" She nodded, though she felt a million miles from being all right. He put out his hand and for a moment she thought he was about to cup her face, just as he would have done in another time, but then he hesitated and pulled his hand back.

She hoped he understood that things would never be the same between them again. But perhaps having Connor as a friend would work better than having him as anything more.

Connor slipped his hand into his pocket. "You were really badly shaken up back there." His eyes bore into hers and she guessed he was curious about her reaction to Edmondo's death.

"I knew Edmondo and I feel for Nico's loss." It felt odd having to justify her reaction to Connor but she knew he was in the dark and would not understand, especially as he had no idea that she was carrying Edmondo's grandchild.

"You're going to the funeral?"

"I must."

"But I thought you and Nico had split up?"

Ava stared at him. "Nico still needs me; he called me. He sounded ... broken. I need to be with him." She refused to answer anything to do with the split.

"Let me know if you want a lift to the airport or anything," Connor offered and then he was gone.

Ava closed the door and wondered what Nico was doing right at this moment. Of course she had to go to the funeral—for Nico, for Edmondo. She would be bound to them once her baby arrived.

They were family now.

CHAPTER FIFTEEN

Elsa had lain awake most of the night, her thoughts a movie replaying happier times with Edmondo during her vacation.

When the first streaks of light cracked through her drawn blinds, she cried silent tears at a new day, knowing that Edmondo would not see it.

Soon after, she went downstairs and powered on her laptop. She sensed that Ava hadn't slept much, either. Her daughter had got up a couple of times during the night. The only thing that had kept Elsa from checking on her was the knowledge that she herself was in no state to comfort her daughter.

News of Edmondo's death had numbed her and she'd felt as though her insides had hollowed out. She had felt emptiness like that once before but she never imagined she'd suffer such a loss again. Even though she and Edmondo hadn't known one another long, nor had anything physical happened between them, it was the depth of the emotional connection they'd shared that now made this tragic news impossible to bear.

When Ava had broken the news, in that instant, Elsa had been taken back to that moment, almost twenty years ago, when the policeman had knocked on her door telling her that her husband had been involved in a fatal car accident. That moment was still as vivid and as fresh in her mind as if it had happened yesterday.

News of Edmondo's passing had opened that void once more and she'd wanted to withdraw from the outside world. She'd heard her daughters, sitting on either side of her, talking to her, and she sensed their concern, but she'd already closed up, preserving her thoughts and memories.

It had taken time to reach a place of peace and to accept the cruel twist of fate that had taken her husband from her. But now this news about Edmondo, as raw, and as unexpected, had been too much to bear. The pain—like an open wound washed with her salt tears—was made even more agonizing because her visit to Verona had only taken place recently. Memories of her short time with Edmondo were still uppermost in her mind and each day when she read his emails, she felt him beside her.

She had never imagined this to be how their story would play out, and she was once again reminded of how fleeting life could be.

Now, flicking through the emails they had exchanged, a fresh sense of sadness fell upon her. Today there would be no new email from Edmondo.

Not today. Not ever.

This thought brought tears to her eyes, and she sat a while at the table, unable to open her email.

After several minutes had passed, she found the courage to make a move. She looked through her mail and started to re-read Edmondo's emails. Her eyes welled with tears that slowly stained her face. She didn't wipe them away.

One email dated less than a week ago, read:

Dear Elsa,

I have arrived back from a visit to a hotel in Ravenna with Nico. It's the same one that Nico took Ava to see when they both went away for a few days. That was around the time we visited the amphitheater. Do you recall we had lunch at that tiny restaurant where you loved the clams?

I am so proud of Nico. He has a passion and great ambition and he so much wants to show me that he can handle the business. I know he can. He had lots of ambition before, but he didn't seem to have that drive, that hunger, to succeed. He was content to take his time.

When Ava showed up, he propelled himself into the fast lane! He wants to prove himself more than ever now. He seems to be in a rush and now my problem is that he wants to take too much on. He wants to do everything. Buy this hotel, build it up into some sort of spa hotel. I can see his vision, I can see what he will achieve by the time it is finished.

You must come when it opens. It will be something to look forward to. Nico is hoping to open around November. My experience tells me that projects of this scale are always destined to slip. I believe it will open much later, and actually, spring of the following year is not a bad time. Would spring be more appealing to you? You would be returning around the anniversary of your first visit here. Perhaps that is an anniversary we could celebrate? And I would happily take you back to that restaurant for more clams.

I digress. Coming back to my earlier point, Nico visited this place with Ava—he said she loved it too. My son has been making plans, and I am certain he has your daughter in mind.

He might try to put on a front that he is working hard, but on more than a few occasions I noticed a more contemplative side to him.

I like to believe he is in love with your daughter and I feel we should do our utmost to see that the two of them realize how much they mean to one another, before they needlessly throw their chance away.

You have already told me how hard you find it to believe the story that Ava is back with that other man.

I would very much like to see this alliance move forward, not only because I know my son has never been happier than when he was with Ava, but because it might give you a chance to come back to Verona!

We still have much more to see.

I hope you are keeping well and that your neighbor has been keeping you busy. I do hope that you are slowly getting back into the social whirl that it sounds like you live in.

I'm tending the garden at my house. The gardener, I am sure, would quite like me out of the way, but I have a fondness for these beautiful growing plants. The lemon trees smell divine.

Fondest,
Edmondo

She read it a second time, but reading it now, knowing that Edmondo would never reply to her again, gave it a macabre overtone. Her chest heaved and her crying broke the early morning quiet.

Through tear-streaked eyes she couldn't help but read his last email. It took on an entirely different meaning now that he was gone.

Dear Elsa,

Did you find out anything more at your end about our twosome? Nico is so busy these past few days and I can't find the right time to broach the subject with him. He tells me the subject is closed, but I find that hard to believe.

How was your art class? Please do send me a photo of the next piece of artwork that you complete.

I have asked the gardener to plant more jasmine near the pergola. I know you like the scent and I am hopeful that at some point in the coming year we will meet again.

I refuse to believe that the one and only time we will have met was that one time you came to Verona. Life is too short and I'm planning on doing more of the things that make me happy.

When you next come, we can sit under the pergola with a jug of lemonade, and you will be able to enjoy the scent of jasmine in the air.

Fondest,
Edmondo

She was going to reply last night, after dinner, as she always did. But last night, everything changed. Even if she had sent her reply, Edmondo would have already been gone.

Time had ceased to move the moment Ava had broken the dreadful news.

A deep sense of loss stabbed at Elsa and she bowed her head, her fingers ready on the keyboard. Only, there would never be another new email from Edmondo sailing into her inbox. Just as she would never write another email to him again.

Quiet tears slipped and fell onto the keyboard. She was so consumed by her sorrow that the first she knew of Ava's presence was when she felt her daughter's warm hands on her shoulders.

"Oh, Mom." Ava's voice was quiet, threatening to breakdown afresh. Her daughter pulled up a chair and sat beside her. Elsa's sobs slowed down and the two women touched hands.

After what seemed like the longest time, Ava tried again. "Come with me to Verona, Mom. Come to the funeral."

Elsa shook her head. "I can't. I don't want to be there knowing Edmondo has gone. But you"—she took Ava's hand between both of hers, and nodded her head with certainty—"you must go."

She searched her daughter's face and saw how rough Ava looked. The news had hit her hard, too.

"Have you spoken to Nico again?" Elsa asked.

Ava shook her head. Elsa looked her daughter squarely in the eye. It had almost been Edmondo's last wish that the two of them would resolve their differences. She'd be damned if she wasn't going to have a hand in making them see the light sooner.

"I called him but—"

"That man needs you right now. You go and put things right between you both."

Ava dropped her gaze.

"He needs you, Ava, even if he doesn't come out and say it."

"I know, Mom. I know." Her daughter's voice was low and Elsa looked at her with concern. Ava looked haunted, dark circles turning her beautiful face haggard.

"Try to get some sleep, honey. I heard you get up during the night." Elsa's maternal instincts kicked in.

"What about you?"

"What about me?"

"I'm worried about you, Mom."

"Don't be. I need to grieve alone. I have a heart full of

memories of Edmondo and I will savor them for the rest of my life. But right now my heart is heavy and I would like to grieve quietly. You do understand why I can't come with you, don't you?"

Ava nodded.

"But promise me you'll make things up with Nico and settle your differences, whatever they were?"

Ava met her mother's gaze.

"Life is too short, Ava, and you don't know if you will have another day of it left, or another hour." Edmondo's words came to her.

"Okay. I will. I'll try, but I'm going to lie down now for a few hours."

"I'll make breakfast when you get up." Elsa shooed her daughter off to bed, and reluctantly closed her laptop.

Now that Edmondo was gone, there would be no pressing need for her to check her email every day.

The sudden emptiness cast a dark shadow over her.

CHAPTER SIXTEEN

Nico sat in his father's chair, in his father's office, at his father's desk, surrounded by the smells and the memories of Edmondo all around him.

He'd been doing this at the end of each day. Late at night, he would come here to sit and reflect.

It had been five days since his father's death; he'd been coming to work for the last three. There were so many arrangements to be made and he couldn't deal with things in the family home.

Family, on both his father's and mother's sides, had started to arrive. Many other friends and acquaintances also came to the family home to pay their respects and all who came wanted to sit and talk about Edmondo.

At first, it helped Nico to talk about this father but after the third day he couldn't take it anymore and he left his elderly relatives to deal with the other guests who came by. He could not listen to the same words of sympathy repeated over and over again, no more than he could tell every person how his father had died.

With each repetition, he found himself falling further into

the abyss that had opened up before him. The only way he could get through each day was to work.

After two days of moping around at home, he was grateful for the distraction of work. A long list of items that he needed to deal with was good for him. A gentle knock on the door caught his attention. "Come in," he said, a little annoyed. This was his escape, why were people disturbing him in here?

His voice and face softened when Gina walked in.

"Nico, I'm so sorry. Your lawyer has been trying to get hold of you; they've moved the meeting to next week."

"Fine."

"I didn't know how important it was. I'm sorry to disturb you."

"You haven't. Come in." His voice softened. The hotel deal was important and he'd had his lawyers go over the details of the potential purchase but the whole thing had now paled into insignificance. It could wait.

There had been many business matters to tend to, and contracts to go through as well as issues relating to the will. It was all too soon for Nico and he hadn't wanted to deal with any of this but the lawyers had been insistent.

That day when he'd taken his father to Ravenna had been the last full day he'd spent with him. He liked to remember that time, for it had been an occasion when his father had been impressed by what Nico had shown him; when his father had seen a glimmer of Nico's vision for the spa hotel.

Except that now his father would no longer be around to see when it opened.

"Have you slept much?" asked Gina. "Shall I get you some breakfast? A cup of coffee?" She wavered before him.

He shook his head. "Sit down, Gina," he beckoned. He needed someone to talk to, and he always felt at ease with Gina, as though he could tell her anything. Andrea had been calling him daily and had visited him on few times, but it felt like too much work opening up to her.

Now that he couldn't talk to Ava, he was desperate to talk to someone.

Gina sat down and kept her eyes fixed on his. She looked at him with concern. "Are the funeral arrangements all sorted? Is there anything you'd like me to check?" she offered, eager to be of help.

"It's all taken care of. You've been a great help just looking after the hotel."

She seemed to dismiss his compliments effortlessly. "It's an emptier place without your father." She kneaded her hands together in her lap and fidgeted as she glanced around Edmondo's office.

"I never stopped to think how much of his soul my father put into this place. Now it all feels so flat and empty." He looked around him gravely, his sunken eyes adding years to his gaunt appearance.

Gina nodded, agreeing with him. "He will be greatly missed, and so fondly remembered, and always loved."

Nico pursed his lips, his composure strained. When people, distant relatives or business associates, talked fondly of his father, it wasn't a problem. But hearing people he cared about talking of his father, the very people Nico knew his father was fond of, brought tears to Nico's eyes, as it did now.

It was another reason that Ava's gut-wrenching response at the news of his death had been so hard for him to hear.

Nico didn't utter a word, but his eyes brimmed with tears that threatened to fall. His chest hurt. He felt a huge void of emptiness inside. The only place where he found a shred of peace was in his father's office. He would ensure that everything stayed as it was, untouched, unmoved, exactly as his father had left it. He found a sense of calm just by sitting in his chair and thinking about things.

It was here that he felt his father's presence the most. After the silence had passed, Gina continued. "Silvia has been inconsolable. She came in yesterday, but you were busy in a meeting."

Nico's gut hardened. He'd bumped into her yesterday evening and she had done nothing but bawl in his arms. In the end *he'd* ended up comforting *her*.

"Are you prepared for the funeral, Nico?" Gina asked gently. He shrugged. It was only two days away and he knew that day was going to be the hardest.

The final goodbye.

He'd experienced the same when they had buried his mother in the family plot on the outskirts of Verona. In a few days' time, his father would be buried by her side.

He needed to be ready for that final day.

"Have you heard from Ava?" Gina asked gingerly.

Nico coughed, then sat up slowly. "Not since I called to tell her." She had called him back but he hadn't returned her calls. She'd sent him an email but he'd read it quickly and then dismissed it, not even bothering to reply. Shacked up with Connor, no more a rumor—it was something he preferred to forget.

"You know she's coming, don't you?" Gina told him. "For the funeral?"

Nico's face remained expressionless. His sunken eyes didn't flicker. "She is?"

Gina continued. "She feels very much that she needs to be here." He could feel Gina scrutinizing his reaction but even though the news came as a complete surprise to him, he managed to maintain a stoic expression. He closed his eyes then and for a moment it seemed he had forgotten that Gina was there. A few seconds later he opened them again. "When?"

"She arrives tomorrow, but I'm not sure. I've given her the funeral details."

Nico moved his back away from the chair and leaned forward, gazing thoughtfully at Gina. "Does she need the pensione?"

"No, no," Gina hurried to reply. "Ava told me she has sorted out her accommodation. She's coming alone and will be staying at the Hotel Cesar. Her mother is deeply upset and is unable to come."

"I see." He clasped his hands so tightly together that the weight on his forearms hurt. His father had spoken so fondly of Elsa, and Nico could only guess at her heartbreak.

Gina got up. "If you need anything, Nico, just let me know."

He blinked, dipped his head, and watched her leave.

So. Ava would be here soon enough. He wondered whether Connor would come along later.

As much as he was touched by Ava's devotion and sense of duty towards his father, he was still puzzled as to why she would come. He understood that she had a fondness for Edmondo but it surprised him that she was making the journey all the way to Verona just for his father's funeral.

He sat in his father's chair, alone with his thoughts.

CHAPTER SEVENTEEN

"Here, let me take that. You sit down. You're out of breath." Connor had parked his car right outside and they were moving the packages into the garage. The cribs shipment should have been here by now, but it had been delayed for some reason. Ava was starting to panic. All ten cribs had been sold and customers were already waiting for them.

She had hoped to have them dispatched before she left for Verona, but at this rate, who knew when they would even arrive in the US?

She sat down at the small table and chair that Connor had thoughtfully put out in one corner of his garage. Her heart was beating wildly. Just a small amount of lifting and shifting of boxes had her breathing heavy. If this was only after two months, what would she be like by the time she reached the end of her pregnancy?

And now, even though her sales had reached a new level and she had high hopes for the future, she found herself worrying about income more than ever. She worried about the time towards the end, when the baby arrived, and wondered how just how she was going to juggle everything: the store and the baby.

She had offered to babysit for Rona once a week and she looked forward to spending time with her niece. It gave Ava the opportunity to try out motherhood even though Rona often told her, gleefully, that babysitting was nothing like being a parent. Her sister constantly drilled into her that it was nothing like the textbooks described.

"Gina Ford? Yeah, good luck with that!" Rona had suffered, but she'd also had her mother and Ava to help her when needed, as well as Carlos, who was a great hands-on father.

Apart from her mother and Rona, Ava would have nobody. She tried to prepare herself for life as a single mom. Unless, by the time of the baby's birth, this whole baby situation could be magically resolved.

She was more determined than ever to tell Nico, but she worried about what his reaction would be. She missed him madly and thought of him more times than not; many nights she had lain awake analyzing their relationship.

If this tragedy had never struck, she would have returned to Verona anyway in order to buy more stock. And she would have visited Nico, for old times' sake.

But now—now things were different. Nico needed her. He'd called her hours after Edmondo had passed away. Maybe his feelings for her ran deeper than she had cared to admit?

Leaving Verona and rushing back to Denver had been the wrong move. Irresponsible and cowardly short-term thinking. It had been her flight or fight reaction. Discovering she was pregnant had made her irrational. She needed a good, honest, loyal man by her side and at that time, she had seen a side to Nico that exhibited anything but that.

It had scared her, the thought that she might make the same mistake twice. First with Connor, then Nico.

But time and distance had given her clarity. Something had shifted inside her and she had started to think that things were not as hopeless as they had at first seemed.

Now was her chance to fix it. Although the circumstances of her visit were sad, she was going to go out there and do the right thing. Or at least give Nico the chance to explain himself and to find out for sure—even though she had no idea how to go about it—whether his feelings for her were genuine.

She needed to know if she was *enough* for him. She had seen a tender and caring side to Nico; perhaps she could coax that out of him again.

Bringing up a baby without its father would be hard. She didn't relish the thought of being a single mother. She had experienced being without a father for most of her life and she didn't want that for her baby.

Sometimes she found it difficult to sleep at nights, worrying about these things and how she would cope. Now that she was preparing to leave for Verona, she had been forced to confront how much she depended on the help of those around her just to ensure her business ran smoothly. She'd had to think about all the tasks she carried out daily and it had taken a lot of planning to feel comfortable about leaving it in the hands of others.

The business depended on her, just as the baby would. She was frightened about letting people down and not being able to cope. Everyone had banded together. Nobody questioned why she was going to the funeral. Even Connor seemed fine with it. And they had all offered to pitch in to help while she was away.

She had worked it so that the final shipment would go to Connor directly. It wasn't ideal since he was at work during the day, but he had offered, and she couldn't really refuse. She had no better option. He'd spoken to his concierge and agreed to take delivery of just that one shipment.

Already today they had moved a few boxes to Connor's garage, in order to free up some living space at her apartment. Elsa had agreed to look after Tori, so that Rona could come over daily to Ava's apartment and then go to Connor's garage to package up the orders before dropping them off at the post office.

Ava didn't want to involve Connor in the nitty-gritty of the business. It was enough that he was allowing her to use his garage space. It wouldn't be on a long-term basis either. Just until she got back from Italy. It was clear that if sales continued at this rate, she would need to hire a second person to work alongside her, if only to work part-time hours.

She would need more help when the baby arrived.

For now, her virtual assistant would continue dealing with customer queries. Between the three of them, Rona, Connor and Kim, she had a network of people to help her just so that she could go to the funeral. A couple of weeks were what she had in mind. Nobody batted an eyelid at the fact that she was off to Verona. In that time, she would be able to restock her inventory, possibly look for other suppliers, not rely solely on Andrea, and sort things out with Nico.

That was the plan.

"You okay?" Connor asked, sweat stained his forehead as he came to a standstill against the table beside her. He had moved the packages from the car to the garage. Ava surveyed the space. Aside from the small table and chair she now sat on, Connor had completely cleared it out for her to use. She was utterly grateful to him.

"Where did all your stuff go?" she asked. From what she

remembered of the time when they'd been together, his garage had been filled to the brim with rubbish.

He winked at her. "I finally offloaded it at the dump yard, just as you used to tell me to."

Ava patted him on the hand playfully. "Better late than never."

"I'll say." He wiped the sweat off his forehead with a Kleenex. "Are you all set for your flight?"

Ava got up and stretched out her legs. "Pretty much. I'll get there tomorrow and the funeral is the day after."

"Once the funeral's over, I don't imagine you'll stay out there too long."

I will, thought Ava wistfully. *If Nico wants me to.* "I might restock my inventory, seeing that I'll be out there." Connor didn't need to know the real reason she needed to stay.

His face twisted. "Why don't you just place another repeat order?"

She didn't like that she always had to explain her actions to Connor. It irritated her, but it wouldn't do to let him know of her displeasure, not after all the help he'd given her. She was beginning to wonder if his so-called "no strings attached" help came at a price.

"Because I need to spend more time thinking about what I need; what's selling well and what new products *might* sell if I took a chance on them. I guessed at the first order and luckily most of it sold. Now I can buy larger quantities and I can also experiment with different products." She saw the displeasure on Connor's face and turned her back on him to move some of the packages around.

She didn't need this level of questioning, not when she had so much to take care of before her flight. Just the idea of leaving her business in the hands of others had her feeling anxious. But she was also nervous because she didn't know how her reunion with Nico was going to fare.

Perhaps reunion was too strong a word. He hadn't been in touch since he had last called, nor had he responded to her subsequent calls and emails. She told herself he was busy dealing with the aftermath of Edmondo's death but it didn't provide any real relief.

It was time to put Connor straight. She turned back round. "Look, Connor. I'm indebted to you for helping me and for giving Rona the key to the garage while I take care of things in Italy. I really appreciate everything that you've done."

He clasped his hands behind his neck and heaved out a sigh. "Don't mention it. Anything I can do to help."

She needed to put it out there. "Connor, I—" she stopped, fumbling around for the right words, the gentle words. For all his reassurances that they were just friends, she was never quite sure if he was toying with her. She had to say the words that weighed heavily on her chest. She had hopes for her visit to Verona.

"What is it?" he asked, crossing his arms and looking right at her.

"We have an understanding that we're just friends, right?" She looked at him and saw his face color. He hugged his arms tighter.

"Go on," he said slowly.

"Are we friends?"

He scoffed. "Yes. Yes, of course we are."

She wanted to add, "That's all we'll ever be," but couldn't force the words out. She got the notion that doing so would crush Connor, and yet he needed to know that she had no romantic illusions about him.

Why was she in this mess?

She should have just steered clear of his help. And yet she couldn't do without it. "I need you to understand we'll never be more than friends." Her angst had forced out the very words she needed to say.

His face turned a deeper shade of red. "I get it, Ava. You don't need to keep reminding me every second. Heck, if this is about Italy, you can stay out there for as long as you want."

She had gotten her message across.

She wanted to be free to go to Italy without worrying about Connor hating her for what might or might not happen while she was out there.

She wanted to be there for Nico, to be his support and backbone and help him in his hour of need, as he had helped her. Beyond that she only had hopes—hopes that when she told him that she was carrying his child, their problems would magically disappear; hopes that she would never have to worry about his roving eye, or the other women.

High hopes indeed. Because, when it came down to it, Ava felt drawn to Nico more now than ever since she'd returned home.

A man could change, couldn't he?

But she also had enough experience to know that reality often did not pan out this way.

It was the final dinner at her mom's place and Rona had come over too. Carlos had the afternoon off and was out with Tori.

Ava had already gone through her list of daily tasks with Rona and spent the morning, with her laptop at the ready, going through the order processing part. Rona had brought her own laptop with her and Ava had set her sister up with the different systems she would need.

Kim was out of the picture, still dealing strictly with customer queries and emails and that was how Ava preferred it. She didn't want her sister and Kim communicating with one another. She didn't need Kim to experience any of her sister's moodiness.

"You didn't eat much, Mom," said Ava, clearing the table once they had all had lunch. The two sisters exchanged knowing looks.

"I'm not hungry, honey."

"You need to eat a proper breakfast, lunch and dinner, Mom. Have you seen Faith this week?"

Elsa shook her head.

Ava sat down beside her. "You should try and get out a little, Mom. You can't stay cooped up inside." It worried her that her mother hadn't ventured out of the house ever since Edmondo's death.

Her mother looked tired, and her skin lacked luster. Ava was reminded of the time back in Verona when her mother had been poised on the steps of the Casa Adriana, about to venture out for another day of sightseeing with Edmondo. She had looked so much younger, full of vitality and vibrant.

That things could change so much in a month frightened her. It was with increasing urgency she now felt compelled to get to Verona. It wouldn't be the right time to have the conversation she and Nico clearly needed to have, but she was buoyed up by what Elsa had told her, of Edmondo's words.

When Elsa still said nothing, the two sisters looked at one another in alarm.

"Maybe I shouldn't go," Ava wondered aloud. She couldn't leave her mother here alone, not in this state. It was all well and good that she felt inclined to attend the funeral, but she was worried. Rona would not be able to look after both her mother and Tori. She had barely managed to get the afternoon free, and that was only because Carlos had a rare afternoon off.

Would Elsa be in any fit state to babysit Tori while Rona looked after her business? She shook her head, agonizing over the right thing to do.

"You go," Rona insisted. "You need to be there, Ava." Now that she and her sister seemed to have reached a better level of understanding and especially after Edmondo's death, Rona had been a pillar of support. At times Ava was tempted to tell her sister about her pregnancy but she knew that Nico rightfully had to be told before anyone else.

"Ava." Elsa turned to her daughter slowly. "Nico needs you. He might not have told you, but he does. Now is your chance to be there for him. Don't worry about me. I'm sad, of course I'm sad. I need time get through this. But, I promise you, I will come out the other end. We all will. We must. That's what life is like. When you fall down, you always have to pick yourself up and carry on." She got up slowly. "Now, who would like some iced tea?"

As Elsa busied herself, Rona squeezed Ava's hand gently. "Don't you worry about a thing."

Ava placed her hand on top of her sister's and knew that her sister was asking the impossible.

CHAPTER EIGHTEEN

T he taxi passed by the road that would have led to the Casa Adriana. A knot twisted in Ava's stomach. She opened the window and breathed in deeply.

Her return to Verona was mired in sadness and she felt an overwhelming sense of loss as they drove along so near to Nico's hotel. Tears started in her eyes. Being here this time around really did feel different. It wasn't only because the occasion was somber. Regret coupled with guilt stared her in the face wherever she looked, now that she was back in Edmondo's beloved city.

It wasn't only the sadness that encapsulated Edmondo's death for her, it was also knowing that Nico was no more than ten minutes away. So near, and yet so far.

This time her flight here had been relatively simple and without any of the drama that had dogged her the first time. Luckily, she hadn't been sick or nauseous on the plane either. All was good. She'd had time to buy a few stretch jeans and a smart pair of trousers for the funeral.

The taxi driver set down her luggage outside the hotel and left. She looked up dubiously at the three-star Hotel Cesar.

The name should have warned her off but she didn't want to spend money on hotels, especially when she needed that money for her business. She'd looked through some of the brochures she had picked up the last time she was here and found this cheap hotel. She'd booked it without worrying too much about what it would be like inside. Now she wished she had been choosier. She would be spending most of the next two weeks here.

If there was one saving grace—aside from the price—it was that this hotel was near the Casa Adriana.

She dragged her trolley bag through the single door. Grease marks on the windows prepared her for the interior.

Inside, the white painted walls and the dull gray lino on the floor confirmed that the place was a million miles from the luxury she had been accustomed to. She sorely missed the Villa Sagranosa. She had briefly wondered about asking Nico if she could stay there again, as a paying guest, but he had never responded to her calls, and so she had let the matter go.

A little while later, she sat in her tiny room. It had an uncomfortable single bed, a small hanging cupboard and a TV, with a small, but thankfully clean toilet and shower at the side. It would do.

She opened her suitcase and then decided against unpacking. Instead she lay down on the pokey, springy bed and adjusted herself. After a couple of minutes of fidgeting around, she realized she would never get comfortable on a bed like this. In defeat, she gave up and curled into a ball, lying on her side. It wasn't just the uncomfortable bed she had to get used to—she also had to mentally prepare herself for being back in Nico's part of the world and all that this entailed.

Her attempts to get hold of him had proved fruitless. In the end, she had resorted to speaking to the ever-reliable Gina. It had made for a pleasant change, speaking to Gina and through her, Ava learned just how devastated Nico was. The way Gina spoke gave Ava renewed hope that her coming to Verona now could only be a good thing. Nico needed her. Gina hadn't said those very words, but Elsa had, which meant she would only have heard this from Edmondo. Edmondo would have had Nico's ear, and if this was true, then Nico *did* need her.

Perhaps their first meeting wouldn't be as awkward as she feared. She was dreading the funeral tomorrow and she wasn't sure what would be worse: facing Nico for the first time since their split or seeing him heartbroken in his grief.

CHAPTER NINETEEN

Ava had arrived early, anxious to blend into the background. Her gaze darted around, searching for Nico, but she knew it wouldn't be easy to get him alone, on this of all days.

She waited alone, outside the church, an onlooker to the rest of the people who arrived at the service. She felt alone and invisible among the many who had gathered together, sharing their sadness.

Most spoke in Italian and she couldn't understand what they were saying. The melancholy mood pervaded the church grounds though she had, so far, managed to keep her self-restraint and hadn't broken down once. Not in public. But it was only a matter of time before she did because only she knew of her secret, only she understood the full significance of the sadness she felt.

She recognized a few faces as people filed past her and walked up the long path that led into the church. She knew Silvia as soon as she spied the bright blond shock of hair. Silvia walked past, tearful and with eyes downcast. She accompanied her parents and as the group passed by, Ava's eyes met Silvia's. Silvia smiled faintly, acknowledging Ava, who nodded back.

There were others she recognized, though it took a while to register where she had seen them. One was the hotel manager from the Cazale Riccione. He even smiled at Ava, looking as perplexed as she did when she could not at first place him.

When the hearse arrived and parked near the church entrance, there was a general commotion as people edged closer that way. The crowds were thick, and she was too far towards the back to see much.

With the service due to start soon, Ava followed everyone else and made her way toward the now crowded entrance. A light tap on her shoulder made her turn.

"Ava. So nice to see you." It was Gina. The women hugged briefly, and Ava felt a sense of relief at seeing a familiar and friendly face at a time when she most needed it.

The one person she had been looking out for had probably already gone into the church. Ava found herself shaking. It was only when Gina took her by the elbow that she felt a little comfort. The two women sat together, taking their seats a few rows from the back.

Only when she had settled into her seat did Ava see Edmondo's open coffin. The sight of him peacefully asleep in the open casket jolted her. It was not something she had been prepared for and it was just as well that they were sitting so far at the back. She could only just make out Edmondo's hair and she shifted her gaze elsewhere, not wanting to remember him that way.

The Edmondo lying there was only a shell of the man she had known in life and she preferred to keep her memories of him as he had been in life. Not as he was now.

His coffin lay on cushions on the floor at the top of the

aisle. It was draped with flowers all around and bouquets of flowers graced the front of it. More brightly colored flower arrangements were placed on steps leading up to the altar.

It hadn't occurred to Ava to bring anything with her. She had only just managed to leave the hotel on time, so fraught with tension as she was.

A feeling of sickness rose deep in her stomach, and she clutched her belly, praying for no displays or drama. As she stared around her, she saw that people stood at the back and along the sides, crowding shoulder to shoulder.

It came as no surprise; Edmondo had been a prominent and well-respected citizen known to many. Today all those whose lives he had touched had come along to say their goodbyes.

A lamenting tune played out and then a slow hush fell upon the congregation. A priest stood up and made an address, but Ava's gaze swept around toward the front, avoiding the coffin, scanning the people for the one she needed to see.

Her heart stopped when she saw him. Nico sat in the first row, in the seat near the aisle, and as he turned to speak to someone, she caught a side profile of his face. She couldn't see much, but it was enough for her to know that it was him.

She found it hard to listen to the service, not understanding a word of Italian. Every now and then she would stare at Nico, and then look down at her hands in her lap. She sat quietly during the service, wondering why she could feel no emotion here in the church, when she had been a complete wreck at home getting dressed.

It was when Nico stood up and spoke about his father that Ava's heart exploded and the floodgates opened. He spoke in English and because she understood every word, she could not hold back.

Gina's arm was firm around her shoulders, but Ava's tears still rolled down easily. Nico talked about the father who loved him unconditionally but who expected the very best from him. The father who strove for excellence and inspired him to do better for himself, his father the friend with whom he had found, only recently, a warm and easy camaraderie. And finally, he spoke of a man who yearned to slow down and enjoy his later years. It was at this point that Nico broke down, his hard mask slowly giving way to inner turmoil.

The last thing he said was that he knew his father had died a happy man, because his last few weeks had been the happiest yet. Ava struggled to compose herself and people in the row in front turned their heads to look back at her. Gina held her and Ava sobbed into her Kleenex, unable to still her sobs or her shaking.

"Ava." She felt Gina's touch on her arm but she could not stop the tears from falling.

"I'll be fine," she mumbled, barely able to get the words out. She wasn't fine. She was falling apart.

When Nico sat back down, silence fell in the church once more. A few sniffles could be heard here and there but none as loudly as Ava's. She was in pieces and she couldn't do a thing about it. She sniffled into her Kleenex, then got out another one. "I'm sorry," she whispered.

Nobody could understand her extreme sense of pain and not one person here would understand her regret. The grandfather of her child lay in that coffin. Edmondo had died yearning for a grandchild, not knowing that his dearest wish was so close to being fulfilled. Maybe if he'd known about the baby, he might have had reason to linger on. He might even have lived. It was irrational, she knew that, but these thoughts tormented her all the same.

Other people stood up and spoke lovingly about

Edmondo. They recalled their memories from when he was a young boy, to the grown man who had built up his hotel business. They all remembered with sadness the shy and lovable man who was so deeply respected by the community.

The rest of the service passed by in a blur for Ava. She sat, dazed and spent.

At the end, everyone rose and the coffin was closed and carried out of the church. People dispersed slowly, leaving the church with shuffled sadness. Ava and Gina followed too.

Once outside, Ava gasped, needing the fresh air to fill her lungs and to revive her again. Gina stood by her, concerned. "Are you all right?"

Ava knew she looked a mess. Her eyes no doubt red-rimmed, she wiped her red nose again. She nodded. She had gotten through it.

But now she needed to see Nico. "Thank you for staying with me."

"Don't mention it."

"What happens now?" Ava looked around her.

"They will drive out to the place where Edmondo will be buried, alongside his wife, not far from here. Everyone is welcome to go."

She couldn't face the prospect of seeing Edmondo's coffin lowered to the ground.

"You don't have to go if you don't feel up to it," Gina said, hurriedly. "I'm not. I'm late, and I need to get back to the hotel. How long are you here for?"

"A few weeks."

"Good. You must come over and see us sometime." She kissed Ava on both cheeks and left.

In the distance, Ava caught sight of Nico. Her heart lurched; her mouth ran dry. He stood in line, with a group of elderly relatives, from the looks of it, receiving condolences from the many who had turned up.

He looked so alone, so tired, so gaunt. She wanted to run to him, and yet she was scared to. A part of her wanted to touch his face and kiss away some of his pain, but he seemed so detached. Looking at him directly, she willed him to look her way, but he didn't.

He seemed lost, as if he wasn't really here, but a million miles away, deep in thought. She could only imagine a sliver of his torment. A dull ache thrummed inside her as she made her way towards him, slowly at first, unsure of herself, and then, as she got nearer, the pull between them resurfaced. She joined the others in line, who took turns to shake hands with Nico and his family.

She moved up the line, shaking hands, not really concentrating on who was before her, only preparing herself for Nico. But when she reached him, he turned around to talk to someone behind him. She waited, causing a bottleneck in the queue. The moment he turned back around to face her, before his eyes met hers, she saw that the woman he had been talking to was Andrea.

His smoldering, dark eyes met hers, his naked gaze seeing her for the first time in months. His eyes widened in slow surprise. But not a word left his lips.

Their hands touched, shook hard, felt warm, felt familiar.

She spoke first. "Nico, I'm so sorry..." Her words were barely audible, her mouth now totally dry. He clenched his lips together, then blinked, nodding his head. She longed to hug him, to touch him, to feel his touch, instead of standing apart as they were, like strangers. But his aloofness kept her from moving towards him.

Not letting go of his hand, she waited, but Nico remained quiet. If he had been surprised by her appearance, he didn't show it. For a moment she wondered if he had known she would be attending. His silence made her quietly uneasy.

It seemed like an eternity, but she couldn't break her gaze, or her hand contact. Finally, when she could bear it no longer, she took her hand away. "I'm sorry," she said once more, and moved on, shaking the hands of the others.

When the line ended, she walked away, only to feel arms around her shoulder from behind.

"Ava, you came."

She turned to see Andrea. The two women shared a hug.

"No Connor?"

Ava shook her head, and the two women moved apart.

"You came." Andrea repeated, but Ava had been so troubled by Nico's coldness that she was in no mood to make small talk.

She smiled weakly at Andrea. "How has he been?"

"Hard to tell. He keeps it all inside."

They faced each other; despondency settling in. "Will you be coming to the burial?" asked Andrea. "You can come with me in my car."

Ava winced. Witnessing such a thing would send her over the edge. This morning had been hard enough. She would have done it for Nico, but he obviously didn't need her around. She had expected him to be inconsolable. But she hadn't been prepared to deal with this level of aloofness from him.

What had she expected? To be able to walk right back into his life?

"It was good of you to come." Nico's sudden appearance took her by surprise. He stood, facing the two women who stood facing each other. He turned to Ava. "It means a lot to me that you did." His tired eyes had long lost the spark she had always seen in them.

Seeing his pain, she felt the urge to take his hand, to stroke his face, to hug him, but making any move towards him right now seemed inappropriate. "My family send their condolences, Nico. Your father was a lovely man, and he meant a lot to my mother especially."

Nico kept his hands clasped together low, before him, still holding onto the program from the day's service.

"It was because of your mother that my father's last weeks were so happy." Such an admission from him meant the world to her. That he had mentioned it when he spoke at the service meant a lot to her, too. Just standing there next to him, she felt him thaw out, just a fraction, and she held on to that tiny sliver of hope, that they could talk things over, at a later time.

"It's time. You should go, Nico. Your uncles are waiting." Andrea placed her hand on his arm and Ava was forced to look away; it hurt, to see the obvious closeness between Nico and Andrea. She saw that the hearse was waiting and that most people were already in their cars.

Nico turned to walk away, then hesitated. He glanced at Ava. "We are having a gathering at my house, after the burial. Please come."

"Yes, do come," said Andrea, and she pulled Nico away.

They left Ava standing alone as they set off to bury Edmondo.

CHAPTER TWENTY

"So sorry for your loss, Nico. We might have not been the best of friends, but we were never enemies. Edmondo Cazale was a worthy and feared competitor and a much respected friend."

Nico listened to Silvia's father. Vincenzo Azzarone and his father went back years. They were completely different types of businessmen, something that Vincenzo Azzarone now attested to. "He was a ruthless businessman, when he needed to be, but he had a huge heart. I admired that in him. He was a better person than I." These words brought a smile to Nico's lips. He was sure they would have brought a smile to his father's face too, had he heard them. While there was no open hostility between the two men, the Azzarones were ruthless in the way they conducted business and his father was on the opposite side of the spectrum.

Nico walked among the people who now trawled through his family home. It was not the norm to have huge gatherings like this, but his elderly relatives had felt that a coming together of some sort should be held. Edmondo was such a prominent and greatly loved man in these parts that it was appropriate.

As he wandered around, many people looked at him with sympathy, not knowing what to say, some hugged him and others cried. Some stopped and talked, needing to get out their words, and he let them. He listened patiently until they had lifted the heavy weights off their chests, until they felt lighter.

It was easier to nod his head and be present for the grief of others. Everyone had something to say about Edmondo, and all of it was good.

Nico suffered his grief in private, not letting anyone in. He didn't want to talk; he didn't want to be surrounded by all these people. He wanted to be left alone. His shoulders ached, and an overwhelming sense of exhaustion pervaded his entire body.

It didn't help at all that he had slept badly these last few nights.

He still woke up in the middle of the night. Sometimes, when he would come downstairs, half expecting to see his father sitting in the kitchen at the table, drinking his morning coffee and reading the newspaper. Or out in the garden he loved so much.

How could a man fill up a home, and a large part of his life, one minute, and just vanish, without warning the next?

Observing quietly from a corner of the room, Nico felt detached, alone amongst everyone. His heart was heavy and his body felt sluggish. He had gotten through this monster of a day in a fog-filled haze—as if he'd been walking through a field of glue.

Andrea came up to him with a plate of food, but he shook his head. She moved in close, gave him an apologetic look and rested her hand on his arm. "You should eat something." Then she slipped away, having taken on the task of looking after his guests: his father's friends and family who were now gathered at his home.

She was good at seeing to the guests and he was thankful for having her around, taking the burden away from him. All he had to do was be seen, make himself be accessible to people. Nothing more.

He scanned the crowds for signs of Ava, but she was nowhere to be found. He wasn't so sure she would turn up here anyway. It was better if she didn't. Touched as he was by the effort she had made to come all the way here for the funeral, it was time to move on. He couldn't move on if she kept turning up. Reflecting on what might have been was painful, and his life was already full of pain as it was.

Seeing her had lifted him, for a mere moment. When their eyes locked, she still touched him in a way that nobody else did.

He observed the people all around him; they seemed to be busy in conversation. He used this opportunity to slip away into the cool sanctuary of the study, a room his father loved and often retreated to himself. If Nico couldn't find his father in the gardens, he knew the only other place he could be. In here.

He closed the door and shut out the rest of the world. It was cool in here, and quiet. A much-needed respite from the cloying hum of chatter outside. He sought solitude. For a while he slumped against the door, holding it closed with his body weight. He inhaled long and deeply, until a light knock behind him shattered his newfound serenity.

His first reaction was to ignore it and he did, holding his breath. If he stayed quiet, whoever it was would go away.

Another little tap quickly followed and then the door

handle turned. He moved off and grabbed the handle, pulling the door wide open, his eyes glaring.

"Nico." Big, blue-gray eyes stared back at him, unsure.

"Ava?" A rush of blood surged through his body. He opened the door wider to let her in. Then closed it immediately and stood with his back to it.

They seemed like two complete strangers standing here in the cool quiet of the room; so different from the happy lovers who had shared such intimate moments together in the past.

Ava looked tired and it was obvious that she had been crying. It had been a trying day for everyone, but to know that Ava had felt that level of sadness today touched him. It was due to her that his father and her mother had spent precious days together.

She stood facing him, looking like a doe-eyed deer caught in the headlights. She kept her distance, a good step away, not daring to come any closer. There was a vulnerability about her, something that he couldn't quite put his finger on. The feistiness he had been so drawn to before had vanished. Like him, she seemed softer, more vulnerable. As much as he assumed she respected his father, this outpouring of her grief took him by surprise.

An uncomfortable silence ensued as they both appraised each other. Ava gripped her clutch bag to her stomach. "I'm sorry for intruding like this. I just wanted to know how you were doing." Her voice was soft, caring. He missed that.

Nico shook his head, dismissing her concern. "I'm getting by."

And I miss you.

He was reminded in this very moment of the woman he loved and had made love to in so many ways and for so many nights, not so long ago.

He'd dreamt of a life with her, toyed with the idea of

having her in his house. Little did he know that the first time she would come here to his family's home would be on the day of his father's funeral.

As she stood there wavering and uncertain, these remnants of past dreams flashed through his mind. She looked as though she wanted to talk and he sensed that it was only his reticence that held her back. He'd put up his guard, held back, forced himself to keep her at bay. He had to.

Things had changed forever between them; it wasn't just that Edmondo had passed away. Something deeper, more fundamental had shifted in their relationship. They seemed to have reached a point of no return.

"It was a beautiful service. The words you said about your father were poignant."

He shrugged, finding it difficult to say anything meaningful because his mind was in chaos.

"How are you?" she asked again, hugging her small clutch bag tightly.

"Taking it one day at a time." *If she really wanted an answer*.

A huge silence filled the gap between them once more. He wasn't making it easy but goddamnit, she hadn't made it easy on him. How dare she turn up like this, just when he was starting to move on?

"One day at a time." She ran his words back to him, but he only looked down at her and kept his gaze cold. He watched her swallow nervously and guessed at her unease.

"If I could change one thing, it would be that I spoke to you before I left that day," she began. She was taking him back to *that day*, when everything had changed, suddenly, inexplicably. One incident, with that troublesome journalist in his office and Ava had slipped out of his life, forever and without so much as a word to him.

It was a bit too late for apologies and explanations now, and it no longer mattered that there was so much unexplained between them. So many words left unsaid, too many things no longer worth pursuing.

She should have thought of those consequences when she made up her mind to return to Connor. There was no reason to delve back into those days long gone. Ava had moved on, and he needed to do the same. His world had changed and he would need to redefine himself again.

She took a step toward him. "Don't," he warned her, his voice quiet. He couldn't bring himself to look at her face, or to stare too long into those searching eyes because he didn't want her to see his truth: that he loved her and that he was still angry with her for leaving him.

She did as he asked and moved no nearer. "Nico, I know the time isn't right, I...I don't know if it ever will be but—"

Her wavering voice caught at his heartstrings and he lowered his head, his gaze settling on her face. It was a mistake, he could feel his guard coming down. He looked away quickly, choosing to stare at a point far away. "Please don't say anything." He didn't want to hear her words. Nothing she could say now would change a thing.

"We need to talk. If not today, then some other—"

"You've made your decision, Ava and I respect that." But the desperation behind her words piqued his interest.

"I'm sorry I left the way I did. If we could just clear things up."

"It's too late for that."

"Too late?"

He didn't answer her.

"Nico?" The voice came from behind, followed by a knock.

With his eyes still on Ava, Nico reached behind him and

turned the handle slowly, then turned sideways to open the door.

"There you are!" Andrea swept in and smiled with relief. "Ava. I didn't think you would make it. How nice. Come." She took Ava's hand and pulled her to the door. Ava looked sideways at Nico as she was dragged out.

"People are asking for you, Nico. It might be better if you came out for a while longer. I know it's not easy. Please," said Andrea.

"I'll be out shortly," he promised. Andrea tugged Ava along and led her away. As he watched the women leave, he saw that Ava didn't turn her head to look back at him.

He closed the door and slunk against it once more. As relieved as he was that Andrea had turned up when she did, his stomach churned at the idea of letting Ava walk away. He was drawn to her like a magnet. Fighting to keep her at bay was not easy.

She pulled at his heartstrings, the way she looked so alone and vulnerable. It made him want to hold her even more. Though he'd made it difficult for her just now, he was curious to hear her out. It killed him to be so cold towards her, and he badly needed to know why she'd left him.

CHAPTER TWENTY-ONE

"Have you had something to eat?" Andrea gestured around vaguely as she led Ava toward the huge dining room. Inside, an enormous table was laden with platters of food.

"I'm not hungry." Ava halted, not wanting to take a step further towards the table. She'd lost her appetite hours ago.

Andrea stopped beside her and then guided Ava out to the garden, where groups of people had gathered and spoke in soft voices.

She needed fresh air and the smell of food just now had almost made her throw up. She was still reeling from the iciness of Nico's behavior. She hadn't expected him to greet her with open arms, but she'd hoped for signs that he wanted to talk, at least.

He had looked anything but pleased to see her. If anything, he'd looked relieved when Andrea had dragged her out of the study.

She followed Andrea to a corner of the garden where they sat on an empty bench under the shade of a Morello cherry tree.

While she was happy to see her friend again, she was touched by a niggling bout of jealousy. Andrea seemed closer to Nico. Had it been that sudden? Or had she never noticed it much before? Andrea had mentioned that she and Nico had had a relationship years ago but had ended up going their separate ways. Ava knew the two of them kept in touch and that Andrea often sought out Nico for business advice.

She also knew she had done nothing to put Andrea right when her friend had questioned her about being together with Connor. Had Andrea been probing to see if Nico was available? Ava had never admitted to Andrea that she and Nico had been more than friends.

If Andrea and Nico were getting closer and rekindling their past, she only had herself to blame.

"I didn't know you were coming to the funeral." Andrea let go of Ava's hand and smoothed down her unruly mane of hair.

"Edmondo and my mother became good friends. He was especially kind to us when my family was here and my mom is still too cut up about his passing." Not that she felt the need to justify to Andrea why she was here, but she hoped that this explanation would suffice.

"It is a terrible, terrible thing," Andrea said quietly. "He went so suddenly and Nico said that when he held his father in his arms, his body was still warm. He feels guilty for not being there." The image of Nico holding his father tore at her. And the idea of the very private Nico telling such close details to Andrea sent her jealousy up a notch.

"I know how difficult his relationship with Edmondo could be, but he thought the world of his father." Ava's voice trailed off. Andrea gazed at her, a ridged line marring her brow. Had their once easygoing friendship been reduced to one-upmanship?

"It has been hard," Andrea conceded. "His family members are here, but they'll be gone soon. He seems to want to be by himself. Sometimes he talks, but I just let him be."

Ava swallowed. The dryness had started at her throat, but now her mouth was parched. The cooling shade of the tree was comfortable, but she was uneasy. Hearing Andrea talk of Nico like that jarred her and the knowledge that she had been complicit in helping the two of them get close, dug at her. She had done too good a job of convincing Andrea that there was nothing going on between her and Nico.

"How is he doing?" she ventured, knowing that the answer Nico had given her told her nothing about his daily routine but everything about him falling to pieces.

"I'm not sure. He keeps his thoughts to himself. He's still the same in that respect. I try to be there for him."

"I want to believe that he will be all right."

"He'll be fine," Andrea was quick to reassure her. "I'm not going to let him sink into depression. Don't you worry." She patted Ava's arm. "Tell me, how is Connor? How are your new products selling? I know we've been meaning to catch up on things. It's just as well that you're here now. Will you stay?"

Ava's insides knotted. It was a mixture of things. The notion that Andrea claimed Nico's well-being as part of her responsibility ate away at her. In addition, Andrea also believed she was with Connor. And if Andrea believed that, so did Nico. But she had wanted Nico to believe this all along. After all, she was the one who'd been feeding this line of lies to Andrea in the first place.

It made sense initially, when she'd panicked about her pregnancy and wasn't sure what to do about Nico—back when she had doubted whether he really was interested in her —but she wasn't so sure it made any sense now.

"I'll stay for a while. My new products are almost sold out, or will be soon and so I need to buy some more stock. I'll need to come to your warehouse again." But she had to find other suppliers and lose her reliance on Andrea. Who knew what the future might bring?

"Anytime. You just come over and we'll see if you can't find another container load of items to sell. It's great that things are working out for you, Ava." Andrea's smile reached her eyes and for a moment it seemed as though things were back to normal between them. Andrea moved in for another body hug.

This was the thing—Andrea was so friendly, so likeable, and such a good friend to her. How would she take the news that Ava was carrying Nico's child?

That was a minor problem compared to telling Nico that she was carrying his child.

The way Nico had treated her made her think that he wanted nothing more to do with her.

A va left soon after, not wanting to run into Nico again just yet. She had to rethink her strategy. While she accepted that today was not the right time to tell him of her news, she still wanted to talk to him.

She deserved the quiet disdain with which he'd treated her. The slight conversation she'd had with him gave her reason to think that her preconceived assumptions about walking back into his life were ill founded, despite what Edmondo might have believed about their relationship. Perhaps Edmondo had it wrong. She felt foolish for thinking it would have been that easy to restart things.

She had been hopeful on her arrival here, she had even

come so far as to think that all would be well after a few conversations, and that there might even be a happily ever after.

How wrong she was.

Nico had tolerated her politely, in the study and at the church grounds. He could barely put up with being in the same room as her.

It wasn't a good sign.

And now Andrea was in the picture; good, kind, sweet Andrea, who seemed to think she had a chance of rekindling an old romance with Nico. Could Ava really stand in the way?

She was confused and hurt and by the time she returned to her hotel room, she was so bone-tired that she fell asleep as soon as her head hit the pillow. Even the springy, squeaky bed, with its broken coils that threatened to jut out of the mattress fabric, had not gotten in the way of her slumber.

She'd left her cell off the entire day and didn't even bother to check whether anyone had called. All worries about her online store were second to her need to shut down and sleep.

CHAPTER TWENTY-TWO

"Thank you." Nico shook hands with Pelosa—a good friend of his father's and his most trusted lawyer. The old man returned the handshake warmly, holding on for a little longer.

"Your father was taken too soon, but he died a happy and proud man, Nico." The old man's wizened skin crackled with lines as he gave Nico a reassuring smile.

All too often now wherever he went, whomever he bumped into in the street, Nico was stopped by people who only had good things to say about his father. Then, as now, he listened and nodded.

But Pelosa wasn't done yet. "We met for dinner only a few weeks ago. He told me of the new ideas you had for the new hotel. He told me that you'd finally found your feet, that you might even be getting ready to settle down." The old man gave him a sardonic grin. "Your father said you were taking on more responsibility; he felt it was only a matter of time before you took over and he would be able to slow down within a year or two. He was proud of you, Nico. Don't ever forget that."

Pelosa didn't need to say all of this, but Nico sensed that the old man most likely felt it his duty to tell him of his last conversation with his father. It warmed Nico's heart to hear that his father had finally started to believe that he was changing in his ways.

"Thank you for sharing that," said Nico and took the brown envelope that the lawyer handed to him. This morning's meeting had been to deal with the possible financing of the hotel. Nico hadn't wanted to discuss anything related to his father's will or his estate, but the purchase of the Ravenna hotel meant that things had to move forward sooner rather than later. Without his father's help, Nico couldn't go ahead and buy the hotel. He needed to know how his father had settled his financial affairs, and only Pelosa could advise him.

Nico left the lawyer's offices alone, and was once again reminded of how he always came here with his father, never by himself. Yet another thing he had to get used to.

He had only buried his father less than a week ago and getting back into daily life, as though everything were back to normal, felt wrong. He felt guilty for carrying on with life in the wake of his father's death.

But he *had* to move forward. He had to stay on the hamster wheel. He had no choice in the matter. The hotel had to be run and managed, just as the other Cazale hotels needed to be overseen. The weekly conference calls still needed to happen. Staff and resource issues needed handling; lawyers, accountants and bank managers still needed information from him. Even on the days when he felt he couldn't face the world, he still had to get up and carry on.

After the funeral, he had allowed himself a day away from work, holed up at home. Nobody visited, and the phone had finally stopped ringing. Gina had ordered him to stay away for the rest of the week, but as head of the Cazale group now, he couldn't just disappear.

Never had he felt the weight of so much responsibility so fully on his shoulders.

The next day he returned to work, much to Gina's annoyance, and he hit the ground running for there had been a glut of things to catch up on. If it hadn't been for Gina, he would have been even more behind.

He had her in mind to train up and become a leading member of his team. She was way too good to be simply heading up the reception desk. She pretty much took care of everything else that he couldn't do. She had become his right-hand person without him giving her the relevant title, status, or salary. It was time he made that up to her; send her on a few management courses and invest in her by offering her training.

Without Gina, he would have drowned. He recalled a conversation with her a few days ago when he'd casually mentioned that Ava had been at the funeral and later at his house, and Gina had, just as casually, mentioned that she would be here for a few more weeks.

Now, as he made his way to a meeting at the bank with the bank manager, his thoughts turned to Ava again. The Hotel Cesar was along the way. He'd been looking out for her when he was back at work but now that he stopped to think about it, why would she suddenly appear at the Casa Adriana? Especially when he had been so mean to her?

He turned left at the crossing instead of right. Hardwired to follow tracks leading to her; she'd been on his mind from the moment he'd set eyes on her. Pushing thoughts of her away hadn't worked and, just like that, while waiting at the traffic light, he turned in the direction of her hotel.

He could turn up casually, to see how she was. She'd been

good enough to fly all this way for his father's funeral; he could make up for his coldness towards her by at least asking her how she was. They had history. They shared a past that was getting harder to bury.

He turned into the stark, ugly car park in front of the cheap and cheerful Hotel Cesar and shuddered. This concrete jungle of a hotel looked onto a main road. It was a two-star hotel that had been given one star too many.

The idea that Ava was staying here horrified him. He couldn't understand why anyone would. Least of all her. Sure, it cost less, and she wasn't about to ask him for the keys to the pensione, even though he knew she would demand to pay for her keep. No doubt her pride was what made her stay at a place like this. That and probably money going into her business. He shook his head, knowing how easily he could have helped her.

Now that he was here, a ball of excitement began to grow inside him. He had mixed feelings about seeing her again. Being cold towards her, knowing he'd hurt her, hurt him. But he'd been in a different space on the day of the funeral and being distant towards her had not been hard to do.

It was only now, when he looked back on it all, that he regretted his actions. Especially considering how upset she'd been on that day. She'd come all the way over here for the funeral.

That meant a lot to him, even if they no longer had a future together. Still, that didn't thwart the rush of excitement he now felt rising within him as he sat in the car, looking at the hideous double-story building in front of him. His breath quickened. It was no later than ten in the morning and he hoped to catch her before she headed out. Andrea had mentioned that Ava would be coming to her warehouse to restock her inventory. Blood rushed through his veins, kickstarting the anticipation which, until now, he'd held in check. When his cell rang, he quickly answered it, hoping to put paid to the call quickly so that he could rush out to see Ava.

A male voice at the other end mumbled something. It was his American accent that gave it a hint of familiarity and it startled Nico into paying attention. He sat back in his seat and took his hand off the car handle.

"Hello? Hello? Is that Nico?" The voice was loud and slightly arrogant. But it was undeniably a voice he knew well.

"Yes." Nico frowned. "Connor, isn't it?" He closed his eyes and rested his elbow against the window.

"Sorry to call you like this." As Connor spoke, Nico wondered where he'd gotten his number from. "I rang the hotel and Gina gave me your number."

That explained it. Nico kept his eyes closed and listened patiently as Connor droned on apologetically.

"I'm really sorry to hear about your dad, man. Too sad. He seemed a real gentleman."

Nico then drummed his index finger along his forehead, tapping away the tension. "It's been a difficult time."

"Yeah, of course. Hey, I've been trying to get a hold of Ava, and I didn't know who else to ask, but could you tell her the cribs have arrived but there's a problem. Customs won't release them. They won't deal with me because, apparently, they need to speak to the purchaser. It has your name on the paperwork and not getting hold of Ava I thought I'd ask you."

Nico opened his eyes slowly. "I'll take care of it." He balled up his hand and lightly punched the soft leather upholstery of the door. His excitement had deflated soon after Connor's "hello."

"That would be great. It's just that we're storing them in

the garage, and I'd gone to take delivery. Ava needed to get these out to her customers as a priority."

"No problem. Leave it with me."

Connor hung up and Nico flipped his cell shut.

Andrea had already told him that Ava was back with Connor. Hell, everything after she left had pointed to the same fact.

He *knew* it, but he'd wanted to see her. He needed to hear it from her, to be sure. This reminder from Connor, so timely, was a sign for him to back off.

She was not his to have any more.

He started the ignition, and his car growled out of the carpark.

He would be early for his meeting at the bank.

CHAPTER TWENTY-THREE

A victorious feeling engulfed Ava as she finished transposing her sales figures into her spreadsheet. Things were looking up, up, and up. Sales were healthy and hadn't slackened off, as she had feared.

She was excited and happy. She needed to order more stock to build on the growing momentum and she hadn't heard from Kim, Rona or Connor, and therefore assumed that all was well back at the fort.

This morning she'd been holed up again in the cafe across the road from her hotel. The cafe had Wi-Fi and decent enough food: the two staples that would keep her going. She'd been here for the past three days, on and off, working on her business and then hopping back to her hotel when she needed to take a break. In the afternoons she found herself nodding off after lunch.

Working hard meant she didn't have to think too much about Nico or worry about how to approach him but, as time went by, she became less sure of how to deliver the news he deserved to hear.

She'd played out so many times in her head how it would

go. She'd even prepared herself for dealing with him being cold and distant towards her but no enactments of such scenarios in her mind really prepared her for being able to deal with the ultimate worst situation: What if she told him and he still treated her coldly? She wouldn't be able to handle that.

Her pregnancy was hardly showing, but she felt fuller all around. No more did her waist feel slim, and her stomach flat and lean. There was still no visible bump yet, but her body had turned soft and fleshy: full, blooming, and rotund. In a few months there would be no denying the fact that she was pregnant.

The ticking time bomb hung over her, coloring her every move.

With Edmondo's funeral over, she was left on the edge of No Man's Land—not sure what to do with her time, not wanting to do the things she had to do. In trying to figure out *what* to do, she had ended up dealing with tasks that she had put off while planning to come here—looking through the sales orders, crunching her figures and analyzing her statistics.

She'd also caught up on Kim's emails. According to Kim there had been no complaints about the new products. Quite the contrary, many of her customers had emailed to express their happiness with their new purchases.

This morning she'd had a look through her inventory to see what stock needed to be replenished. It was time to go to Montova, back to Andrea's warehouse, but she'd put that off until tomorrow because it would mean having to listen to Andrea go on about Nico.

A fleeting thought of visiting the Casa Adriana tempted her; she could walk there easily, if only to sit in the spacious and airy conservatory. She missed the Casa Adriana with its ambiance and its genteel sense of old elegance. She imagined that now it would be all the emptier because of Edmondo's passing.

Having crossed off half the items on her to-do list, she packed up her laptop and walked back to her shoddy hotel room. Now that she was used to it, it didn't seem as bad as it had at first. She had even figured out how get a better night's sleep by placing a folded-up towel over the part of the mattress where the spring coils bumped out.

As soon as she entered her room, the flashing light on her cell grabbed her attention. She'd forgotten her phone here in the morning and as a result she'd had a few uninterrupted hours without it. But now she saw that Connor had called her a couple of times. Only Connor—nobody else. She listened to the voicemail message and on hearing his panic due to some customs problem, she called him right back. It was late, almost two in the morning at his end.

Wearily she sat on the edge of the bed with her elbows on her knees. "Hey, Connor. What's this about the cribs and customs?" She was aware of how much this call was going to cost her, so brevity was of utmost importance.

"Sorry, I didn't mean to alarm you. I've spoken to Nico and he's going to take care of it."

Ava froze as he spoke. "You spoke to Nico?"

"I had to when I couldn't get hold of you," Connor replied defensively, no doubt reacting to the irritation in her voice. "You said the cribs were a priority."

She backtracked. "Yes, they are. Thanks. What did Nico say?"

"Who?"

"Nico."

Connor scratched his chin. "He said to leave it with him and that he'd deal with it. Can you let me know when the problem is cleared up so that I can pick them up and take them to the garage? I hope it's this week but I'm away on a conference next week."

Damn it. Ava scrubbed her forehead. She couldn't have a bottleneck in her delivery process. Connor carried on. "Rona's beside herself. She says that the customers are screaming out for their orders."

Ava rolled her eyes. It was typical of Rona to exaggerate. From her own experience customers didn't mind waiting if they knew when the products were likely to be dispatched. A couple of courtesy emails to them would soon alleviate their anxiety. But Rona was not to know this because Ava had shared the work processes out. She had given each of the—Rona, Kim and Connor—little pieces to do when the whole conveyor line should have worked together in harmony. Having work split out like this was asking for trouble, but she had no choice. She'd had to leave things quickly and it was the best working scenario she'd come up with at the last minute.

Maybe it was time to return home.

"Thanks, Connor. I'm so grateful to you for dealing with this for me." He was going out on a limb for her. The man had corporate law responsibilities to take care of, and the fact that he was going out of his way to help her, wasn't to be taken lightly.

"I'm glad I could help. Are you all right? You seem a little down. If you're worried about this stuff, don't be. We've got it all under control here." Connor's comforting voice soothed her, and then it left her feeling sorry for herself.

"I'm fine," she replied, her voice wavering, because she felt anything but fine. "I have complete faith in you guys and I know I owe you big time."

"Don't worry about it. Just let me know as soon as the custom clearance problem is fixed. Like I said, I'd like to get these picked up in the next few days."

She assured him that she'd get on the case, made more small talk, and hung up. And then, she buried her face in her hands. Her opportunity had come sooner than she'd anticipated.

It was time to go to the Casa Adriana and face Nico. Maybe she would go later this evening. Maybe they would end up having dinner together.

Anything was possible.

CHAPTER TWENTY-FOUR

No sooner had he made the call, than Nico regretted it. Andrea had happily accepted.

After the support and help she'd given him lately, he'd feel a total bastard if he canceled on her now. Just because they had been lovers once, a long time ago, didn't mean they couldn't be good friends.

He ripped off his tie as he paced around his office.

The meeting with the bank manager had gone well. All his meetings and business dealings usually did. Now Nico understood just how much weight the Cazale name carried. His father had been an honorable man who had conducted business ethically. He never rode rough shod over anyone and in return he had garnered the deep respect of all the people he'd had dealings with.

It was from this very respect for his father that Nico now reaped the benefits.

His father had handled the bigger things, but out of necessity Nico had had to take over. With his father's death uppermost in most people's minds, Nico was treated with a mixed sense of reverence and empathy wherever he went.

He hoped to continue in his father's footsteps.

Irritation chewed at his insides as he flung his tie onto his chair. Connor's conversation had played on his mind and he was anxious to clear up the problem at customs. Calling Andrea just before his meeting at the bank to confirm a few details, he'd acted on the spur of the moment.

He'd asked her out to dinner.

He'd detected a hint of surprise in her reply and it had made him instantly regret his offer. While he didn't want her to get the wrong idea—because he didn't want to hurt her—he also needed to get his mind off Ava. This had been the underlying reason for him asking Andrea out.

He had spent the last month trying to forget Ava but goddammit if the woman didn't keep turning up when he least expected it.

That draw towards her, the one he had almost succumbed to, was still too strong. Even now, after she had left him cold, without an explanation, and returned to her ex, she still managed to reel him in. The worst part of it? She never had to do anything. He went running to her at every opportunity.

The call from Connor had promptly put him in his place. Now he needed to stay there. What better way would there be to do this than to go out for a simple, no strings attached dinner with a good friend?

It had been a long day of meetings and the huge backlog of business matters to deal with had worn him down. Dinner and some company would be a good distraction.

He estimated that he had half an hour to get home, shower and then meet Andrea at their favorite restaurant. He tutted. Maybe he should have picked somewhere different, a more neutral place without the memories. He didn't want her to get the wrong idea.

Roughing his hand across his hair, he decided to leave the

office now. He yanked the door handle in frustration but his eyebrows lifted to find Ava standing on the other side, equally as shocked to see him as he was to see her.

Her closed fist, poised in mid-air for the knock, remained suspended, until she withdrew her hand quickly.

Looking at her standing to close to him took his breath away. The split-second feeling of sweet surprise quickly turned to bitterness as he remembered his resolve to forget her.

They stared at each other and he didn't know what to say. He knew what he *longed* to say, and do, but he was determined to be strong, to look unaffected, even though his insides were in turmoil. "I was just leaving," he said, making an apologetic start and hoping that she would take the hint.

Disappointment framed her face, and she moved her hand to her handbag.

Standing so close to her he detected the slightest hint of the flowery scent she wore; the one he knew so well. The one he smelled on her when he'd loved her all over, when he'd explored every curve and orifice of her body, when he'd taken his sweet time tasting every last inch of her.

These things were not so easy to wipe clean from his memory.

"Oh." She sounded disappointed. "I was hoping we could talk."

He stepped backwards to distance himself from the smell of her perfume. This time she appeared to be a little more determined, a little less vulnerable than the last. By stepping backwards, he'd given her permission to enter, and she did. She swept past him like a woman with a mission.

He tried again, leaving the door open, with his hand resting on the handle, getting ready to leave himself. "I really can't stay long. I've got a ... meeting."

Somehow, telling her he had a dinner date with Andrea didn't seem right. He would have given anything to have had the dinner date with Ava instead. But he forced himself to shake that thought right out of his mind before it took a hold and brought him more misery. Frustrated by the obvious effect she still had on him, he promised himself to listen to her for a minutes only.

"Connor said he spoke to you," she said, speaking softly.

"Yes. It's all taken care of." He opened the door wider. *Better to get out now while he could.*

"Thank you. Do I owe you anything? Was there a cost involved?" She seemed ready to delve into her bag and this riled him up further. With Ava it was always about settling the score and being equal. About not having to owe him anything. If his hopes had been raised when she'd told him she wanted to talk to him, they'd just come crashing to the ground.

He waved his hand dismissively, irritation seeping from his skin. "No. They needed a signature, that's all." He glanced at his watch. He now had ten minutes less to get home and shower.

Ava didn't move. "Thank you, anyway. I'm sorry Connor called you—"

"As I said, it doesn't matter. I really must go."

His sharp tone slammed into her at the same time as it crushed him to be so callous towards her. He told himself it was only for the good of them both.

"This isn't a good time, is it?" she asked softly just as his cell rang. He answered it immediately and watched Ava's face as she looked away. She stared toward the window, a faraway look settling over her face. Andrea spoke at the other end, telling him she was already at the restaurant, having arrived a little early.

He hesitated before answering, but Ava had already turned towards him. She whispered, "Sorry," before slipping away. By the time he answered Andrea, it was already too late to stop Ava's hurried exit.

Goddammit.

He didn't want her to jump to the wrong conclusion, and yet it would help him with his quest.

Then why did it hurt so much?

He slammed the door behind him and stormed out to get ready for the dinner he no longer wanted, with a woman he no longer cared for.

CHAPTER TWENTY-FIVE

A va fought back the suffocating breaths that came short and fast.

She had to get as far away from Nico as she could. After leaving his office, she didn't wait around for a taxi or risk the walk back to her hotel, knowing that he might see her on his way out to meet *a woman*.

Her hopes had been crushed the moment she'd heard the faint soft tones of a woman's voice on his cell. She'd wanted to vanish into the air there and then.

And it had taken all her might to hold on and display a calm exterior she didn't really feel.

The idea that he was cutting her short to meet another woman devastated her as much as the fact that he had no time to listen to her anymore.

Deep, satisfying love had given way to loathing.

Could she blame him?

If there was anyone to blame for this mess, it was herself and now she was paying the price for her stupid strategy, not just of running back to Denver but of also trying to make him believe—as he clearly seemed to—that she was back with Connor.

This cruel world sucked.

She'd been silly to stay here after Edmondo's funeral. She would have saved herself a lot of painful humiliation if she'd returned home soon after. Why had she even thought that Nico would be remotely interested in her?

This man could have any woman he wanted. He didn't care for her. He had moved on. She'd been wrong to think that telling him of their child would be the glue that would fix things and help them get back together again.

Anger took over, and she now seethed with the pain of humiliation because of the way he couldn't wait to get away from her.

It colored her thinking. If she returned home now without telling him, could she live with the secret forever? Just as she had come to regret leaving in a rush the last time, she didn't want to make the same mistake again.

Or did she?

Would she be able to look her child in the eye in later years when he or she asked about his or her father? It was one thing to tell her child the father didn't want to know. But if she kept the father in the dark, could she look her child in the eye and say anything then?

She had to decide. Tell Nico no matter what, or hide the truth from him forever and sever all ties. Right now, she felt like doing the latter, but she owed it to her unborn child to try harder.

Her strategizing occupied her mind and in her desire to avoid Nico outside, she hung around the hotel, ending up in the airy lightness of the conservatory which was in stark contrast to the dark mood that enveloped her.

Her stomach rumbled and having a bite to eat in this

lovely room won over. The waiters recognized her and she smiled and exchanged pleasant small talk with them. Ordering the seafood pasta, she excitedly looking forward to the heavenly cooking of the Casa Adriana kitchens which were a far cry from the plastic panino she'd been having from the cafe near her hotel.

The steamed clams in a tomato and wine sauce were sublime and sated her both emotionally and physically. Immediately invigorated, she was in a much better frame of mind and when Gina walked in, clearly overjoyed at seeing her again, she felt even better.

A familiar and friendly face was the equivalent of dessert right now, especially since she had no room left in her stomach for the latter. She liked Gina and immediately brightened at the prospect of talking to her.

"I thought it might be you. It's great to see you again, Ava."

"The smell from the restaurant enticed me. I have no willpower when it comes to food," Ava replied. The women smiled warmly at each other. "Sit down a while, why don't you?"

Gina did, seemingly thrilled by the invitation. "Are you feeling better now?" she asked. Ava remembered the way in which she'd fallen to pieces in front of Gina at the funeral. She nodded. "It was too much that day, too much sadness all around."

Gina nodded in agreement. "Did you come to see Nico?"

"Yes." Her gaze flicked up, rested on Gina's face. "I was hoping we could talk. We've not had the chance to catch up."

Gina nodded, it seemed she was waiting for Ava to continue.

"But he was in a rush to get away."

"He has much to deal with." Gina tried to reassure her.

"There are so many things to handle: the estate, the new hotel, the other hotels. Everyone wants a piece of him. Always questions, so many questions. They forget that he is still sad." She placed her elbows on the table and bent forward slightly. "Don't feel bad because he had to rush off."

Ava understood that Gina was trying to make it sound better than it looked. She had a feeling that Gina knew more about her and Nico's relationship than anyone else and she found herself wondering if she knew everything. "I upset him. I don't know if he wants to get together to talk anymore, not after I left him the way I did ..."

"He was hurt when Connor returned the bracelet."

The bracelet. Back then, she'd never intended for Nico to think she was going back to Connor. But asking her ex to return the bracelet had maybe painted that picture.

"And don't forget," Gina trilled along, obviously eager to paint a different picture, "he's also busy now with the purchase of the Ravenna hotel. He will be living in Ravenna once the building work starts."

A shiver shot up Ava's spine. If Nico disappeared to Ravenna any time soon, it would be even harder to get hold of him. Time was running out and she needed to act quickly— even if it meant risking getting shot down by him again. "He's going ahead with it then?" she murmured, more to herself, thinking back to the time when he had shown her the hotel.

"Yes. He's anxious to start work on it soon. It will keep him occupied and prevent him from dwelling too much on the sadness all around. There is too much of Edmondo here at the Casa Adriana. Nico feels it, you can see he feels it, you can see it in his eyes. You know what he's like, Ava. He puts on a brave face even though he's falling to pieces inside."

Gina's words landed on her like a heavy cloak, weighing down her spirits. "I know," Ava replied softly. She understood him very well; this man she loved and cared so much about. Her thoughts were filled with Nico and his sadness, and her heart ached to console him.

Gina glanced at her watch and frowned. "I must get back to work. Even when Nico is not around, I swear that man has eyes at the back of his head." She got up to go, but before she did so, said, "I hope we will see you before you return to Denver."

Ava assured her she would. She might have a few more trips back to this hotel before she went. As Gina rushed back to duty, Ava felt even more anxious about her dilemma. She paid the bill and left, preferring to walk home.

Walking helped her food to digest and gave her time to think. She was so engrossed in her thoughts that she didn't at first hear her cell ring. When she did, she fumbled for it frantically and rushed to answer it.

"You're impossible to get hold of!" Rona squawked on the other side.

She dismissed her sister's squawking. "Hi to you, too." She looked carefully both ways as she crossed the road. "What's up? I'm walking back to my hotel. Can you call later?" She hated talking on her cell phone when she was outside.

"No. I'm getting my hair highlighted this afternoon and I'm dropping Tori at mom's now."

Ava sighed. "What's up?"

"The baby backpacks and the nursery storage sets have completely sold out and we have orders placed. You need to order more. What's happening with the cribs? Connor's going mental."

Aaaah, that was what she'd forgotten to tell her. "The problem with the cribs is settled. Nico's signed the paperwork so Connor should be able to pick them up."

"About time too. Your customers are going crazy, and we've had another six orders for them."

"Another six?" Ava questioned. "Since when?"

"Today."

"Six orders in one day?"

"Six orders in one day," Rona parroted. "Can't you hear me? 'Cause I can hear you pretty well." Rona sounded irritated.

Ava laughed out in pure joy. Her evening was turning better by the minute. *Six orders today.* It was unheard of. Then she remembered about the ad she had placed in one of the major mommy sites. Usually, when she had tried ads like that before, she'd seen a blip in traffic to her site and she was lucky to get one order out of it.

But now that she had products that were *this* hot, it was *beautiful*.

"Can you hurry the hell up and order more? 'Cause at the rate we're going, we're going to need them. And all your stock is going down fast. I went to Connor's garage earlier and it was empty."

The news made Ava giddy with excitement.

"Ava! You there? I gotta go." She heard the hurry in Rona's voice.

"I'll order more right away. Thanks, Rona. How is everyone?" But her sister had already hung up.

Ava was starting to wonder whether she should have kept the wrong order quantity of one hundred cribs since it seemed to be closer to what she needed. She shook her head, excited by the heady prospect of her sales. The cribs were guaranteed hot products. Maybe this time around she would order forty. She couldn't afford to let a sales spike go to her head.

She walked with more than a spring in her step. Tonight she'd get knee deep into her spreadsheets and speak to Kim.

She would also call Connor to tell him that it was fine to go ahead and pick up the cribs now that Nico had taken care of that problem.

The evening sky looked glittery, as though it was specked with mirrored fragments.

It was breathtaking.

For a second, she wished Nico were walking beside her.

CHAPTER TWENTY-SIX

"Forty cribs?" Andrea repeated, tapping away on her calculator. "I'm excited your sales are going crazy, Ava, but just be prepared that the stock and shipping on that alone is going to cost a lot."

"But it's what I need." Ava had been up until well after midnight analyzing exactly what she needed to order this time around and the costs involved. She had gone through her figures three times.

Her sales were great, but she wasn't sure yet whether this was a temporary glitch or whether it was the sign of something more long-term. But either way, she was going to ride this wave while it lasted. Chances were good that she was going to be a single mother, so she needed to earn as much as possible, as quickly as possible.

She finally settled on placing an order of forty cribs and twenty of everything else that she had ordered before. While she was at it, she had thrown caution to the wind and taken a gamble by ordering new products that had caught her eye.

"What about clothing? Did Natale's clothes sell well?"

"They're selling, but I want to focus on the real hot sellers for now." Ava had checked this and though the clothes were moving, the nice-to-have and quirky items, such as the nursery organizers and closet cubbys were selling consistently and well. However, it was the essentials, such as the cribs and baby bathtubs that moved the fastest and it was on these products she chose to concentrate her efforts, as well as the cribs.

Andrea cocked her head, "You're being careful and wise," she said, nodding approvingly. "You can always scale that side up later." Which was exactly what Ava had thought. She could only concentrate on specific areas for now. Maybe later, when she got nearer to her due date, she'd have to take on more staff. If things continued to grow at this rate, she would need to get more hands on board.

It wasn't only her waistline that was growing.

Andrea furiously made some more calculations. "You're doing very well, my friend. I'm so happy for you. You deserve every success." Her smile could not be any brighter and Ava accepted her friend's compliments happily.

"Thanks, Andrea, but it's all down to your products. It's because of your stock that my sales have gone to another level and I can't thank you enough."

"You've already thanked me by buying more. If *you* do well, *I* do well."

"Like I said, these new products are what have helped my sales, and the cribs are selling faster than I can get them shipped over."

"Such a pity that you didn't stick to the order with the typo in it!"

"That's exactly what I thought. I wish I had. But ten was good to test with. For now I'll stick with forty." She wondered what advice Nico would have given her. His input would have helped now when she really could do with some solid advice, instead of making these big decisions herself.

Andrea closed her notebook. "Now I see the real reason why you look so good. We were talking about how well you looked, despite the sadness of this visit."

Ava's heart leapfrogged. "We?" Any news about how "good" she looked instantly put her on alert.

"Nico took me out to dinner last night, and naturally the conversation got around to you. I commented on how well you looked and he agreed."

So that was where he had rushed off to?

Anyone else she could have handled; Silvia, or the journalist, or any other floozy she could have dealt with because they were easy enough to direct her wrath on. But Andrea? Andrea was her good friend, and it now seemed she was also a confidante of Nico's, with the potential of becoming something more. They already had a history of a love relationship, and who knew what could happen when the passionate embers of a dying romance were rekindled once more?

Ava's newly jubilant outlook on life stuttered to a halt. Andrea sauntered back to her table, oblivious to the heartache her simple admission had caused. Ava wanted to leave; she didn't think she could handle listening to news about Nico and Andrea but at the same time she willingly gave herself to the torment as she found herself eager to know more.

"I didn't think I constituted business advice." A nervous laugh emanated from her throat.

Andrea giggled as she set down her books and pulled out a chair for Ava. "Oh, I'm not sure it was a business meeting. He called me yesterday, out of the blue, and asked if I'd like to go to dinner."

Ava swallowed and sat through it, a smile grazing her face. She feigned enthusiasm.

Like a schoolgirl talking about an adolescent crush on a boy, Andrea was all smiles and shiny eyes, savoring each moment where she got to relive events and talk about Nico. "I've been calling him and visiting him, you know, because we were friends. I mean he was there for me when I needed business help. When Edmondo died so suddenly, Nico broke down. Nobody else could see it, because he has that metal armor, that bulletproof shield around him to guard his feelings, but I could tell. I know him."

As do I, thought Ava, miserably. She'd have given anything to have been by his side in his darkest hour. But she had failed him, as she had failed him on so many occasions. It was only a natural progression that he'd grown sick of her and moved on. Her smile slipped, exposing the real sadness she felt as she recalled the memories.

Andrea stopped talking. "Ava ... " She faltered and put a hand to her lips. "Did you, *do you*, like Nico?" The silence cut through like a scythe.

How could she tell Andrea to back off her man, when her man no longer considered himself to be her man? When her man now believed that she was back with her ex?

But now was also the only time she could put an end to these lies that had grown and mushroomed. She saw anxiety claw at Andrea's face and something else too—pity.

Ava cleared her throat, her tongue stuck to the root of her mouth. "Me? No, of course not." She let out a high-pitched laugh and hoped it didn't give anything away. Memories of their days in Ravenna flashed before her and her eyes shone as tears lined up. "He helped me to see how I needed to grow my business, that's all."

"Then why do you look as if you're going to cry?"

Ava let out another short laugh. "I'm just so happy for you." It killed her to say it, but how could she say anything else? Nico didn't want her, so why should she stand in the way of Andrea's happiness? She gulped back a sob and forced the smile to stick.

Andrea's face relaxed, but only a little.

"Go on, so he called you to dinner?" said Ava, smiling widely, knowing her heart was bleeding, knowing that it would soon be time for her to go. In the faint far distance she heard the grating noise of shop shutters coming down.

Andrea relaxed back in her chair. "You know we were together once?"

Ava took the stab easily and forced herself to sit through it. She nodded, when she realized Andrea was waiting for acknowledgement.

"I thought we were over. I don't know. He just needs a friend right now. He was stressed out when he first arrived, but then he gradually relaxed and we ended up having a great evening." Andrea twirled a thick curl around her fingers. "I can be that friend, and more, if he wants. I've never really stopped caring for him."

With her heart mashed to a pulp, Ava could barely breathe. She longed to get out and take some air in. "He's a very kind and caring man," was all she could say.

"Shall we have dinner?" suggested Andrea.

The idea sank faster than quicksand. It was the last thing Ava wanted to do. Rising to her feet, she announced, "I'd love to, but maybe another time. I have to get back and catch my VA first thing in the morning, and I need to tell my sister of the new stock I've ordered."

Andrea looked crestfallen. "Perhaps we'll go out soon?"

Ava nodded and kissed her on both cheeks, then made her

escape. "Could I just use your bathroom first, if you don't mind?"

Andrea pointed the way. Ava's escape to the toilet provided instant relief, not just from emptying her bladder. These days it seemed as though she needed to go every couple of hours.

She wondered how much worse things would get by the time she reached nine months.

CHAPTER TWENTY-SEVEN

Elsa's neighbor, Faith, had been most persistent, but one trip to the mall had been more than enough for her.

Starting back on her art classes recently had been a huge stretch for her but once again, she no longer felt like attending. She could have helped at the voluntary shelter, too, since helping others always made her feel better, but this time, her lethargy overpowered her.

Perhaps she should have told Faith. But she couldn't bring herself to. She'd told her friend everything about her trip to Italy, but she'd left out Edmondo. That had been when he was still alive. For some reason, Elsa didn't think her friend would understand the connection she'd made with this man. And so she hadn't mentioned him at all, preferring to keep him to herself.

Now that he was gone, it was worse. Far worse. Not only did she not want to do anything, she also couldn't bear to be around people where she had to put on an act. She was hurting inside and suffering the most gut-wrenching sense of desolation.

She couldn't talk about it. Not even to Faith. None of her friends knew anything about Edmondo and they would never understand the special bond that the two of them had shared.

Her connection to him was so sacred to her that she refused to tarnish it by sharing it with others. It was for her; for her moments of deep and dark reflection, and she often went to a quiet spot in the nearby park to reflect on the beautiful few weeks this man had given her.

No, it was better not to say anything to her friends at all, until she was in a better frame of mind to deal with things outside. She was still trying to pull herself together.

Getting out today had been a good thing and she didn't mind leaving her apartment to clean Ava's. Not that her daughter had asked her to. Ava had only wanted her to check in on her place but Rona had mentioned that Ava's apartment was a mess.

As soon as Elsa had set foot inside, she saw for herself just how huge a mess it really was. There were boxes everywhere, many of them empty but still taking up space and adding to the chaos. The dust was thick and settled like a spray of dirty gray all over the surfaces. She gave it her best shot but after a while she wasn't sure if she was just adding to the mess, merely displacing the dust from the windowsills and surfaces onto the floor. She couldn't vacuum either because there were too many boxes everywhere.

After a while, she stopped and slowly sat down on Ava's bed, shaking her head as she placed the duster on the floor. At least she had cleaned out the refrigerator. She'd done something worthwhile.

She looked around the bedroom in dismay and stared at the boxes and magazines piled everywhere. Elsa still didn't understand what it was that her daughter did exactly, except that she sold things on the internet. She had a feeling that Ava worked for Amazon, or that she had, and was now trying to sell products herself by getting them from the warehouse in Italy.

Italy.

Edmondo.

Verona.

She wrung her hands together as memories came flooding back. She hadn't touched her computer in days, ever since the funeral. In the days leading up to it, she found herself reading all over again the emails that she and Edmondo had sent between them, just to feel a connection to him. But since that final day, she couldn't bring herself to do that anymore.

If Edmondo hadn't gone so soon, who knows what might have happened? She lowered her head. It was pointless thinking about it now because she would never know. She had lived two decades content with her life and had tried to make the most of it.

She had never so much as looked at another man.

There had been suitors. There had been men who had shown interest in her but she'd never been interested. Raising her girls had been her life. But then Edmondo had appeared and she'd been left thinking that perhaps second chances were possible.

Some women were lucky to meet such a man once in their lifetime. She considered herself especially lucky to have met two.

But now it was time for her to accept things for the way they were and move on.

As the sadness welled up again, she willed herself to pick up her duster and keep busy. Always keeping busy was what had gotten her through this malaise the first time. As she bent over, she stole a look under Ava's bed and frowned at the bags and boxes stacked underneath. Flickers of unsettled dust flew at her and she coughed. It wasn't healthy sleeping with so much dust caked around under the bed. Did her daughter never clean here?

She crouched down on her knees and reached out. This would need a good vacuuming but she would only be able to move the bed a few inches each way because of the boxes arranged all around the bed and the edge of the room like a border.

Wait until you get back, Ava, vowed Elsa. She was annoyed that her own clothes were covered with dust. As she pulled out bags, boxes, and whatever she laid her hands on, she soon found herself amid a swirling ball of dust that had risen around her, like a mini typhoon. She coughed and decided to fetch the vacuum and give it her best shot. All the items she had retrieved could do with a wet wipe too, she thought, screwing her nose up. She felt a sneeze coming on, and when she sneezed, it was loud and with enough force to empty her lungs. As she blew away the dust that had been disturbed, she caught sight of a paper bag with the address of a shop in Verona at the bottom. Reaching out, she pulled it towards her, but it had a rip in it and its contents spilled out onto the floor.

A flutter of joy spread through her as she picked up a few leaflets and saw that they were brochures from Verona. A fire lit inside her, warm and glowing, and she sat on the floor looking at pictures of the Duomo, the Giusti Gardens, Castelvecchio. For a forgetful moment, she was transported to the very places that had cast an imprint on her heart. Just holding the papers in her hands set her soul on fire and she sat, closing her eyes and inhaling deeply.

There it was: the faintest smell of outdoor scents, of dry grasses, lavender and rosemary. She breathed in again, holding on to the scents and memories of Verona as tears tumbled down her cheeks.

She sat like that for a few minutes, stilling her mind and finding a sense of peace inside. When she opened her eyes, she drew in a long breath, then tidied up the pile, putting the brochures back into the ripped bag as best as she could.

She would return another day and finish off. But as she put the leaflets back, she found a small folded up note. She unfolded it, wondering what tourist attraction this might be.

Her newfound joy stilled when she realized the paper was nothing to do with Verona. With her hands shaking, Elsa scanned through, reading quickly.

It was a leaflet from a pregnancy test kit.

Her hands trembled and the paper slipped to the floor as a small cry left her lips.

This was it.

This.

Was.

It.

The thing that made everything click into place.

It all made such perfect sense now if this was true.

Her skin prickled, and a small burst of electricity spread all over her body, making her nerves dance with joy, and excitement, and fear and laughter, all at the same time, unleashing the dark sadness that had been living inside her.

She had known there was a bigger reason for Ava's return than the one her daughter had told her, but she'd never imagined it would be as life changing as this.

Elsa couldn't stop trembling. It wasn't just her hands but her whole body had started to shake. It took her a few seconds to understand that her grief was surrendering to a sense of joy.

If this was true, it meant that she and Edmondo would share a permanent connection forever. Her grandchild would also be Edmondo's grandchild.

She burst out crying at the thought of it. But this time the tears that fell were tears of pure joy.

CHAPTER TWENTY-EIGHT

Nico rammed his foot down on the accelerator. He was scheduled to meet with a highly revered architect at the Ravenna hotel later this afternoon.

There was one final factor that would decide whether he proceeded with the hotel purchase: he needed to know how much space he could allocate to the new building, the one that would become the spa center.

With the top to his sleek convertible down, he sped along, the wind smacking him head-on. He raced along with his shades on, hair whipped back, adrenaline surging. He felt free and away from the cloistering confines of his office.

For too many days he had worked hard. Sleep came a little easier these days but waking up to an empty house was still difficult. Nobody else knew, not even Gina, but the first hour of each day he sat at his desk paralyzed. He could do nothing. It was only because so many people depended on him and needed him that he kept moving forward.

If he hadn't had anyone depending on him he wouldn't have even bothered to get out of bed. But too much work was also dragging him down and even when he managed to forget about his father for a while, images of Ava slipped into his mind, unbidden. Knowing that she was just around the corner from the Casa Adriana haunted him. He'd had the perfect opportunity to talk to her yesterday, when she'd showed up at his office, and all he'd done was push her away.

It was a self-preservation tactic but it hurt all the same to be that cruel to her.

This was why reaching back into his circle of old friends to distract him was something he welcomed. It was also partly the reason he was on his way to see Andrea now. He had paperwork for her that had only come through this morning and since he would pass Montova on the way to Ravenna, he could easily drop it off in person.

Of course, he could just as easily have scanned the documents and emailed them to her, but the dinner date last night hadn't been as awkward as he had anticipated.

Friends they could be, perhaps something more, in time. For now, though, friends would do.

It hadn't helped that Ava had come by his office just moments before he was about to leave. As a result, he'd turned up at the restaurant in a pissed off mood brought on by the short meeting with Ava. He was more annoyed with himself than with her. Her sudden appearance rattled him still because he cared for her, no matter how hard he tried not to think of her.

He wanted to be with her. He wanted her. And he was trying so goddamn hard to forget her but how could he when each time he turned a corner, there she was? It was obvious that she had wanted to talk but he'd pushed her away again and had gone to meet Andrea instead. Yet all through dinner with Andrea he wished he'd heard Ava out.

He owed her that much at least.

A couple of drinks had soon loosened his mood and Andrea was easy going anyway. He'd enjoyed dinner more than he thought he would.

If he was ever to get over Ava, the only way would be by spending more time in the company of other women. And pray that they didn't read too much into it. Right now, he wanted to let some light into the darkness that was his life and hanging out with old friends enabled him to do just that.

He parked up close by Andrea's warehouse and strode toward it. A handful of visitors walked around inside as he entered and in the far corner he saw Andrea talking to a customer. She looked over at him, and he put up his hand, indicating that he could wait. Her beaming smile was infectious and he couldn't help but smile back.

He walked around the warehouse, looking at the goods she had on offer, but when they reminded him too much of Ava and the times she'd come here looking for exactly these things, he walked away. Everywhere he went memories of her seemed to follow. He tried to push these thoughts away and waited patiently by Andrea's table.

"Sorry about that." She smiled at him, the way she always did when she saw him. It was another reason why he found himself looking forward to being around her. She lifted him out from his shadow of gloom.

"It's fine. You're busy." He handed her the papers. "Some paperwork for the cribs order. I wasn't sure if you needed them or not."

She rifled through them. "I didn't need them but I'm sure I should be filing them away. Thanks." She placed them on the table. They stood facing each other, and he found himself caught in a sudden, silent moment that was turning awkward. "I enjoyed dinner last night, Nico."

"Me too." They smiled through the awkwardness. He was lost as to what to say and instead his gaze roamed over her face. "I should get going," he said.

"You're always in such a rush." She took a step toward him and his eyes fell to her lips, but all he could think of were Ava's lips and the feel of them against his own. Andrea was staring at him oddly, but his mind was elsewhere. And then, with more boldness than he'd ever known her to possess, or perhaps she mistook his inaction for something else, she lifted her hand and brushed her fingers lightly across his face.

He was too stunned to move away. When her fingers skipped over the side of his cheek, he lifted his hand to clasp hers as she moved closer to him, this time lifting her mouth toward his.

He started to object. "Andrea, I—" But his ministrations went unheeded. Andrea lifted up onto her tiptoes, her lips fluttering lightly across his. He moved his hands to her shoulders to try to push her away.

Ava stepped into the waiting taxi and remembered she'd left her inventory list at Andrea's warehouse. She stepped out quickly, stuck up her hand at the driver, indicating that she would be five minutes. Then she half-jogged back to Andrea's, ready to dash in, but she stopped in her tracks.

A gasp escaped her mouth, and her fingers rose to her lips. She felt like a voyeur. If she needed proof that the man she loved had moved on, here it was.

She stood transfixed, knowing it was wrong to watch, knowing she was only prolonging the torture by staying a second longer. But she couldn't move.

It was only when Nico placed his hands on Andrea's shoulders, that she felt suddenly nauseous. Holding her hand to her mouth, Ava turned around and silently ran back in the direction from where she had come.

CHAPTER TWENTY-NINE

The floozy in his office had been nothing compared to this.

Ava had intruded on an intimate moment and now she had to walk away. The only saving grace was that Nico and Andrea hadn't seen her and so they would never know what she knew.

She ordered the driver to get her back to her hotel as fast as possible and the whole time during the journey she tortured herself by rewinding the scene of Nico kissing Andrea over and over in her head.

If it wasn't Andrea, it would have been someone else. The very thing she had been worried about he had just confirmed.

Her lower lip trembled. She was never going to be enough for a man like Nico. Never. He was so over her and who knew —maybe soon he would be over Andrea and move onto the next woman?

How could she even contemplate telling him about the baby now? In that moment she decided that he could never know. The last thing she needed was to force him into something. If she now told him of his child, she felt sure he would feel a sense of obligation and responsibility, at the very least. That wasn't the right reason to get back together. The sudden thought that he could use his money and power to take the baby away from her, terrified her.

Unable to sit still in the taxi, she looked through the emails on her phone. They had piled up in a matter of hours and it made her wary. A storm was brewing. Rona had made a few mistakes with a couple of deliveries, sending the wrong items to customers and Kim had taken the brunt of it by dealing with the unhappy customers. Somehow, Kim and Rona had ended up exchanging more than a few choice words between them despite her best intentions to keep the two women apart.

She rushed to her hotel room and crashed onto the bed; this was the last thing she needed on this most terrible of days.

Now she would have to wade into the mess back home and sort it out but she didn't even have the strength to open her laptop.

Outside, the constant drone of the traffic made it impossible for her to lie down and get any rest. Images rushed at her at the speed of light and the pandemonium inside her tired mind made her restless. She sat hunched up on the bed, before realizing it probably wasn't a good position for her baby and she immediately straightened out her legs.

Suddenly she longed for the peace of the Villa Sagranosa; the pensione Nico had made available to her the last time. When things had been good, they had been very good. She shivered as she looked around the tiny, dingy hovel of a cheap hotel room that she had confined herself to.

The time to leave Verona had come. This time when she left it would be forever and there would never be any reason for her to come back. Nico would never know about his child and she would never ever tell him.

She would never tell anyone. She'd think of something to tell her family, they would of course know it was his, but she would swear them to secrecy.

Now that she had witnessed what looked like the beginnings of a romance between her own supplier and her ex-lover, finding other suppliers was more important than ever.

She could no longer rely only on Andrea. Doing so would only mean more trouble, and heartache. With the weight of the secret she was going to have to carry for the rest of her life, she didn't want to cross paths with Nico ever again, and that meant cutting out the people he was involved with.

The sight of Nico and Andrea together had dealt her a more painful blow than she had been prepared for. Trying to keep Nico at bay, as she had first intended, had backfired on her badly and now seeing him and Andrea kissing had been like a stab in the back.

She clutched her stomach and found relief. Her baby was the one thing that belonged only to her. The baby gave her strength.

The problem was she also needed her inventory list of the products she had just ordered from Andrea, but she didn't want to return to Montova.

Ever.

Jerked into reacting, a burst of energy propelled her to the table and she fired off an email to Andrea for a scanned copy of it. An email from Rona was already sitting in her inbox and she quickly read it. Rona had threatened to quit, telling her that it was all getting to be too much. Ava could pacify her sister and get her to hold out until she returned but her days in Verona were numbered.

Just as she was dwelling on the current problems, her cell phone rang, interrupting her. This time it was Kim and she answered it right away.

Kim charged in, guns blazing. "Ava, I hate to say this to you, but either your sister goes or I do." It was like a punch in her stomach. Ava was too stunned to talk as she visualized her business falling to pieces.

"Let's talk about it, Kim. Please don't make any rash decisions." She couldn't afford to lose either one of them at such short notice or even risk there being a bottleneck in the system. Kim was super-efficient and could work well without supervision. Ava had found a rare diamond in the haystack when she had signed her up to be her virtual assistant. Having Kim dealing with all customer queries was a godsend.

It was a job that her big-mouthed, cocky sister would never be able to do in a million years.

"Your sister is rude and obnoxious. She's a total pain in the ass." Ava had never heard her super cool assistant sound so worked up. *What had Rona said to her?*

"You're right. She is." The best defense, always. To agree. "I can't do this without you, Kim. I really can't. I'm still in Italy but I'll be back soon. I really, really need you to hold the fort for me a little while longer. Please stay. I can't afford for anything to go wrong." A silence at the other end gave her the confidence to continue. "I'll call my sister and tell her not to bother you. Please, if you two can just hold out until I get back."

"All right," Kim replied, slowly. "But if she interferes with me again, I'm not taking any shit from her. I'm warning you now, Ava. I *will* walk."

Temporary victory. "Thank you. Are there any other problems I need to know about?" Ava massaged the back of her neck.

"Apart from your sister, no."

Okay, heard loud and clear. "Leave it to me."

Ava walked over to the bed and sat down; she summoned her energy. It was time to call Rona and get her version of events. She braced herself. She knew her sister well enough to know that the problem lay with Rona. Ava had never had problems with Kim, ever.

She held the cell to her ear, nursing her forehead with the palm of her free hand but instead of Rona, Elsa answered the phone.

"Mom? I was after Rona. How are you?" It all came out jumbled because she'd psyched herself up to speak to her sister.

"Hey, honey. Rona's out, she's gone to the post office to deliver your packages. I'm babysitting. I was just thinking of you. How are you?" Elsa's warm and loving voice instantly calmed Ava down. She suddenly longed for home.

"I-I'm...fine, Mom." It couldn't have been a lousier day.

"How are you keeping? You sound tired."

"It's been a busy day. I bought some more products for my store." She was about to mention the rift between Rona and Kim but decided to keep her mother out of it.

"And how's Nico?"

Ava's voice hitched in her throat. "He's ... fine."

"Have you two sorted out your problems?"

God, no. Ava had forgotten the wise words her mother had dispatched her with. "He's been busy and I have, too."

"You haven't fixed things?"

Ava sighed, she hadn't fixed things because things were unfixable and today, of all days, she had no desire left in her to try again. "No, Mom. I don't think that's going to happen."

"Not going to happen? Why not?"

Ava didn't know where to start and when she kept silent,

Elsa jumped in. "Honey, don't leave it too late. You know, after what happened to Edmondo, you can't let things fester." The phone went silent and Ava restrained herself from replying. "Honey, please don't bear grudges. Whatever happened between you two can be sorted. Life is far too short to spend it being miserable."

Ava rested her forehead in her hand and stared at the dirty floor. She was in a pit of misery both hypothetically and literally.

Things weren't going to get better between her and Nico. Maybe it was time she set the right expectations for her mother. "Mom, he's seeing someone."

"What do you mean?" The indignation in her mother's voice went up a notch.

"I mean he's with someone. I saw them kissing today. Don't be so surprised." *I was only a temporary summer fling for him. The man doesn't even want to know me anymore.*

"But I don't understand."

"What's there to understand? It's no big deal, Mom."

"No big deal!" Elsa's voice went up another octave. "Are you sure it was Nico?"

"You don't believe me?" Ava was indignant. She got up and paced around the room, not caring how dirty the floor was. "Mom, I'm coming back home soon. I tried to do the best I could. I know all the stuff you said about Edmondo, but Nico is not the same person as his father was. I've tried talking to him a couple of times but he's not been interested. He doesn't want to give me the time of day and after today, I know why. He's got his heart set on someone else."

Elsa let out a low muffled noise at the other end. "I find that hard to believe." Then she quickly retracted. "Of course, I believe you but I find the whole thing morally wrong."

"Why? I left him, remember? He's hated me since then. It's too late now."

Elsa let out an irritated groan. "Such a mess, all of this."

Ava narrowed her eyes. "Why is it such a big deal? I can move on. I did before."

"Nico was a good man." Her mother wouldn't let it rest.

Ava wanted to end the conversation. "Mom, I get that you're hurting over Edmondo but please don't get your hopes up about me and Nico sorting things out. It sounds as if you badly want it to happen, but it's not going to happen."

Elsa breathed loudly again. "If that's your final decision."

Ava ran her hand over her hair in exasperation. Outside, cars beeped and hooted. It happened a lot around here especially around lunch and dinnertime, when local teenagers hung out at the cheap pizza places and ice-cream parlors on the main road. She hated this place so much and many times she longed for the peace and quiet of the pensione.

"Yes, Mom, it is. I've got to sort out a lot of things before my business collapses. I'll speak to you later."

She hated being so upfront with her mother, but she'd never known Elsa to be so insistent about something before. Usually, Elsa left her and Rona alone, not interfering with their lives. Though so far, Ava knew she'd made a real mess of hers. Her mother was dead set on Ava settling the score with Nico. And suddenly Ava knew what drove her to it. Edmondo's unexpected death had hit her mother harder than it had all of them.

Her mom was grieving.

With a jolt, Ava knew her place was back home, by her mother's side, helping her to get through this dark patch.

She wished her mother would stop going on about her and Nico getting back together again, because that was never going to happen. Picking up her laptop she moved over to the bed.

Her love life had nosedived for good. It was time to make sure her business did not.

CHAPTER THIRTY

The sale would go ahead, just as Edmondo would have wanted. Nico vowed to build the best spa retreat along the eastern coast of Italy.

One of the things he would have in it, as well as the lap pools, treatment rooms and relaxation areas was a beautiful garden in his father's name, with the plants and flowers that Edmondo loved.

He walked around, admiring the flowers just coming into bloom in the gardens at the Casa Adriana. It was something he found himself doing more since Edmondo's death. His father had loved this garden so much and he would often go for a stroll in it at least once a day.

Nico had never been particularly drawn to it before but now he found a deep sense of peace when he was out in it.

The smell of lavender and jasmine enlivened his senses. It was peaceful here, and solitary, and it soothed him, giving him a break from the chaos that was his life. It also gave him precious quiet time to remember his father and his words and the advice Edmondo had given him.

During the day Nico didn't have time to think about

anything else but work. Daily he was assaulted by emails, calls from accountants, lawyers and bank managers. Then the hotel managers would offload their problems to him, usually staff related. It was a lot to handle.

He needed to assemble a management team and wondered why his father had never done so before. For too long his father had, with his help, somehow managed the hotels himself. He had employed great managers, most of them, who were able to function effectively, but they still looked to Nico or his father for guidance. Nico wanted the onus off himself. The next few years would be the busiest yet for the Cazale group. He couldn't expand and build new hotels while also effectively managing the existing portfolio.

If he had a small team, he could delegate more and get more done himself.

Whenever he came out here to think, he felt clearer, as if the solutions he sought presented themselves easily to him. Maybe unconsciously this was also part of the reason he came here more.

He sat down at the bench near a lemon tree and sat back with his arms sprawled out on the top of the backrest. The visit to see the hotel in Ravenna had proved fruitful and he'd instructed his lawyers to move forward with the purchase. A lot of his time would be spent out there now, with him possibly working there three to four days out of the week. He needed to oversee the work on the new building that would be the spa center as well as the refurbishment of the existing hotel.

He would have no time for anything then, and the idea pleased him. He wouldn't need to seek out distractions, or the company of friends for comfort. The hotel would suck up all his time.

He wouldn't make mistakes like the one he made when he

had let Andrea kiss him. For all his hopes that she wouldn't get the wrong idea, she clearly had. It had been partly his fault too—a mad, last minute crazy notion to accept her kiss, a pathetic attempt to erase all memory of Ava but the instant Andrea's lips had touched his, he'd had his answer.

Kissing Andrea had meant nothing to him. There had been no feeling, no thrill, nothing to complete him. Nothing, compared to the way his heart exploded whenever he kissed Ava.

She excited him physically, but it went way beyond that. Ava ignited his soul and being with her was something he couldn't easily forget.

If he could get the lawyers to move forward with the hotel purchase by next month, he would do his utmost to ensure that work started on it as soon as possible. The sooner he was away from all the memories that the Casa Adriana tortured him with, the better for his peace of mind.

It all made sense, this plan of his, but he still felt restless. Something was incomplete and he couldn't rest until he found the answer.

It was something that kept him awake at night.

Why did Ava go back to Connor? He'd never understood it and it baffled him more than he let on. Perhaps if he found the answer to this question, he *could* move on. Not knowing was the thing that kept him stuck.

With Ravenna looking hopeful, it was something he needed to do now. He jumped up and rushed inside.

"Nico, I need to talk to you about the—" Gina raised her hand as he shot past her into his office, stopping briefly to grab his car keys.

When he appeared again, like a whirlwind, he put his hands up to silence her. "Not now, Gina, please."

"Where are you going?" she asked.

He inclined his head a little and his lips curved up slightly. "To find out if I have a future or not."

In less than five minutes, he was back at the car park outside the Hotel Cesar where Ava was staying.

Completely energized, he was ready to take on the world but just as he rushed toward the hotel doors, Ava swept out and dazzled him with her radiance.

He stopped in his tracks, his eyes raking in her appearance from top to bottom while his insides danced somersaults.

"Nico?" Surprise painted her face fleetingly and his excitement rose at seeing her. His gaze lingered on her face. It was softer, more rounded than he remembered, and the dark circles underneath betrayed signs of tiredness.

He wasn't the only one suffering sleepless nights. She wore a pale lemon-colored knee-length shift dress and he kept his white-knuckled hands close to his side lest they give in to his inability to refrain from touching her. He wanted to tell her she looked beautiful and that he loved her but the words that came out instead were, "Going somewhere?"

She didn't answer; alarm shadowed her face, and he knew he had overstepped that mark, the line that delineated between him having the right to know what she did versus the fact that it was no longer his place to know her business.

They stood staring at one another, with Ava's hand on the open door, as a few people filed past them.

"What are you doing here?" There was a sharp edge to her voice that hadn't been there before.

"I was hoping we could talk."

Incredulity floundered across her features as she craned her neck towards him. "You want to talk? *You?*" Sarcasm dripped from her words making him rethink how to play this. Things weren't going the way he had imagined them to.

"Are you upset about something?" he asked, then immediately regretted his words. She had every right to be upset with him, after the way he had treated her so badly on each of the occasions she'd tried to reach out to him—when she'd been the one to want to talk.

He watched as she kept her mouth clenched tight, no doubt locating the right words to throw in his face, words he knew he rightly deserved. He moved forward, blocking the doorway so that nobody could pass through. "Look, Ava. A lot has gone on, not just with my father, but with us. Can we at least talk in private?"

"No." She stepped back a fraction. "I've got to go. I'm running late."

He had to know where she was going dressed up like that. A stab of jealousy sliced through him. "I'm not going until you let me talk. All I'm asking for is five minutes."

"Talk quickly. You've got four and a half."

"Not here, somewhere private."

She made a low angry noise in her throat and if looks could kill he'd be lying on the floor like a wounded animal. She stormed off down a long, narrow corridor and he followed her willingly.

She opened the door to her room and let him through. "Four minutes. Start talking," she hissed at him, glancing at her watch in annoyance. He stepped into her drab little room. "What are you doing *here*?" He looked around at the tiny room, his gaze taking in the muck-colored carpet, the uneven bed, and the dirt-colored walls.

She'd stayed here the whole time? Guilt surged through him and he wanted to put his hand to his mouth in horror, but he didn't want to belittle her. He should have offered her the pensione as soon as Gina told him she was coming.

He'd messed up.

She watched him with a look of mild irritation, then looked at her watch again. "The clock is ticking."

"You can't stay here," he said, not caring that he had no right to tell her what to do.

Ava glared at him. "I am staying here. Two minutes." She tapped at her watch face. She seemed distant, as though she couldn't wait to get him out.

He slipped his hands into his trouser pockets and stood at the center of the room, not bothering to hide his disapproval as his gaze took in her shoddy surroundings. It pained him to know she was staying here. When he faced her, she glared back at him.

It saddened him that things had come to this. There had been a time when they couldn't bear not to be together, all night long. It hadn't even been that long ago.

"I need to know the answer to one thing," he said quietly. "It's been bugging me ever since you left." His eyes locked onto hers.

She tilted her head upwards, throwing out her chin in defiance, and those blue-gray eyes blazed at him. "What is it?"

"Why Connor?"

She snorted at the question. "Are you serious?"

"I'm being dead serious." His voice went lower as he shifted closer to her. This time when she stepped back she was up against the table. He watched her chest rise and fall quickly, her eyes not meeting his as confidently as they first had. Already, that told him a lot, that her coldness was just a front.

"Why does it matter to you?" She forced herself to look at him.

"Because I was crazy, madly, deeply in love with you." He took a small step closer and this time she was stuck. He lifted her chin upwards, and when he looked into her eyes, he saw confusion. He was still in love with her but he couldn't tell her that, yet.

"You *were?*" She sounded surprised. Then in a second, her eyes narrowed. "And yet you couldn't keep your hands off that woman when I walked in!" Her voice dripped with malice.

"What woman?" His brows inched together, creasing his forehead. "You mean the journalist? The woman who demanded a story from me, about you, about us? The one who wanted to post pictures of you all over the press and social media unless I gave her a story? The one I threatened never to come near me again?" *Was this what she had been so mad about?*

She frowned in response. He could smell her scent, and it took all his might not to crush her soft, warm and luscious body against his; he fought to keep himself from giving in.

"Ava, that woman was trouble. She wanted to hurt me by hurting you and I couldn't let that happen. I wasn't making a move on her. I was warning her to stay away!"

"That's just one woman," she shot back. "What about the others?" She tilted her head again, staring at him with menace that spiked his curiosity.

What other women?

"Let's sit and discuss this properly, Ava." He reached for her with his hand, but she moved her head back, as if the very touch of his fingers was abhorrent.

"What about the others?" she asked, angrily.

"What others?" There were no others. Not now, not since he'd met Ava. "Tell me you love him."

She looked away. He grabbed her arms, then loosened his hold quickly because the touch of her warm skin sent his senses into overdrive. When she didn't flinch from his touch, he moved so close, that only fabric separated their bodies.

His hand moved towards her face and he made her look at him. Desire drove his need to kiss every inch from her forehead to her chin, and more but first he needed to know how she felt. "Tell me you love him, and I'll walk away forever," he demanded. Her eyes were so clear, so shiny, he could see his reflection in them. When she didn't say anything, he knew it was because Connor didn't matter.

She was so tantalizing that he couldn't hold back anymore and his lips ached to touch hers. He dipped his head and pressed his mouth over hers, tasting her sweet, soft lips. She fought back, for all of two seconds, then gave in to him completely, the warm familiarity of their closeness driving him crazy. When she moved her hips toward him, he knew she felt the same. In answer, he pressed his body into hers, the feel of her tongue against his, the smell of her, the things he missed so much making him react and not question. His hands trailed down, encircling her waist while his fingers moved over the rounded contours of her hips while they kissed deeply, their hot tongues lashing together like long lost lovers.

Lost in the warm wetness of her mouth, he didn't want to come up for air, afraid that doing so would break the bubble. His heart soared with hope as she reacted back, grinding her body against his hardness. This was a moment he had dreamed about for months.

When at last they needed air and broke their kiss, he smiled at her, knowing he had the answer he had suspected all along. The idea flashed across his mind, to take her back to his, and to make up with her properly, to show her how much he had missed her and how much he loved her and needed her.

But Ava pulled back, her lips swollen, her eyes dark, breathing heavily, recovering. "What others?" she snarled. "I gave you a chance to tell the truth for once and you couldn't. You ask whether I love Connor? Do I need to spell it out? I love him. Of course I love him. He hurt me and I'm still hurting but I feel happier for having known that kind of love. I loved him before and I love him still. Is that enough of an answer for you?"

Nico stumbled backwards as she twisted the blade deeper, each word like deadly shrapnel. She moved towards him slowly, as if taking pleasure in her attack. "I never stopped loving him, if you only knew how much." Her voice broke at the end and she walked past him and out of the door, leaving him alone in her hotel room.

He staggered around, his heart thudding violently as he lunged towards the table and placed his hands on it, steadying himself.

She had made up her mind. She loved Connor. Her admission had made his heart crumble and he knew it would be a long time before he managed to put it back together again.

CHAPTER THIRTY-ONE

Out of breath and gasping for air, Ava jumped into the first taxi that came along as she ran down the road, trying to get as far from her hotel as fast as she could.

Her heart thumped and she didn't turn around once to see whether Nico had come after her. She couldn't be with him a second longer, otherwise she would never be able to resist the temptation he offered.

She hurriedly showed the driver a piece of paper on which she'd scribbled the address of a new supplier she wanted to visit. As the man nodded and drove away, she leaned back into the seat and took in deep, long breaths, trying frantically to still her breathing. Dabbing at her eyes she looked out of the window trying to avoid the furtive glances from the driver.

Her mind was in chaos. Nico affected every single emotion in her body, from pure lust to hatred and many places in between. That he could control her like a puppet on a string only proved to her the depth of her depraved devotion for him. The man was a psychopath who played with her emotions. If she hadn't witnessed him kissing Andrea, she would have fallen for his lies just now.

He had so easily explained away the situation with the woman in his office that she was left feeling like the village idiot. But she still loved him, and loving a liar was a surefire way to a life of heartache.

That was the sad part of her situation. Nico was a master manipulator who could twist and bend his words to suit him. He played with her emotions, tossed them this way and that without any regard for her well-being.

How dare he turn up on her door and demand to know if she loved Connor? And why had he turned up at all? His need to know had thrown her completely. Unlike him, she wasn't the consummate liar. There was no way she could have convinced him that she loved Connor. But the knowledge that he had so flagrantly kissed her friend and now demanded the truth from her, well, that just plain riled her up.

She'd given him a chance to come clean and to own up about Andrea, and when he hadn't she was left wondering of the kind of life she would have with him; one where she would fret each time he went away on business.

Life with him would only be a pack of lies. She would always be suspicious of how many mistresses he had and she didn't want to live her life like that.

But when he'd kissed her, oh good God, she was a goner. She'd fought it for a nanosecond but knowing it would be her last kiss with him, and unable to draw back from his magnetic pull, she had yielded to him and let him take over. The feel of him up close and so flush against her body had intoxicated her faster than a glass of champagne ever could. Her head spun, her senses whirred up to dangerous, seductive levels, and her body had responded to his pure animal rawness.

It had taken all her might to stop. Right in that moment, her body was so hungry for him she would have done anything he demanded, but somehow she had managed to make a stand.

Reliving that kiss between him and Andrea had given her the armor she had needed to plunge the knife deep into him.

And she had spoken about the man she loved.

Only, she hadn't been talking about Connor.

It had choked her to say those words, knowing that the object of her desire, the man so plainly wrong for her, *was* Nico.

She had to make sure she hurt him enough so that he would never, ever come looking for her again.

For the second time in months, she was done with Verona. This time for good.

She had a couple more visits to make during the next few days, having scoped out new suppliers, and then it was homeward bound to Denver. The way things were looking between Nico and Andrea—and knowing that it would be a while before she got over Nico—it would be better to avoid all form of contact with Andrea, since that risked having contact with the man she was trying to forget.

The sooner she found suppliers she could reliably source her products from, the sooner she could sever ties with all that had meant so much to her here.

Elsa might never forgive her, but her mother had yet to find out that Ava was carrying Edmondo's grandchild.

Somehow, Ava would find a way to convince her mother to keep this secret from Nico. It wasn't going to be easy, but she would worry about that problem when she got to it.

CHAPTER THIRTY-TWO

"I thought you might like it here."

"I love it." Elsa slipped her arm through Edmondo's and they wandered around the art gallery slowly, standing in front of each of the paintings and looking at them. They were back in Castelvecchio, admiring the art in the museum.

She looked from the portrait back to Edmondo's face and basked in the warmth of his smile, feeling wanted and happy as they paused to admire another portrait.

"I like this one." Elsa stared at the image of a woman standing between two trees.

"You do?" Edmondo pressed his arm against hers and stared at the painting pensively. "What is it in particular that you like about it?"

"The colors. The green and the gold and how the gold brightens the whole picture."

Edmondo continued to stare, then after a while added, "I like the green and gold, too." They admired the portrait a little longer.

"Shall we move on?" she suggested.

"As you wish." He was always content to let her lead the way.

They shuffled along to the next portrait but the distant cry of a baby poked into the hallowed quiet of the room. The cry turned louder, forcing them to look and see where the noise was coming from but when Elsa turned back, Edmondo had disappeared and the baby's earsplitting scream pierced through her.

Tori's yell carried across from her nursery, forcing Elsa to shoot wide awake. Startled into a gray reality, disappointment rained over her. She would have sat and wallowed in the bleakness of her misery, had it not been for Tori's loud insistence for company.

Wearily, Elsa got up from the couch and went into the nursery where she carefully lifted Tori out of her cot. She held her granddaughter in her arms, gently rocking her back to sleep. When calmness finally ensued once more, Elsa carefully laid the toddler back down and tiptoed out.

She returned to the couch and gazed at the TV screen blankly, willing time to pass. The clock showed it was already way past midnight, causing Elsa to frown. She was tired and she wanted to go home. Lately, Rona had become a little too used to her babysitting services, and these days both she and Carlos almost always went out on the rare occasions he had a night off.

Eager for Rona and Carlos to spend more quality time together, especially now that they had Tori, Elsa had been more than happy to step in and babysit. But this was the second time this week. Once a week had been her offer. Perhaps she needed to emphasize this point to her daughter because she didn't want Rona to make this a regular occurrence.

Try as she did to get into it, this week's *Murder, She Wrote* didn't grab her attention. Elsa's mind was elsewhere, entangled with nagging worry and she switched the TV off in irritation.

She'd been feeling troubled ever since the call from Ava.

Nico with another woman? She shook her head, unable to comprehend such a thing. It couldn't be true. Yes, the man was good-looking to a fault but she had seen enough goodness in him that she found it difficult to reconcile his actions with what her daughter was now telling her.

She closed her eyes in despair, in a vain attempt to get some peace to collect her thoughts.

For days now, she'd felt an urge to return to Verona. Not to gain closure over Edmondo, for she carried dear memories of him in her heart, but because she wanted to discover the root of the problem between Nico and Ava.

Why was it that these two people, who seemed so right for each other, couldn't find a way to sort out their differences?

But returning to Italy just for this purpose was alien to her. Unless she was asked, Elsa kept out of her daughters' problems. Of course, she worried about her girls, and had experienced many a sleepless night because of them, but to interfere so blatantly? It wasn't in her nature and yet this time it felt different. She just *knew* she needed to be there.

More was at stake here than just love.

The fate of an unborn child lay in the decision that these two would make. Even though Elsa didn't know for sure whether Ava was pregnant or not, everything about her daughter in the last few weeks certainly pointed to the fact.

There was no way that Elsa was about to let Edmondo's grandchild go undiscovered by its father. It was bad enough that the poor man had not known.

Tears pooled in her eyes as she remembered their conversations when he'd shown her around Verona. It was then that she'd come to know of Edmondo's deep-rooted longing for grandchildren. The man had waited patiently for years, and the way he spoke, Elsa knew he'd had his heart set on Ava making a decent man out of Nico.

Now that there was a chance that Edmondo's wish might finally be realized, Elsa wasn't about to let the opportunity waste away.

The grating sound of the key in the lock indicated that it was time for her to go home. Elsa rose and collected her belongings together. By the time Rona and Carlos had stepped into the room, she'd had her jacket on and handbag at the ready.

"Off so soon, Mom?" Rona tripped in on her heels, wearing low-slung jeans and a short T-shirt that showed off her slim waist.

"Thanks for taking care of Tori, Mom." Carlos moved over to give his mother-in-law a thankful kiss on her cheek.

She nodded at them both, her car keys ready in her hand. "She was as good as gold. She had her milk on time and went back to sleep. How was your evening?" she asked even though it was quite evident from Rona's flushed red cheeks and that silly grin on her face.

"It was great!" Rona sank into a heap on the sofa.

"Stay for some hot chocolate," Carlos offered.

"No, I best be going." Elsa made her way towards the door, then stopped before she opened it. "I'm thinking of going to Verona," she announced. "In the next week or so." She pulled the door open.

Rona jumped to her feet instantly, wobbled around, then collapsed back onto the sofa. "Mom, you can't," she blubbered.

"Why not?" Elsa waited patiently for the explanation.

"Because," said Rona slowly, "I've planned a weekend away, just me and Carlos, and I was going to tell you."

"When?" Elsa dropped her head in consternation. Now that she no longer socialized as much as she used to, her daughter seemed to think she had nothing better to do with her time than babysit on demand.

Carlos and Rona looked at her in surprise. Her tone had been a little sharper than she'd intended.

Carlos spoke up. "It's okay. We can change our trip to another time. Sorry, we should have checked with you first." He glared at his wife. Rona opened her mouth in protest and closed it again without saying a word.

Elsa shrugged off his reply. Maybe Ava might stay over there a while. Perhaps she ought to let her daughter sort her own problems. It would be for the better. Then she relented. "No, you go. I'll look after Tori. I don't need to go to Verona."

"You could go once we get back," Rona offered.

Carlos made to speak again, but Elsa put her fingers to her lips. "You'll wake your daughter up. Now, you two get to bed and we can talk tomorrow. Verona can wait. I'm a little tired and irritable. Don't mind me." She left them with her smile and slipped out of the door, thinking about Verona and Edmondo and the lovely time they'd had together.

She missed those blissful days, wandering around Verona, listening to Edmondo's stories of the places they visited. She missed their lunches and dinners and stops for milky lattes. She missed his eager smile, his friendly laughter and most of all she missed the way he made her feel.

CHAPTER THIRTY-THREE

Intricate burnished gold and silver metalwork held in place pearls and gemstones of different colors. Nico ran the tips of his fingers lightly over the Flamentagostini bracelet. It was an amazing display of craftsmanship.

She had worn this.

And then she had given it back. Worse, she'd gotten Connor to give it back for her.

If she had slapped him then it would have hurt less. He had it now—the answer to the question that kept him awake at night. She had told him, in no uncertain terms, that it was Connor she wanted.

It had left him stunned when she had walked out on him, leaving him alone in her hotel room and it had taken him a few minutes to get over the beating she'd just delivered.

But then again ... her kiss said one thing, her words another. He tossed the bracelet onto the table. It was over. Finished.

When Gina knocked on the door on the dot of the hour, he ordered her in, eager to have something else occupy his thoughts. "Don't look so scared, Gina." She looked so nervous that he immediately tried to put her at ease.

She mustered a forced smile. "We don't usually have formal meetings." She sat down slowly.

"Don't think of this as a meeting then. Think of it more like our usual conversations." Nico gave her an encouraging smile. He had already looked through her details, but he opened her personal folder again and placed it on the table in front of him.

"You've been with us for quite a few years now." His gaze shifted from the papers before him to her timid eyes.

She nodded in agreement. "And I've enjoyed every minute of it."

Nico smiled and closed the folder. He couldn't do formal, not with Gina. He pushed the file away and placed his hands on the table, interlacing his fingers. "I've sacked Alphonso." The man was hardly ever here, and on the rare occasions he showed up for a full day's work, he caused more problems than not. If it hadn't been for Gina, the Casa Adriana would have suffered many problems.

"He came in?" Gina frowned.

"No. He hasn't been in for a long time, claiming some sort of long-term illness. I made him a deal: if he didn't come back, I wouldn't give him a bad reference. He has a month's wages. That's quite generous, given that he's not been here and you've been doing his work for months anyway."

Gina gave him the kind of look that indicated she had no idea what any of this had to do with her.

"I don't consider working only when the mood grabs you to be the trait of an exemplary employee. That's not the type of person I want working for me."

Gina kept quiet.

"I've found the perfect person for his job. *You.*"

"Me?" Joy slid slowly over Gina's face as his words sank in.

"Yes, you. I've told you before. You've been doing this job anyway for so long now. I needed to clear it with my father, and I'd have told you a lot sooner. But ..." He didn't need to finish the sentence.

Gina's lips bordered on turning into a smile, but something stopped her. "Thank you for this opportunity, Nico, but I'm not properly qualified. I don't have any formal training, I left school at—"

He shrugged away her concerns with a wave of his arm. "You've got common sense, a quick mind, and you work hard. Above all, you're reliable and I trust you implicitly."

Gina reddened at the praise he heaped on her.

"It's true and you should absolutely be proud of all you have done."

Her eyes shone. "Thank you."

"I'm not done yet." He placed his elbows on the table, unlocked his fingers and gave her a serious look. "The new hotel is going to take up all my time now and I'm going to be extremely busy from now until the end of the year. I want to open in November, a month before Christmas so that we'll be able to iron out any problems in time for the big holiday season next spring."

Gina listened intently.

"Not that I see the new hotel being a strictly seasonal operation. Being a spa retreat, I want to target corporates and attract that kind of guest. I see it as an expensive gift, a treat, if you will, something that is available all year round."

"That's an excellent idea," Gina commented. She sat back in her chair and loosened up for the first time.

"I don't know how my father managed to look after everything, but I'm going to need people I can trust by my side." Gina smiled at him, but he could tell she didn't understand the significance of what he was at driving at. "You'll need to look after this hotel when I'm away. As I mentioned before, I intend to be in Ravenna for two to three days every week."

She appeared unfazed.

"In time, I'll need to rely on a few people to be my trusted management team. I know it's early days, but I'm looking for you to be a part of that team."

Gina looked dumbfounded. Now he had her. He could see her hesitation. As far as he was concerned, she was more than able to carry out the tasks and she had already been doing them. He was running out of time. Work in Ravenna would begin in a matter of weeks and he had to get the ball rolling.

"I can do the work, it's not a problem." She chewed her lip. "I just don't have the qualifications that you—"

Nico shook his head quickly. "I would take learning through experience over pieces of paper, anytime."

She didn't look appeased.

"Don't worry. If you need training as we go along, I will make sure you go to courses. I'll make sure you have the training you need. Or you think you need. I know you can do this, Gina. If I didn't I wouldn't have asked. Right now, I'm telling you I need people to look after the Casa Adriana for me, report any problems, tackle any issues and bring things to my attention if you feel you can't deal with them for whatever reason. I'll also need you to keep an eye on the other hotels, beginning with the weekly conference calls. Do you think you can do it? We can go over all the tasks at length, later. I'll spend a few days with you, going through it all. I'll make an announcement to the other managers informing them that they need to deal with you instead of me."

"So soon?"

Nico nodded. "Don't look at the job title, it's not important. Look at the tasks you've been doing. And I promise you, you've done most of the things I've mentioned."

The frown disappeared from her face.

"We haven't even discussed terms and conditions and your new pay grade but here is what I propose: go away and think about it. And later this afternoon we'll discuss anything you want to. Sound good?" He pushed a white envelope towards her. She took it unopened.

"Open it in your own time. We can meet later to discuss and finalize the details."

She smiled. "Thank you so much." Her voice was overcome with emotion, and then her gaze settled on the bracelet lying on the table. She looked at it and then at Nico. Admiration and questions abounded in her gaze.

His jaw tightened, in preparation.

"It's a beautiful bracelet."

"It is." He tried to look indifferent.

"And its owner no longer wants it?"

He had no answer for that. He picked up a pen and tapped the end of it on the folder. "It doesn't matter anymore; she has gone back to Connor."

"It doesn't make any sense," said Gina, her timidity fast disappearing.

"What's to make sense?" His irritation climbed.

"Ava came here for dinner last week."

Nico shifted and sat up straight. He wasn't sure what point, if any, Gina was trying to make. "She likes our chef and our restaurant. And after seeing the hell pit she's staying at, I don't blame her for coming here."

"You've been to her hotel?" Gina's eyes widened in surprise. Nico could almost see her brain working in overdrive. Just like that the power had shifted and now that it was moving into personal territory, Gina appeared to have the upper hand again.

He shifted uncomfortably in his chair. He admired Gina for her foresight when it came to getting to the heart of the matter. She was so skilled at eliciting feelings from others. While he appreciated that this might be a handy skill to have when she was on his management team, he wasn't so keen to be the one under her spotlight. "Yes," was the best he could offer. When she gave him that knowing look, he shrugged under her all-knowing gaze. "What?" The edge in his voice gave away his defensiveness.

"Don't you see?" Gina waited as a smile spread across her lips.

"I don't see a damned thing." This meeting had been over ten minutes ago.

"She's there, and you're here. That must tell you something." She hovered in anticipation. "You can't keep away from one another. It's just that you keep missing one another or saying hurtful things when you get together."

Nico looked at her pointedly. "I don't have a clue what you're talking about, Gina. But if you could find the time to look through your contract and let me know when you are ready to discuss it, we can move on."

Gina smiled at him sweetly. "Of course."

CHAPTER THIRTY-FOUR

The light spray of early morning rain had spritzed the roads and buildings until everything looked and smelled fresh again. Soon spring would bloom into summer. On a day like this, with bittersweet sunlight sprinkling the barely wet streets, drinking a warm, frothy latte out on the pavement was a treat.

Ava would remember this day forever. She would hold this memory dear when she was back in Denver again.

Andrea stirred her coffee lazily, and the flush of a new crush stained her cheeks. It was a conversation that Ava dreaded. But at Andrea's insistence, she had reluctantly agreed to a coffee in a café in the town center since Andrea was coming into town on other business.

Coffee would be shorter than lunch. She readied herself for Andrea's love talk, but her friend had other things on her mind.

"Are you sure there's nothing you have to tell me?" Andrea asked.

What could Andrea be referring to? "No, there's nothing." Ava tried to bluff her way through it.

"Really?" Andrea stopped stirring. "I've been trying to work out why you've been avoiding me. We've become quite good friends; at least that's what I've come to believe. Why, when you've now been here for so many weeks, is it that every time I suggest we meet for lunch or dinner you avoid me? What could you possibly have to hide from me?"

The insides of Ava's stomach felt as if they had fallen out. Nico wouldn't have told Andrea about their kiss, would he? She paled, and her heartbeat accelerated to a sprint. It might be best to come clean with the whole thing; to just tell Andrea what had happened and that she was going back to her one true love in a few days' time. Okay, so she'd be lying about that last point, but once a lie, always a lie.

Lies, lies and more lies.

"Andrea I don't know what to say." She tried to find the best way to start.

"Got you." Andrea pointed at her and laughed. Recently Ava had witnessed a more childish side to her friend. "I really had you then, huh?" Andrea beamed one of her huge full smiles at Ava, who instantly deflated with relief. Good job she'd kept her mouth shut. "At first I was going to be angry," continued Andrea, "but then I thought, if I were in your shoes, I'd most likely do the same thing, too."

Uh-oh.

Ava waited with a mixture of fatigue and anticipation. This simple coffee morning had turned into an event of high drama that had her nerves on standby. "What would make you angry?" She fiddled around with her spoon.

"Different suppliers," replied Andrea. Ava looked up.

How did she know?

Andrea continued, "You must know that we all know each other around here. So you didn't go to Montova, but you went a little further. All the tradespeople there know us too. I don't mind that you looked for new suppliers; it was a surprise to hear it from my friend, Geraldino.

Geraldino. One of the two new suppliers that she had recently discovered.

"We got talking. I buy my stock from there too. He mentioned he'd just had a large order from a lovely American woman. He described you to perfection. Between you and me, I think he likes you." She dipped her head and winked at Ava who breathed a sigh of relief.

That's all it was? If she were any further in her pregnancy she'd be at risk of breaking her waters early.

Andrea patted her friend's arm playfully. "I really don't mind. You're free to go to as many different suppliers as you want. I want you to branch out and sell lots of everything. I want your business to be a huge success. I just wondered why you hadn't mentioned anything to me. We've been sitting here drinking coffee and you've not said a thing."

Ava sat back in her chair. "I'm sorry. I didn't think it was that important." How could she tell her friend that she had sought out new suppliers because she was hoping to stop using Andrea for good? That she could no longer tolerate Andrea's non-stop chatter about Nico? That she didn't want to hear another word about their dinner dates, or God forbid, soon enough, it would be about him in bed with her.

Luckily, this seemed to appease Andrea. "Okay, forgiven. Just a word of advice: next time, you can drive Geraldino down on price more. He adds on a huge markup to his products."

"I wish you'd told me that before!"

"I would have if I'd known." Andrea reminded her gleefully. "So this really is goodbye?"

Ava nodded her head. She looked around her, as the people spilled out onto the cobbled streets, gently ambling by.

The Casa di Giulietta, just around the corner from here, had been a point of interest, on her first day out in Verona—back at the time when Nico had pretended to be the hotel driver. She had come full circle.

She smiled in spite of herself but it was a smile weighed down with a touch of sadness.

"Why do you look so happy?" Andrea asked, "I'm already feeling sad about you leaving."

"I love it here," Ava replied almost without thinking. It was the truth. Verona had become like a home away from home, even in her misery. There was something about the place that anchored her to it. While she couldn't get away from her sleazy hotel fast enough, she was sad to be leaving. Everything about Verona, its lush green landscape, its cobbled streets and sense of grandeur, and the people—most of them—rooted her here.

Though Denver beckoned, Verona felt more like home.

Her unborn baby would never know about this place if she never revealed anything to him or her about its father. A pang of guilt shot through her, knowing she had failed in her mission of coming clean with Nico.

It had been impossible to see that task through.

"Then you must come back again. Nico will miss you too. I'm not the only one."

"Oh?"

"He came to see me. He had some papers to drop off to do with your cribs order. He's very proud of the success your store is having."

Ava made a low noise in her throat.

Andrea perked up a little. "We kissed." The look on her face made Ava's heart stop.

"Oh?" Ava forced herself to sound as excited as Andrea looked.

Andrea bobbed her head excitedly. "He's a great kisser."

Ava felt a pain in her chest, possibly heartburn, most likely not. She blinked at her friend.

"We just ended up...in this ...kiss."

Ava felt her face flush and was reminded of her own encounter with Nico's lips a few days ago. The image of his body pressed against *hers* raised her temperature. She lifted her hand to the waiter and when he stopped by, she ordered a glass of milk.

"Heartburn," she said when Andrea looked at her.

"I don't know if it will lead to anything. He hasn't called since. I know he's been busy with the new hotel. Did you know he bought it?" Andrea chirped along happily.

Ava nodded. "I thought he might." The hotel purchase was the furthest thing from her mind. Now that she had recalled it, she couldn't remove memories of his kiss or stop that familiar ache between her legs. But along with the yearning and the seared memories, came the guilt and the anger, that he could so easily kiss his way from one woman to the next, treating each as nothing more than instant relief.

But he hadn't called Andrea back and this was news to her. In fact, since then, he'd come to see *her* at her hotel. He'd wanted to talk. A tiny thrill gave flight in Ava's chest.

"He'll be staying mostly in Ravenna soon. Apparently he has this insane desire to open the new hotel by November; at least that's the plan."

November?

She'd have his baby that month.

She clasped her stomach. No longer flat, the slight roundness of her belly, noticeable only to her, was a comfort.

Perhaps this promise of a new life was the very thing she needed to make meaning out of everything that had happened to her up until now.

That chapter of her life that had started when things with Connor had ended had now come to a close. Things with Nico had ended and perhaps it was for the better.

Her baby's birth would herald another new chapter in her life. Maybe this baby was the gift she was meant to have.

CHAPTER THIRTY-FIVE

It was turning into a day of goodbyes.

First Andrea, and now back to this hotel she had come to love so much. As the taxi drove off, Ava stood in the car park and stared lovingly at the front of the Casa Adriana.

She hadn't set out to come here when she left her hotel this morning. But after sitting at the pavement café with Andrea, all kinds of memories stirred within her. She'd felt compelled to return to the place where it had all started.

She told herself she would come to take a final look at the hotel that her child would never know was part of its legacy. And because she knew she would never come back here, she allowed herself the gift of a final goodbye.

She needed to say goodbye to Gina who had been so good to her and given her the support she had needed on the day of the funeral.

And then she convinced herself that a last goodbye to Nico was in order.

The glass entrance doors glistened in the sunlight, bringing back memories of her mother and Edmondo the last time she had seen Edmondo alive.

She breezed through, her heartbeat already ratcheted up tenfold. The sight of Gina tapping away at the keyboard gave her relief. As soon as Ava approached the desk, Gina stopped typing and turned to acknowledge her. A cry of surprise left her when she saw Ava.

"Ava. What a lovely surprise." She left her keyboard and turned to face her.

"Good to see you too, Gina." Ava placed her hands on the high wooden ledge and looked around. Her heart skidded at the idea that Nico might be around. She hoped he would be. The anger she felt toward him recently had melted away once again in the knowledge that she was here to say goodbye.

"What brings you here today?"

"I came to say goodbye."

Gina's face dropped. "Goodbye?"

Ava nodded. "Yes, I know it seems as though I'm always saying goodbye, and then I show up again, or extend my stay. But this time, it really is goodbye."

Gina looked genuinely sad and shook her head slowly. "I thought you might stay longer."

So did I. "I have so many things to take care of back at home." Ava smiled again, despite feeling sad at the prospect of returning to Denver. She looked forward to seeing her family again, but the idea of resolving issues between Rona and Kim, and navigating around Connor, just seemed like more work than she wanted to handle.

Gina pursed her lips together. "I hope you will come back here again someday. I feel we could have become better acquainted."

"I have the same feeling myself," replied Ava warmly.

"Would you care for some tea in our dining room?' Gina offered suddenly.

"Thank you, but I'd better not. It was only a quick visit.

I'm not very good with goodbyes." Her hands still stuck to the wooden ledge. She hesitated, wanting to ask about Nico. She felt she owed him an apology, at the very least.

Finally Gina said, "Nico isn't here, but he might be back soon."

Maybe she would have that cup of tea after all. But, seriously, who was she kidding? She was so confused about what to think anymore, and being here, at the Casa Adriana, she was right in the thick of it all.

Her thoughts spun a hundred and eighty degrees. Perhaps going now would be best. "It might be better if I went now, anyway."

Gina pulled an apologetic face.

"Goodbye then." Ava dragged her hands down and turned to go.

"He has your bracelet on his desk—you know, the one you returned." Gina's parting words forced Ava to turn back. The two women looked at each other.

"It *is* a beautiful bracelet." Ava sighed, remembering the first time she had held it in Venice, when Nico had come after her.

They had been so beautiful, those precious days in Venice.

"It's not my place, but that woman in his office, a long time ago, just before you returned the bracelet ..." Gina waited, needing assurance that Ava understood what she was saying. Ava nodded dutifully. "That woman was a journalist. Nothing more than a troublemaker."

"I know," Ava replied. She believed him, at last.

Whatever it was that had prompted Gina to make a last-ditch effort of salvaging their relationship, it was too late. Ava doubted that Gina knew of the Andrea and Nico love match either. Though from the sounds of it, that looked to be cooling down, too.

Men like Nico, too handsome for their own good, dripping with sex appeal, were dangerous for women like her to be around. She was better off with someone who would offer her security and loyalty.

She thought she had that with Connor once. And look how that had turned out.

Maybe she was better off alone.

Nobody could hurt her then.

"I must go, Gina. Goodbye." Ava made an effort to be decisive before Gina tried to find more reasons to stop her from going.

"Goodbye," said Gina sadly.

Sadness gripped her chest, crushing it in a vise-like grip as she rushed across the tiled white-and-black marble floor. In a rush to get away, she pushed out of the double glass doors and skipped down the stairs, exhaling fully, now that she was out.

But the thin strap on her sandal gave way and she lost her footing. She buckled, flinging out her arms as she fell forward, but her hand smacked the floor at an awkward angle. She slammed onto the ground with a thud. A sharp pain in her head made her cry out—just as a burning pain shot up her wrist.

And then her world turned black.

CHAPTER THIRTY-SIX

He'd heard the scream first, and then, in that instant he froze when he saw Ava lying at the foot of the steps.

He'd reached her in no time and cradled her head in his lap, checking for her pulse, his insides quivering. Gina burst through the doors and gasped when she saw Ava's pale face lying in Nico's lap. She had scrambled back inside and rushed to call the emergency services.

Ava had only lost consciousness for a few seconds, but it was enough to scare him to pieces. She had come to but was confused and dazed, and in a lot of pain, her wrist swollen alarmingly.

Now at the hospital, Nico refused to move from her bedside, sitting back while the medical staff tended to her. First they rushed her off for an x-ray, and then they checked her over properly. The concussion worried them the most.

In the end they diagnosed a bad wrist sprain. She was lucky nothing had been broken.

With his heart in his mouth, Nico felt as helpless now as he had when his mother had lain here, just like this. He'd been unable to help her then.

This was different. Ava wasn't going to die. She would be fine. He left the room at the nurse's request since they needed to put a splint on her injured wrist.

He waited outside in the hallway, his legs shaking uncontrollably. The waiting was giving him the jitters. The doctors had said everything was fine, but he wanted to be sure. That strike to the head must have been painful and she had a nasty raw gash on the side of her forehead.

When he went back inside, Ava had fallen asleep. They had given her a little something for the pain, but it had made her drowsy. He didn't want to disturb her and sat down quietly by her side.

After a while, he leaned over and ran his fingers lightly down her face, stroking it with feather light touches. He traced a line from her forehead, passing the angry red scrape on the side, outlining the curve of her dark eyebrows, down the center, along her too perfect nose, and finally, he traced his finger over her luscious lips, before slipping down to her hand again.

She stirred, and he stopped, wanting her to rest. But her eyelids fluttered slowly open, and huge, blue-gray eyes looked up at the ceiling, slowly moving around, before settling on his face. His heart melted and he slipped his fingers over her hand again and smiled at her.

She looked at him, confused, and lifted her hand up to touch her face, her brow crinkling.

"You're fine," he said softly. "You've got a badly sprained wrist and slight concussion."

"Owww!" she moaned, looking down at her right hand, now sheathed in a fingerless black glove.

"Don't try to move it," he warned, seeing her grimace.

"It hurts a lot." She squinted, indicating the pain.

"You'll need to let it rest for a few weeks."

He felt the draft behind him first, before the doctor appeared beside him. "Good," the man said, looking over the splint she wore. He flashed a light in Ava's eyes. Nico ducked out of the way. He had a million questions to ask but let the doctor carry on with his tasks. Ava still seemed a little dazed, but the doctor made all the right noises.

"Good. Apart from the sprained wrist, you'll be fine." He put away his light. "How's your head, Ava?" he asked, bending over with a careful smile.

"A little groggy. It hurts."

"I'd like to keep you here overnight at least, just for observation. I'm happy that everything is fine but with a concussion, we need to make sure."

Nico breathed a sigh of relief. He would stay with her for as long as she was here. Or as long as she needed him.

"You'll both be happy to hear that the baby is fine, too." Nico heard the doctor's words first and he froze. The doctor gave Ava a comforting smile, then placed a placating hand on Nico's shoulder before he left.

Pale as a ghost, Nico's eyes riveted on Ava.

What baby?

She was watching him, and one step was all it took for him to reach her side. He looked at her face, and then his gaze dipped to her stomach. "What baby?" he whispered, frozen in place.

Ava's eyes grew wide and she placed a protective hand over her stomach.

"What baby, Ava?" he repeated and when she said nothing, he asked with urgency. "What baby?"

Silence seared the awkwardness of the moment, until the door burst open and Andrea breezed in. "Oh my goodness, Ava! Look at you." She swept over to the side and gave Ava a kiss on her cheek, then her gaze scanned over the wrist splint and the dressing on her forehead.

As though she had only just noticed him, she turned to Nico and acknowledged him, her face brightening as she did so. "Hey, Nico." She tucked an unruly curl behind her ears.

His eyes still on Ava, Nico barely uttered a mumbled greeting back.

"What happened?" Andrea turned her attention back to Ava.

"It looks worse than it is. My sandal strap broke and I fell down the stairs and then I passed out. It's not a big deal, really." She gave Nico a small smile, but he couldn't reciprocate. She was chattering on as though everything was normal but his world had just been rocked.

"Thank goodness you're fine." Andrea's cell phone rang and she held up a finger to Ava. "I'll be back, I have to take this." She breezed out again.

"That's why you went back to him isn't it?" Nico demanded, this time leaning over her and bringing his face close to hers. Her eyes, smoky now like a river, captivated him while he held his breath anticipating her answer. She gazed back at him, staring deep into his eyes while his blood simmered. "I couldn't believe you went back to him, but now it all makes sense."

He felt the blow to his chest, followed by a sharp pain of regret. Then the realization hit home and he scanned her face, hoping to intercept hidden signals beneath the surface.

Whatever had taken place between her and that idiot, whatever had possessed her to give him a second chance, had ended up cementing her to him. She was romantically minded enough to want to do the right thing.

"Nico—" She started to get up, but he didn't want to hear any more words from her.

"Sorry about that. Damned suppliers." Andrea breezed back in again.

"I'd better get going." Nico stepped away. "Goodbye," he said, over his shoulder, not even turning around to look at the two women who stared after him as he walked out.

CHAPTER THIRTY-SEVEN

"If this is what it takes for us to spend the day together, then so be it." Andrea sat down on the uncomfortable plastic chair and dropped her handbag to the floor.

Ava smiled tiredly in response.

"To think our coffee this morning would lead to this."

Ava winced. Her head hurt and the pain from her wrist was unbearable. But that pain was sweet relief compared to how she felt inside. It had been one of the hardest things she'd had to hear—that Nico assumed the baby was Connor's.

What did he take her for?

She would have put him straight there and then, but she'd been so shocked by his assumption that she couldn't find her voice, and then Andrea had returned. She had never imagined it would come to this. Whenever she'd imagined telling Nico about the baby, their story had ended happily.

Andrea babbled on, but Ava's mind was elsewhere. She closed her eyes, trying to block out the pain inside her chest and she lovingly pressed down gently on her stomach. The small bump seemed a little rounder each week and soon, she'd have to start shopping for maternity clothes.

"You fell at the steps outside the Casa Adriana?" her friend asked.

Ava rolled her eyes. "There of all places, would you believe?"

"Gina said you passed out cold."

"How did you find out?"

"I was passing by the hotel, like you. If I'd known you were going there, we could have gone together," said Andrea.

She was going to see Nico? Ava didn't like the sound of that. "Mine was a spur of the moment decision. I wanted to say goodbye to Gina." *And see Nico for the last time.*

"When I got there, the emergency services had just left, and Nico had gone with you," Andrea told her. "Gina said Nico didn't want to leave your side."

Ava raised her hand to her forehead, not daring her fingers to touch the red mess.

"Does it hurt?" Andrea asked, making a face as she examined the gash on Ava's face.

"It hurts like hell." Ava braved a grin. "I must look like hell, too."

"No." Andrea shook her head slowly. "You look gorgeous, you always do. Nico couldn't take his eyes off you even when I interrupted you both by turning up." Her voice was somber and she looked at Ava then swallowed slowly, the corners of her lips straightening. "I've been thinking." Andrea's brown eyes darkened with worry, and she paused.

"Thinking about what?"

"Thinking that I've had it all so wrong, this thing with me and Nico." Ava's breath hitched in her throat. Andrea's face was somber. "Even now, when I came in, it was all wrong. I had it wrong. He barely looked at me."

"I don't think that's true," Ava countered, knowing that news of her baby was what had kept Nico transfixed.

"No." Andrea shook her head again. "I've read it all wrong, even the kiss. If I'm honest with myself, looking back, he moved away. It's only me who's been feeling the vibe. It's all been in my head. It's all been one-sided. Nico doesn't have it—those feelings, the vibe, the desire or attraction—none of it, for me." She looked squarely at Ava, who shrank beneath her friend's gaze.

"But this morning when we were having coffee," Ava said slowly, "You were so happy when you spoke about him."

Andrea's expression remained dull, just like her voice. "That's it, don't you see? I convinced myself that we were rekindling an old romance. We've been good friends, and now, with this dark time in his life, I wanted to help. He seemed so alone and so sad and I made the mistake of imagining something that wasn't there. He let me in, but not because he wanted me. He let me in because he needed a friend."

"But you went to dinner together? And the kiss? You said he kissed you. He wouldn't do that unless it meant something."

Andrea shook her head slowly. "The kiss was more my doing than his. But I can see it clearly now, it's nothing compared to the way he looks at you."

The pain from Ava's wrist almost made her pass out but she couldn't turn away from Andrea's words. She hung onto them, like a child clinging to its mother's fingers.

"He looks at you the way I wish he looked at me," Andrea's voice was barely a whisper. "That's the look of a man who'd give his life for you."

Daggers danced around Ava's temples and left her no voice with which to answer back. She was speechless, and in pain, and yet her heart was starting to dance with joy.

"I care for him," said Andrea. "I'll always be here for him, as a friend only because I don't think he wants anything else. It's strange to see, really."

"What's so strange to see?" Ava asked, grimacing.

"Strange to see Nico Cazale want the one thing he can't have."

Ava tried to shake her head, but it only made it hurt more. Andrea stared at her knowingly. "I know you don't want to talk about it and I don't know what's gone on between you both, but something *has*. I've been blind to have not seen it. I've never seen that man look at anyone the way he looks at you."

Ava's face crumbled and her mouth fell open.

"You look like you're hurting. Do you need something? Shall I get the nurse?" Andrea asked.

"No, they'll start making their rounds soon."

"I shall leave you to get some rest." Andrea picked up her handbag. "I'm going out to grab some food. Can I get you anything?"

"No, thanks. I'm not hungry," Ava managed, now that the pain was hurting more than ever. "Will you come back again?" She hoped Andrea would return. She didn't want to be left alone with her thoughts for it hurt too much to think.

Andrea nodded. "For you, I have all the time in the world. Get some rest."

CHAPTER THIRTY-EIGHT

Nico bumped into Gina as he walked back through the hotel doors. "How is she?" she asked.

A muscle flexed along his jaw. "She'll be fine. Concussion and a sprained wrist. They're keeping her in for observation."

"I can't believe it. She only came by to say goodbye." Gina's expression grew sad. "She asked for you, you know."

What for? Nico wasn't in the mood to talk much. He had driven back numbed by this latest revelation, by the news of Connor's baby. For a second he'd dared to think that it might be his. But they had both been so careful, it would be a miracle if it were.

Her whole time here, she really had hated him. Even that day when he'd kissed her, he'd been a fool for thinking she felt something for him. Now he understood the malice in her voice when she'd confessed love for Connor.

He'd been stupid for thinking they could work things out.

"I'm going to pay her a visit on my way home." Gina seemed to be waiting for his reaction. He only caught the end of her sentence and frowned. "I really like Ava. She's all alone here, it would be nice to let her know someone cares."

He swallowed. "Did you get hold of Elsa?" They still had her contact details on file. Nico felt it was his duty to let Ava's family know that she was in the hospital. Gina shook her head. "I called a few times but no-one answered, so I left a message."

Perhaps he would call Elsa later. He wasn't in the mood for speaking to Connor, not now or ever, and he figured Ava would let him know that she and the baby were fine.

He rubbed his face with his hands. He'd written off his working day to stay by Ava's side at the hospital, but then she'd dropped the bombshell and he'd had no choice but to leave.

What a God-awful mess this was.

He thought he understood women, thought he knew all about them, their ways, their moods, their quirks, their odd reasoning. He thought he had it all figured out.

And then he'd met Ava.

That woman was an enigma to him and, it seemed, would always be. He'd gotten the whole thing so obviously wrong. He believed he'd found 'the one.' But for her, it was nothing of that sort.

How wrong could he have been?

"Can I go with you when you go to visit her this evening?" Gina asked.

"Who said I'm going back this evening?" he replied gruffly. Gina eyed him with a look that made him think she could read his mind. "I'm busy, and I don't want to be disturbed for the rest of the day." He stormed off and heard a sarcastic, "Yes, sir," from Gina.

Slamming the door shut behind him, he sank into his father's chair. He hoped the mere action of sitting in the seat where his father spent much of his time, would impart some of his father's wisdom to him. Or give him the sense of peace that he craved now that his emotions had been so heavily shaken.

But as he sat, he suddenly ached to hear his father's voice again. This time he wouldn't care if his father was annoyed with him for being too ambitious or complained about a task he had forgotten to carry out. Right now, he would gladly accept any telling offs no matter how harsh, just to hear his father's voice again.

The void in his chest hadn't diminished as time went on. Each day Nico felt more and more as though he was falling apart. He drove himself harder than ever, traveling back and forth between Ravenna, keen to get the building work started. After all, he was now armed with a plan and a timeline to work against. But he knew what it was all for; a form of distraction to keep him from wallowing in the emptiness of his world.

With Edmondo gone, and Ava too, his world of safe and familiar loved ones had disintegrated and he was now more alone than ever. But when he'd seen Ava lying so awkwardly and unconscious on the ground, it had brought back those strong emotions of what it was to truly love and care for someone. In that second he'd felt as though his insides had been ripped from him, and he hadn't breathed easy until the ambulance services had arrived and told him she would be all right.

He'd been ready to stop running on his hamster wheel, and to take time out, just for her.

But now that he knew about the baby, and Connor, his decision had been made for him. They would never share anything together; there would never be any hope for reconciliation.

He pulled out the project plan for the work on the Ravenna hotel. With an opening date scheduled for the end of November, there was much to be done. The Cazales had never owned a spa retreat before and he was going into unknown territory. It was a risk, but when he pulled it off, the reward would be all the sweeter.

Edmondo's absence hurt him deeply, and it was only now that he realized just how much his father's guidance meant to him. Just when things had started to pull together, they had splintered and fallen apart.

He had to accept the ways things had worked out and he had to have the faith that it was all for the best.

Wearily, he picked up his phone and called the architect. There was much work to be done.

W hen he left his office later that evening, the reception desk was manned with the usual late-night clerk.

Gina's shift had finished long ago and Nico breathed a sigh of relief that she wasn't around to ask more questions. Lately he found himself answering a lot of them.

With a nod of his head, he decided that tomorrow he would ask her what she thought of the new role he had offered. It was time he went over some of the tasks he needed her to take care of, because soon he would be staying over at Ravenna a couple of nights.

As he stepped out into the cool May evening, his stomach rumbled loudly. He had been so busy going over the architect's drafts that he had forgotten to have lunch. He didn't want to go home either. Maybe he could call Andrea and go for a bite to eat. But he shook his head and got into his car.

Andrea as a friend was what he needed, but the more he relied on her, the more she seemed to get the wrong end of things. He didn't want to hurt her and he still wanted her friendship but maybe it was better to lie low for a while. He didn't feel romantically inclined towards her, but he got the feeling that she did. There could be no more dinners with her until he told her. He would have to let her down gently.

For a good while, close on twenty minutes, he sat in his car, unsure of where to go or what to do.

He had turned the music off, preferring complete silence to still his thoughts. When his mind wasn't busy on his work, his thoughts drifted to Edmondo, and Ava, and things that could no longer be.

He sat quietly, pondering the visceral nature of relationships and the frail thread of connectivity that sometimes held people together—or pulled them apart.

It made sense to go home, but the constant buzzing inside him made it impossible for him to ignore this feeling he could not make go away.

And so he did the one thing he felt compelled to do.

"You?" He had forgotten she would be here, just as she had said she would.

"You told me you weren't coming back here tonight," Gina retorted, no less with a smile on her face.

Nico's gaze fell to Ava, who now sat upright in the bed with her sheets up to her waist. She looked at him in surprise, before letting out a slow smile. She seemed better and rested compared to how she had been when he had left her earlier.

He smiled back at her, relieved to see that she seemed in less pain. When he looked back at Gina, she was gazing at him expectantly. Nico frowned. With Gina here, this wouldn't be the quick get-a-load-off-his-chest visit that he wanted it to be.

"I'm going," announced Gina, and he wondered if the woman had telepathic powers.

"But you only just got here," Ava cried in disappointment. Gina got up with a look of determination. "I remembered that I have an exercise class tonight."

"It was good of you to come and see me. And thank you for the flowers and the fruit."

Gina gave Nico a knowing look as she charged past him. It had been the speediest exit from her that he'd ever seen.

"She literally just arrived about ten minutes before you did." Ava made small talk and he could tell by her forlorn expression that she was a little unsure of how to react to him. Things had been a little strained when he'd left her earlier, but he'd had time to think things through.

What he had to say now was important and he needed to get the noise out of his head. He needed a clean slate before he lost himself in the plans for the new hotel. Ava would return to her life and leave him to get on with his, but not before he had said what he needed to.

"Why don't you sit down?" Ava asked. She seemed more at peace, a little less cranky. Maybe keeping her news from him had been hard and now that she had come clean, things were on a more even keel between them.

He declined her offer to sit and stood near enough but not close enough that her scent and the nearness of her would remind him of what he had lost. "You seem a lot better now."

"The pain has gone down. I refuse to take painkillers because of the baby..." She stared at him oddly and he couldn't quite read her expression. "I tried to get a hold of your mother earlier. I left a message and Gina did too."

Ava nodded. "She told me. My mom's fine. I called her on

her cell. She's been out and about, keeping busy as usual. It's a good thing. She found it hard to leave the house after Edmondo..."

Nico nodded, then turned his head away, avoiding her gaze. "Was Connor worried?" he asked.

"Connor?"

"About the baby?"

"Oh." She breathed out loudly, adjusting herself in the bed. A nurse walked in just then and looked at her watch, "I'm afraid it's time to leave. Visiting hours are over."

"Please, just five minutes. It's important," Nico urged. To his surprise, the nurse agreed. Silence fell again as soon as she left. He took a calming inhale, preparing himself. "You'll be gone soon, and I'll be spending a lot of time in Ravenna from now on—"

"Congratulations. I heard you were going ahead with buying that hotel we saw."

He nodded, trying not to think about their time in Ravenna. This had become much harder than he had imagined. He tossed aside her comment, wanting desperately to get out the words that were choking up his throat; interruptions he could do without. "It's going ahead, the whole spa retreat and lots of building work."

"That's wonderful news." She looked happy for him, and the gray in her eyes flecked blue again. He looked away because it was getting painful for him to see her sitting there, and to recall their past times together.

"I have to go now, but..." He thrust his fisted hands deep into his pockets and looked down. "I want you to know..." His voice choked up and suddenly he found it hard to tell her the words he wanted her to hear.

"Nico—" Ava's voice was a whisper.

He composed himself, and with a determined effort,

looked at her. "Please, let me say this. I want you to know that I'm thrilled for you ... about the baby. I really am. And I wish you every happiness with Connor." He struggled to steady his voice, thankful for her silence.

Her gaze was solemn as she heard him out. When she tried to speak, he put his finger to his lips, motioning for her silence. "It might not seem like I'm happy for you ... but I am ... because I know what a great mother you'll make."

"Nico—"

Again, he held his finger to his lips, his eyes pleading with her to let him have his say. "I hope it all works out for you. But ..." He took in a deep breath. "It might be wrong, very wrong, of me to say this, but I'm going to say it anyway." He looked intently into her eyes. "If Connor ever does to you what he did before, I'll be here waiting for you and the baby. I'll raise your baby as my own, if you'll let me. If you want me, that is."

She looked shell-shocked, her mouth gaping open. It was when the tears stood along her lower lash line, that he knew he had overstepped his boundary; there were some things it might have been better to keep to himself.

"Oh, Nico—"

But the doors swung open and the nurse was back, looking sterner than ever. "It really is time to go now, please."

Because he was now done with what he had to say, he stepped towards Ava, leaned over, and kissed her gently on her forehead.

She seemed lost for words.

"Goodbye, Ava."

And without saying another word he walked out of her life.

CHAPTER THIRTY-NINE

His words had moved her and she'd let the tears roll down, unabated.

It had been the last thing she had expected, and the very thing she had been waiting for.

Confirmation that he really cared. That he really wanted her. And now she knew, without a shadow of a doubt.

The only thing that had stopped her from telling him about his baby, was because she had so desperately wanted to hear his words first. But she need not have worried because he'd told her that he loved her no matter what. She hadn't slept at all last night and it was only when the birds started to chirp outside that she finally felt a light sleep crawl over her.

Her eyelids flew open when the doctor came in first thing the next morning. She couldn't rest or stay here another day; she would make her escape somehow.

In her sleepless disquiet, she had been forced to think. For too long now, Ava had kept too many lies, and the web of deceit she had woven around her had turned into a beast that now threatened the very structure of her life.

If Nico hadn't said those words, she would have gone back

to Denver and bumbled her way through life, accepting help from everyone, finding more lies to bind her life together and agreeing to Connor's help but nothing more. There would probably have been many moments when she would have thought of Nico. Her child would see to that, probably. She sometimes wondered which of Nico's features her baby would share.

But now she needn't wonder anymore. Things had changed. There was a chance. There was hope.

"I'm sorry to have kept you waiting." The doctor smiled as he checked through her medical notes.

"Can I go now? I feel very well." She couldn't get out fast enough.

"You certainly can, young lady. If you get your things together—"

"I've already gotten everything together." With her good arm, she slipped the strap of her bag around her neck. She didn't have anything else; she was leaving in the same clothes that she had arrived in.

"Go easy on that wrist. The paperwork will need—"

"Done, I signed it while I was waiting for you." She was relieved she'd had full medical insurance in place.

The doctor checked the notes again and gave a shrug. "You really are in a hurry." He stared down at her through his bifocals and gave her a warm smile. "Best of luck." Ava shook his hand heartily and almost ran out of the door.

A short while later, the taxi stopped outside the Casa Adriana and this time when she went up the stone steps, she walked carefully. The hospital slippers, the only footwear she had on her, were just as dangerous but she wore them anyway.

She flip-flopped her way across the beautiful white-and-black marble floor, anticipation swirling inside her. A warmth enveloped her and she felt as though she'd grown a pair of wings and was ready to take flight. Even the pain of her wrist didn't deflate her spirits.

Gina threw down her pen as soon as she saw her. "They've discharged you already?" she asked, surprised. "How are you feeling?"

Ava nodded happily, a smile dripping from her lips. "I'm feeling a lot better now. I couldn't have stayed there another day."

"It looks painful. Come, sit down. Let me get you something nice to eat—" Gina was about to walk around from behind the reception area, but Ava stopped her.

"Wait," she said. The idea of Casa Adriana cooking made her mouth water, but she had more important things to tend to first. "Is he here?" She nodded towards the office door.

Gina shook her head, delight spreading slowly across her face, in anticipation. "He's in the gardens."

"The gardens?"

"He spends a lot of time out there these days."

Ava beamed at her. Wordlessly, she went through to the conservatory, to the door that led out to the back. She walked out, excitement buzzing all around, as she rushed as fast as she could in her slippers along the garden path, disturbing the peace that spilled over everywhere. She craned her neck in all directions, looking for signs of Nico but all she saw were evergreens, flowers, potted shrubs and bushes. She followed the garden path and walked along until she saw the pergola.

Sitting in the corner, on one of the wicker chairs, was Nico. He turned his head in her direction and it seemed as though he was a million miles away. But she didn't care. She would bring him back to here and now.

To her.

She rushed, walking faster, and he stood up, a perplexed look decorating his face.

"Ava?"

"Nico."

She stopped where she was, the distance between them no more than his height. She was breathless, more from the excitement of seeing him, and from knowing that she carried the news that would make his heart sing.

"They discharged me this morning."

The initial relief and happiness on his face were quickly replaced by his cool, and unflappable mask. She watched as he dug his hands into his trouser pockets. "You look well. How're you feeling?" He nodded at her arm.

"It's fine," she answered, shaking her head dismissively. She felt happier than she had in a long time. Now was the time to lose the lies. She wanted to tell him and knew she would never forget this moment. But for these precious few seconds she loved the anticipation of keeping him in suspense.

He stared back, looking more confused than ever, as if he couldn't understand why she was here. She guessed that he had a hundred questions, but with his jaw set so defiantly, he was clearly holding back. "Everything's fine?" he asked.

She let her lips curve upwards. "Yes. *Everything* is fine." She stepped toward him slowly, taking small, hesitant steps and all the time she watched the muscles tighten on his face. He let out a slow release of breath and in a voice low, husky, peppered with confusion, said, "That's a relief." His hands were dug deep into his pockets.

"Your baby is going to be fine, Nico." She watched the words fall and waited for his reaction. He inclined his head, unable to speak, and his hands slipped out of his pockets slowly.

"*My baby?*" Confusion crept across his and he crossed his arms over his chest. "But, I thought you said ..."

She shook her head and closed the distance between them so that they were an arm's length apart. "I didn't say anything. You *assumed.*"

He looked confused. Happy confused. "But why didn't you put me straight?" She stared deep into his eyes, needing for him to hear what she had to say from the depths of her heart, and because she also needed to hear his truth; because a lot rode on it—her future, theirs, the baby's. "I needed to know how you felt about me. I needed to know that it was *me* you wanted."

His eyes glassed over. "It was always you. Only you, Ava." She looked at him, holding her gaze, unable to speak. He stared back, unblinking. "From the moment I met you, it was only ever you."

At last, she allowed herself to breathe, and smile.

"My baby?" He uncrossed his arms, readying himself. "But I thought we were safe?"

"So did I, but you remember the couple of times in Venice?"

He tilted his head back, as if recalling the memories and the tightness on his face melted away. He smiled at her properly then, for the first time in a long time. "May I?"

She nodded.

Gingerly, he reached out and ran his fingers over the roundness of her stomach. She had on a loose shirt, so when he found the roundness, surprise resurfaced once more. He splayed his hand out against her stomach and she liked the feel of his hand on her skin. "Venice?" he asked, still looking puzzled. "So you're—"

"Almost three months pregnant."

His face broke out into a big, wide ear-splitting smile and

he laughed, still touching her stomach. Then, "What about Connor?"

"What about him?"

"All these rumors about you and him getting back together."

"They were just that. Rumors, and nothing more."

"But he returned the bracelet. Why?"

His hand felt warm and gentle across her stomach, and in all that time he'd not moved it an inch. She had forgotten how sensual he made her feel.

"I couldn't accept the bracelet when I'd seen you with that woman."

Nico looked away, as if trying to remember who she was talking about. A line deepened between his brows. "I've already told you about her."

"But I didn't know that then. I hated you. After we had spent those days together in Riccione and Ravenna, for me to then walk in and see *that*. Can't you see how I felt? I didn't want your bracelet or you. I couldn't even bring myself to return it to you. I didn't want to hear more of your lies so I asked Connor to return it. I realize now that it was the wrong thing to do. I should have given you a chance to explain."

His face softened. "I'm sorry, for what I put you through."

"I'm sorry, too." She moved closer to him. "I shouldn't have run away like that. I was a complete mess that day, crying all the time. That was the day I found out I was pregnant." She looked into his deep brown eyes and sought comfort in them.

"I'm sorry, Ava."

"Me too."

"Nothing happened between you and Connor?"

"Nothing." She shook her head, but a delicious burst of excitement pooled in her nether regions. He could do this to her just by stroking her belly. She would never let this man get away—ever. She reassured him. "Connor's just a friend. He makes a better friend than a fiancé."

"An ex-fiancé."

"Yes," she agreed. "An ex-fiancé. I made up all these little lies because I didn't know where your heart lay. I had to protect myself, and the baby. I love you, Nico. I have loved you ever since that time in Venice, but you're a hard man to love and you've broken my heart many times."

"I never intended to hurt you." He moved his hand from her stomach to her waist. She lifted her good hand to his jaw and ran it gingerly over his skin. Prickles of excitement sprang up all over her body.

He looked down at her splint. "We have to be careful."

"Not that careful," she replied and moved her lips to him. He bent down and melded his mouth with hers, until they both drank from each other's kiss as though they hadn't tasted water for days.

She had missed *this*. Happiness settled all over her, leaving her secure in the knowledge that he would be hers, forever.

"Come on." He took her hand and led her gently around to the swing chair. The weight of the world had been lifted from her chest and her heart was once more filled with light, just like it had been when he'd come for her in Venice.

He fussed over her, making sure she was comfortable, propping her arm up on one of the cushions. "Do you need to put your feet up?" he asked, moving over to get a chair for her so that she could.

She laughed. "No. I'm not that incapacitated yet. I can still do a lot of things."

"Really?" He turned to her with a suggestive glint in his dark eyes. The sizzle in them heated her to her core, and pure carnal lust stirred within her. She laughed again. It was infectious, this feeling of happiness that he had unleashed.

She settled back into the swing chair and stared out at the lemon trees straight ahead. A sense of peace descended on her as she sat in this perfect little spot and she decided right there and then that she would come out here more often. It was so obvious to see why Nico had started to spend so much time here.

She imagined that Edmondo had probably spent many summer days here. As she patted the empty space beside her for Nico to come and sit, he looked distracted, and was staring out past the swing chair.

"I don't believe it." His voice broke and wavered, incredulity layered on thick. Ava tried to turn around, but the canopy of the swing chair obstructed her view.

Nico threw his head back and smiled. "Thank god you came," he mumbled, more to himself, and then he walked out of Ava's view.

CHAPTER FORTY

As her gaze locked on Nico, at the very same spot where she and Edmondo had last sat, Elsa rubbed her eyes.

For a stark, split second, she thought she was looking at the young Edmondo, standing tall and handsome as he smiled at her with his arms outstretched. She blinked away the tears that choked in her eyes and quickened her steps as she made her way to him.

But he was coming to meet her. A few strides were all it took for Nico to reach her. "Elsa." He covered her in his huge arms. "I am so happy you came." When his arms wrapped around her, she broke down, and sobbed uncontrollably, letting the floodgates open to tears that she had so far managed to hold back.

She cried long and hard in his arms, finding his embrace the safe haven for her sadness. He held her and when she looked up, his eyes were also glassy. They looked at one another quietly for the longest time.

"I'm so sorry for your loss, Nico," said Elsa, when she had regained the strength to continue.

"As I am for yours." He looked down at her, his hands gently placed on her shoulders.

"Mom?" The sound of Ava's voice rang out and Elsa moved away from Nico, a worried frown crossing her face when she saw her daughter's hand.

"What in god's name happened to you?" Elsa rushed towards her and gave Ava a careful hug, her eyes glued to the splint she wore.

Ava examined her mother's face. "I fell. Isn't that why you're here? We called you and left messages."

Elsa looked over her shoulder at Nico who also looked confused at her sudden appearance.

"You fell? I had no idea. What happened?"

Her daughter explained. "I tripped and fell down the hotel steps. It's fine now. The hospital discharged me this morning."

Horror struck and Elsa felt the color drain from her face. "Are you all right?" She touched her daughter's arm as though it was made from porcelain.

"Yes, Mom. I'm fine. It looks worse than it is." Ava gave her a reassuring hug. "But if you didn't come because of my fall then why are you here?"

"The baby. How's the baby?" Elsa asked, sounding fearful.

"How do you know about the baby?" Ava asked slowly.

A look of triumph and relief spread out over Elsa's face. "I didn't, not one hundred per cent, until now. But a mother has an idea about these things."

Nico had kept his distance, as if he wanted to give mother and daughter time to have their moment. Now he walked towards them, catching the last couple of sentences. "You were *also* in the dark?" he asked her.

They both turned to Ava, who blushed, looking helpless, and said nothing.

"Let's sit down at least, shall we?" Nico gently pointed the two women back towards the pergola. Ava sat back in her swing chair with Elsa beside her.

Elsa looked at their faces and saw the confusion. "I was worried," she began, sitting back in her seat, remembering the last day she had sat in this very chair, when Edmondo was still alive. It had been the last time they were together and she savored the memory, reliving it again as though it had only happened yesterday. It had been a day like this, almost. Only not as warm as it was now.

Distracted, she sat quietly, almost stepping back into the precious memory she often carried with her.

"Mom?" Ava touched her lightly on her knee. "You were worried?"

"I was worried about you both." She looked first at Ava, then her gaze traveled to Nico. He was listening carefully to her every word. She nodded her head back in Ava's direction. "I was especially worried about you and the baby. I wasn't sure at first, but I suspected." She turned to Nico. "But now I see that I didn't have any cause to worry at all."

Nico reached over and put his hand over hers. "You've no cause to worry at all, Elsa."

Somewhere near the bushes, birdsong broke out. It was midday and the sun's scattered rays warmed them. "Edmondo loved this garden," she said, the tears welling up in her eyes.

"He did," Nico agreed quietly.

"He would have been so happy to see you two back together, to know about the baby." She dabbed at her eyes and felt Ava's arm around her shoulder.

"I know, Mom. Not a day goes by that I don't regret keeping this from him."

"Don't." Nico reached out and put a hand on Ava's thigh. "You weren't to know. None of us could have known that he would be taken as quickly as he was."

"I like to believe that he knew this was going to happen all along," said Elsa. She wiped her tears away and felt a little better for coming here. She had announced to Rona and Carlos that she had decided to go to Verona anyway, and that they could either postpone their trip or take Tori with them. That had settled things fast enough.

She looked around her, gazing at the lemon trees, and breathed in the faint smell of jasmine in the air. In time, she would go and visit his grave, but she felt Edmondo's presence more strongly here in the garden.

She had done the right thing by coming. And in the end, Ava and Nico hadn't needed her to put things right; they had managed fine by themselves. Life always had a way of working out. "Lemonade," she said, getting up. "That's what's missing."

"I'll get it," offered Nico, standing up before she did.

But Elsa shook her head, "No. I can see the two of you need to spend time together. I'm going for a walk and on my way back, I'll bring a jug of lemonade."

She set off, following a path she recognized and walked slowly, taking her time.

"Let her go, Nico," said Ava, stretching out her hand to him and beckoning him to sit by her. "She needed to come, to have closure."

She watched her mother disappear past the lemon trees, happy to have her here, but more than that, she knew Elsa needed to be here.

Nico hugged her close to him. "I'm never going to let you go again."

"You said that once before," she reminded him.

"So I did. I never let you go, willingly. You walked out on me." He kissed the side of her head.

She turned to him and gazed up into his eyes. "I will never, ever do that again."

"And I promise never to throw that in your face again but —one last thing." His face was serious.

"Yes?" She waited, for now there would be no more lies.

"That time in your hotel, when I asked you if you loved Connor—you told me you did."

"I told you of the man I loved. It had nothing to do with Connor. I was speaking about *you*."

The twinkle in his eyes returned and he kissed her lightly. "Now that we've had the honeymoon, and we're having a baby, we're going to have to do something about a wedding."

The hairs on her neck tingled. "A wedding?"

He nodded, smiling as he watched her face closely.

"*This* is your idea of a proposal?"

"I can do extravagant, if you prefer, but then again," he stroked her cheek softly, "a shared panino on a bench somewhere could be just as fitting."

She relaxed. "A shared panino on *that* bench *would* be perfect."

"I thought so." He kissed her again.

"About that honeymoon, is it over?"

"No," he whispered, his lips hovering near hers. "It never, ever ends."

She liked the sound of that.

EPILOGUE

In Verona, 2 years later...

"I think it's time." Ava clung to the door for dear life and breathed in slowly as a wave of pain lacerated her lower back. She closed her eyes and tried to focus on her breathing.

"Time for what?" Nico looked up from his desk. He'd been deep in reading his financial reports. The Cazale Ravenna had made an excellent start.

Ava breathed in again, looking at her watch. The contractions were ten minutes apart, but they were lasting for longer, and getting more painful. She had been forced to abandon analyzing the figures for her US and Italian operations. It was only when she couldn't bear to sit any longer that she got up and paced around.

She let go of the door and took relief when the pain subsided. Maybe not. She wasn't sure. "I thought it might be time to go to the hospital." But then again, maybe she could finish analyzing her figures first. This might have been a false alarm, and she still had two weeks to go until her due date.

"Are you sure, sweetheart?" Nico watched her carefully. "We can go now."

"It's probably a false alarm." She waddled over to him and sat in the chair opposite. She had heard it was easier to push out subsequent babies but she still wasn't worried, after all, Elisabetta had gone eight days over the due date and had taken three more days to come out.

Ava hoped this second baby would be quicker. Two weeks early was good. It was May time and it was just starting to turn hot. A birthday in May would be wonderful. An almost summer baby.

"Are you sure?"

"I'm sure," she said, confidently. She could do with getting the figures out of the way. "Where's Elisabetta?"

"With your mom, in the garden." It was a good day to spend in the gardens, though probably not for painting, if Elisabetta was around. Elsa split her time between her two daughters. When she was in Verona, she often sat in the gardens at the hotel or the house and painted.

"Why are you in today?" Nico asked, moving his papers away. "You said you were going to take it easy."

"I wanted to get some things done here while I could. I'm going to be stuck at home for a few months once the baby comes."

She'd moved into Nico's office and he'd moved into Edmondo's. With the option of working from home or here, at the Casa Adriana, Ava alternated her days, not wanting to be cooped up in the house all the time.

She spent a lot of time in Montova or with the suppliers and now had a unit in Verona for storing her huge shipments.

Most of her products sold in the US, and she flew there

every quarter overseeing operations at that end. Kim had been recruited full-time and managed a lot of it, and they spoke many times during the day.

Rona had found the juggling of work and a child too much to handle and had reverted to full-time mothering.

Carlos worked harder than ever. He needed to, since they had a second one on the way any time now.

Ava had come in today because she had planned to work up until the last minute and she hoped the small contractions she had just experienced were Braxton Hicks.

She cast her eye over his reports, which were scattered all over the table. "How's it looking?" She noticed it was data from the Cazale Ravenna Spa Center and Hotel.

Nico sat back, weaving his hands together and placing his arms behind his head. Satisfaction was written all over his face. "It's doing great. Just great."

The Cazale Ravenna had started taking bookings as soon as it opened. By the time of its opening, word had already spread about its personalized spa treatment rooms, outdoor garden showers and seashell infinity pools, not to mention the facials and body treatments from the Far East. It hadn't opened on time; Nico had put Ava and the baby first, for the birth had been the highlight of November that year, almost eighteen months ago. But the opening had taken place the following spring, and Nico need not have worried.

Ravenna had seen nothing like it and the hotel drew praise from the moment it opened.

"It was just as you imagined it, wasn't it?" Ava looked at him proudly, knowing how tirelessly he had worked to make his vision a reality. "Your father would have been so proud of you."

"I wish he'd been here to see it." Nico unclasped his

hands and sat forward, suddenly somber. They held hands across the table.

With an excruciating cry of pain, Ava pulled her hand away and winced. Nico shot around to her side and placed his hand on her lower back but she screamed when he touched her. With her whole body racked with pain, she didn't want to be touched, not on her lower back or anywhere else.

"Don't," she said through gritted teeth. He moved his hands off at lightning speed and she closed her eyes.

"Hold tight, sweetheart." He was still fussing around her even as she managed to slowly stand up. It felt easier to stand than to sit and she suddenly wondered if she could bear the twenty-minute journey to the hospital in the car. She had forgotten this pain the moment she'd held her daughter in her arms. But now that it was back, she wondered how she could have ever forgotten a pain so intense it felt as though her body was being ripped apart.

She closed her eyes and inhaled slowly and deeply.

When the contraction had passed, she relaxed her hold on the table and opened her eyes.

"Tell me what I can do to make it better." Nico looked at her with soft brown eyes, his boundless love for her pouring out of them. He didn't want to see her in this pain, not after the long drawn-out birth when Elisabetta had made her entry into the world.

They had married, just three months before Elisabetta's birth, in the searing hot heat of August, at the church in Montagnano, where Nico's parents had married.

By the looks of it, the entire village had turned out. Her family had flown over, too.

She had felt like a beached whale, wearing cream for her wedding dress and six months pregnant, but the way Nico had looked at her, when she had joined him at the altar, she knew she looked beautiful.

Another pain shot through her and she winced, knew this was it, and grabbed her chance to lay down her rules. "I'm sorry, I can't bear to be touched; the pain is too much. Bags are packed, in my car. We should go. Tell Mom."

Nico panicked. "I'll get her."

She tried to breathe through the pain as he rushed out of the room. Trying to recall a pleasant memory, she thought of their first-year anniversary when they'd returned to Venice. She was now reaping the rewards of that celebration. She only had to cough in Venice and she got pregnant.

Once more, the pain started to build up again and her stomach turned rock hard. She couldn't move.

Good God, were they five minutes apart?

She braced herself and started to pant, short quick fast breaths in and out while she tried to block out everything, groaning as the pain started to rise to a crescendo.

Nico walked through the door, this time with little Elisabetta in his arms. The beautiful plump little girl with her mother's eyes and her father's dark hair, squeaked with delight when she saw Ava. She held out her arms towards her mother, straining away from Nico.

Ava groaned. She couldn't let her daughter see her in pain. She tried to smile, but it only scared Elisabetta, who hadn't seen her mother pull a face this scary before.

Elisabetta began to wail.

"Not a good time?" Nico started.

"No," growled Ava, she bit down on her teeth as waves of pain shot through her and she was forced to pant once more. She closed her eyes and heard Elisabetta howl.

While the other one strove to push out.

"Not a good time, honey," Nico cooed to Elisabetta. Lost

in the abyss of her pain, Ava clung onto the edges of the table again, pushing down. This man could run a string of hotels with cool efficiency, but he seemed to go to pieces when he saw his wife in pain. He left the room and she heard him holler for Gina as the last touches of pain shuddered through her. At this rate, they wouldn't make it to the car, let alone the hospital. She shouldn't have come in today.

In the next moment Nico appeared, without his daughter this time, and Elsa trailed closely behind.

"Shall we go, sweetheart?" he rushed to her side and was about to move her hair out of her face, but a stone-cold look from her stopped him.

"No time."

"You said it was time. Let's go."

"No time. Baby coming … now!" She started to pant again; the contractions were a minute apart.

She hadn't been prepared for it being this fast.

"Honey, you'll be fine." Elsa moved to her side, and Ava automatically felt a little comforted. "Nico, fetch me towels, a sheet, a shower curtain or tablecloth, whatever you find, hot water too, and call the doctor."

Ava suddenly felt as if she needed to use the washroom and just as she started to think about walking towards the door, a spurt of liquid gushed out, as though a bucket of water had emptied onto the floor.

Thank goodness they had wooden flooring.

"Bring me a mop, too," cried Elsa, "Now!" she hollered, her voice stern as Nico stood there, immobile.

"Now? The baby's coming now?" He stared at Ava in shock.

"*Now!*" Ava yelled, fighting the urge to push down.

"Can you move over to this side?" Elsa asked. Slowly Ava

shuffled over to the space behind Nico's chair. There was room here, for her to bear down.

"Kneel down," ordered Elsa. "I've got you, honey. Don't you worry about a thing."

"Need Nico," Ava panted.

"I'm here." Nico rushed to her side. And then he yelled for Gina.

Alessandro Edmondo Cazale was born less than forty minutes later, in Edmondo's office.

A few hours later, the family returned to their home.

"How's Elisabetta?" Ava asked, relieved that the birth had been over so quickly.

"Fine, tired. She thinks her baby brother is a plaything. Your mother is putting her down for her afternoon nap." Nico sat with his son in his arms, in their room, while Ava lay in bed, recovering. "He's so good, isn't he?" Nico's face had been fixed with a permanent smile ever since his son had been born.

"So far," replied Ava. She knew what was to come; the two-hour feeds would start soon, and she could kiss sleep goodbye for the next few months.

"He's perfect." Nico lowered his lips lightly to the top of his son's head.

"Your father would have loved him." Ava watched father and son sitting quietly by the window.

"I know," he said softly. "He would have loved all of this— the children, you and me together, your mother here." A flicker of sadness crossed his face until Ava smiled at him, and he smiled back.

It would have been perfect, but life was like that

sometimes; a trickle of bittersweet mixed in with a burst of happiness. And that was fine too.

Thank you for reading HONEYMOON BLUES! Nico and Ava's story continues in HONEYMOON BLISS when they finally seal their commitment to one another.

Please note: The Honeymoon series was initially a trilogy (which was why I wrote an epilogue for this book), however, due to reader demand, I wrote a further two books continuing Nico and Ava's story. **HONEYMOON BLISS takes place shortly after the end of HONEYMOON BLUES but it does not go as far as the epilogue mentioned in this book.**

On their honeymoon at last …
Life has never looked better for the newly married couple as they embark on their honeymoon, but even in paradise, problems from home creep into their lives. In dealing with the highs and lows of love, Nico and Ava try to pick themselves up at every opportunity. But sometimes life has other plans.

HONEYMOON BLISS is available everywhere

SIGN UP FOR MY NEWSLETTER to find out when new books release!
http://www.lilyzante.com/news

You read an excerpt from HONEYMOON BLISS below.

Thank you and happy reading!
Lily

"Nico, I'm sorry but I won't be able to make it to your wedding."

Hot on the tails of Bruno telling him about the problems with the treatment rooms in the new spa center, one of his closest friends not coming to the wedding was the least of his problems.

"That's a shame," Nico replied, slowly. He'd been looking forward to meeting his friend.

"I hate to let you down like this, especially since you asked me to be your best man, but Chiara's ankle is bad, she was lucky not to have broken it, and there's no-one to look after the twins."

"Your wife comes first," replied Nico, understanding the man's dilemma. "Don't even worry about the wedding. What happened?"

"She fell down the stairs last night while carrying up the laundry. She's resting now but the twins are running riot. You know what they're like. I'm sorry if I've left you stranded."

"No," said Nico, closing his eyes. "Please don't worry about it." He wondered who else he could ask. "You take care of Chiara and the twins and you take it easy." If such a thing were possible. "I hope we can all meet up sometime."

Nico didn't have such a tight knit circle of friends; from his younger days he'd had many hangers-on, had known many women, but when it came to close friends and people he could trust, he could count them all on one hand. Romano was one such person, they went back a long time, and had been his first choice for a best man.

Now he was a best man short.

He stared at the wall in front of him, at the picture of his father that hung there, as he adjusted the cuffs of his shirt. He tried to think who else could stand in Romano's place.

The memory of his father still held strong in this room which had once been Edmondo's office before Nico had taken it over. He felt his father's spirit strongly in here, as if his essence was imprinted everywhere within the four walls and ingrained upon the leather chair in which he now sat. Deep in thought, he clasped his hands together; not quite praying, but sitting in silent remembrance.

A faint knock at the door was followed by the slow opening of it and instead of Ava entering, as he'd expected, he was surprised to see his future mother-in-law, Elsa, walk in.

"There you are," she said, as if she expected him to be somewhere else. "Why so glum? That's not how a prospective bridegroom should look. It's time for you and Ava to get ready for this big day of yours."

He attempted a smile and watched as she walked over to examine the photo of his father. She always did this, as if she was drawn towards it. He'd put it up there but wasn't sure he liked to see his father staring back at him all day long, watching over him with an almost stern expression on his face. Yet sometimes, even looking at that stern face gave Nico comfort.

Edmondo was never far from his thoughts, and having that photo close by always took Nico back in time to memories that were tinged with sadness. He tried not to show his grief to others, but he missed his father sorely and knew that only time would heal the wound left by his untimely death.

"There is so much of you in him," Elsa said quietly, still staring at the picture.

"There is so much of him I want to be like."

She turned and faced him. "You *are* like him," she insisted. "You have his warmth, his eyes, his ability to make people feel at ease, and to trust in you. You are already so much like him, Nico. Perhaps you don't see it, but I do. I'm sure others do, too."

He remained silent because nothing would ever bring his father back. Even though four months had passed since his death, sometimes Nico imagined his father sitting in the kitchen or the study at home and tortured himself with the thought of Edmondo walking through the door to his office. Of course, that would never happen. But it didn't stop him from wishing.

The absence of the man he had clashed with for so long— and whose respect he had at last begun to earn—was sometimes hard for Nico to acknowledge. And there wasn't a damn thing he could do about it. It made him want to hold onto Ava more tightly than ever. It taught him how much could change in one second and this thought frightened him. It was a constant reminder to him that nothing lasted forever. Even the new life Ava carried, and the new start he'd been given, could all be taken away from him in the blink of an eye.

Sadness surrounded Elsa too. This gentle woman, the mother of his fiancée, tried to mask her grief, even from him, yet it was plain for Nico to see straight through it because their grief was almost identical. He knew she still missed

Edmondo and her visits back to Verona were hard for her because she lived alone and had nobody to spend her time with, nobody to distract her from her sorrow and only the memories of the golden days she'd shared with Edmondo months earlier to haunt her.

"Look at you, Nico," she said, disapprovingly. He unclasped his hands and picked up a pen, twiddling it around in his hands. "Your father wouldn't have wanted you to sit here like this. You can't bring him back, Nico. And you mustn't let the darkness of his passing pull you down. Your father would have been happy that you and Ava were getting married."

"I know," replied Nico, remembering how much his father had adored Ava. "I wish he were here, that's all."

She looked down and nodded. "I wish he were here every day. We would have been outside the whole time. Or he would have shown me more of Verona." She chuckled softly to herself. "If there was anything else left to show me."

Nico swallowed. His father had died a happy man—happy for Nico, for he had seen the effect that Ava had had on him, and happy to have met Elsa—and to have shown her this wonderful city he'd loved so much.

There were times when Nico wondered, as he knew Ava did too, what might have happened between her mother and his father had a fatal heart attack not claimed his life so cruelly.

"My father had the happiest time showing you Verona," he said, sitting up in his chair and putting the pen down. He knew he had to let go of the past so that he could embrace the future but it was always easier said than done. Ava tried to do her best to keep his mind from sinking too much into the sadness but he was aware that things weren't so easy for her. She was juggling far more on her plate than a six month pregnant bride—soon to be married in four days' time—ought to. "There is a lot to be done."

Elsa laughed. "There's not a lot to be done, but a lot of enjoyment to be had," she said. "It's time to get it all together. You're getting married! I don't understand why the pair of you find it so difficult to detach yourselves from your computers."

He couldn't wait for it to be over. For months he had been dealing with all the documentation and the religious paperwork required by the church where his parents were married. Despite his initial concerns, the priest had agreed to allow the ceremony with an obviously pregnant American woman. But until he had a ring on Ava's finger and until they walked away as husband and wife, Nico would not be able to rest.

It was the wedding reception, and the long honeymoon that he was looking forward to the most.

"I was checking a few things."

"That's what Ava keeps telling me. How many things do you both have to check? And why is this checking taking place constantly? What will go wrong? We were far luckier in my day than you are now. We didn't have these things." She pointed at his computer and at his cell phone which lay on the desk. "Nobody had a computer at home, or a phone they carried around with them all day long. We got by just fine."

"I'm sure you did." He got up and stretched out his shoulders. His body was stiff from sitting around for the past few hours without moving. He couldn't wait to take Ava away from all of this. Just having the time to themselves—that was what he wanted more than anything.

"Come with me." Elsa moved towards the door. "Help me to remove your fiancée from her desk and unplug her from her computer. It's going to take both of us to achieve that."

"You might be right."

"I'm sorry. I...I..." Ava stammered. "No. Mi dispiace," she apologized. "I don't speak Italian. Non capisco. I wanted information about your furniture...um...for the children. Bambino? Parla inglese?" She rested her forehead in her hands. "Nessun problema. Ciao." She couldn't put the phone down fast enough. "Impossible," she wailed, massaging her temples gently. "It is *so* hard trying to get through."

"You *are* in Italy," declared Rona. "It seems only fair that you speak the language."

"I thought English was universal."

"So what if it is? You're in Italy and you plan on living here. I'd say it's time you learned Italian."

Ava groaned again.

"Do you know you put on a false Italian accent when you're talking?"

"I do?" Ava was shocked.

"It's not going to make them understand you."

"I know," Ava mumbled to herself. "I didn't know I was doing it. Oh, god. I hope they don't think I'm being offensive."

"Your children will be fluent in Italian, Ava, so you might want to think about taking some lessons." Rona pulled open the filing cabinet and rifled through it. Ava considered her sister's advice, not that she often took it, and groaned even louder, causing Rona to drop the file she was holding. "What's wrong?" Rona asked, looking worried.

"A new language, new places, new customs, a new life, new country, new husband and a new baby."

Rona's features relaxed. "I thought the baby had kicked or something. Your point?" Rona crossed her arms, waiting.

"I'm scared."

"About what?"

"Of everything happening so fast."

"You should have thought of that when you had unprotected sex."

"I don't mean about the baby," retorted Ava. "I..." She didn't know how to explain it. Her whole life had changed ever since she'd come to Italy and now she was taking the next step up, a real commitment, with a man who loved her. But the magnitude of the change still overwhelmed her.

"You have Nico. There's no reason to be scared. And they also drive on the same side of the road, so that's a bonus. One less thing to worry about."

"Some days I miss Starbucks. Sometimes I crave Dennys and IHOP."

"What for?" Rona shot her a confused look. "You get nicer, tastier, and classier coffees and pancakes here."

"But it feels strange to know that I am leaving it all behind —the places I grew up in."

"You miss Denver?" Rona picked up the file and slipped it back into the cabinet.

"I have, lately." This was what happened when she started to slow down at work in readiness for her wedding. Not being crazy busy gave her the time to sit and reminisce and to consider the life changing step she was about to embark on.

She wasn't only getting married, she was emigrating and bringing her children up in a new country. A country she had come to love, but a country that was still as new and as unfamiliar to her, as it was beautiful. It would be home to her children and her Italian husband, but would it ever feel like home to her? She'd thought so the whole time, had fallen in love with the place as deeply as she'd fallen in love with Nico. But now she was beginning to wonder, and the doubts had started to creep in. She would miss her mom, and Rona and

Carlos and her niece, and her friends in Denver. She would see them, but perhaps once a year, maybe less?

"I've never seen you happier, Ava." Rona tried to assure her. "These are just last minute wedding jitters. It's natural."

"But what if I'm making a mistake?"

"Marrying Nico?" Rona stared at her in surprise.

"Not Nico," Ava replied. "He's the one constant in my life." She exhaled loudly. "Maybe you're right," Ava sighed. "Maybe I'm being nostalgic because it's getting so close to the wedding. I keep remembering the things I've left behind." She rested back in her chair and let her hands fall to her lap, as she stared down at the bump that now passed for her stomach. Being six months pregnant, it resembled the size of a small rounded watermelon. "I'm scared about the baby. I don't know *anything* about babies; I've only looked after Tori and I must have changed her diapers a handful of times. Mom isn't going to stay here forever. What'll I do if I'm stuck? Who will I call?"

"You can call me." Rona sat down at her small corner desk. "And as a mom, it's all second nature. I didn't have a clue but it kinda comes to you."

Ava listened to her sister but felt a strong urge to go for a walk in the gardens and to forget her troubles.

"Hey." Rona's voice turned soft. "What's going on? You're not having second thoughts about moving here, are you?" She walked over to Ava's side and placed a hand on her sister's shoulder. Ava reached up and put her hand over it.

"No second thoughts," she replied. "I'm happy. I really am," but she was beginning to well up. One lousy call to a supplier whose nursery furniture she'd seen online, and a few minutes of non-communication had left her almost in tears. Lately, she'd been mulling over things. In the early days she'd been caught up in her roller coaster romance with Nico, and then she'd fallen pregnant not long after they'd met, and with the news of her pregnancy, then the shocking news of Edmondo's passing—all of the months leading up to now had been filled with one drama after another. She'd never had time before to think about the change that had taken place in her life in the space of less than a year. But now that she was starting to slow down, with her wedding only days away, she found herself thinking too much about many things and it often left her feeling sad. She wasn't sure why.

"Hey," Rona kissed the top of her head.

A quick rap on the door commanded her attention as the door opened and Elsa and Nico walked in together. They both stared at her.

"What's wrong?" they both asked in unison, as two pairs of eyes descended on her. Ava smiled. "Nothing," she replied, staring back at Nico and feeling heat radiate through her chest. She loved the way his eyes shone full of love and concern each time he looked at her. That was all it took for her fear to disintegrate.

"Still working?" Nico asked her. She'd bet ten dollars he'd been at his desk until a minute ago.

"You told me you would stop today." Elsa looked at Ava's cluttered desk with disdain.

"It's no use," Rona appealed to both of them. "You're going to have to physically remove her."

"Ava, honey. Time to unplug and remove yourself." Elsa's voice was firm.

Nico stepped forward, the warmth emanating from his relaxed smile. "Come on, Ava. Time to go. We've got a few things to do yet and I've booked you into the spa tomorrow, once you've got your wedding dress fitting out of the way."

Ava looked horrified. "But I don't have the time—"

"And that's exactly why you need it."

"A bride with no time to unwind?" Elsa asked her, in that simple and effective way she had of dealing with her girls, with her usual healthy dose of common sense and kindness.

"Why don't you close the office for a few days?" Rona suggested.

"I can't," replied Ava, testily. "You're going to have to keep an eye on things until the wedding day." She wanted to knock that idea right out of her sister's head.

"I was hoping to go sight-seeing with Carlos and Tori." Rona stuck out her bottom lip.

"Lose the pout, honey," said Elsa. "Don't go giving Tori ideas."

With her attention still on Nico, Ava listened to the exchange between her mother and her sister. Rona going sight-seeing with her husband? This was news to her. Things between the couple had been icy lately but after Tori's temporary 'disappearance' a few days ago; she'd noticed that they seemed to be more attentive towards one another.

"If you could work a few hours between now and Thursday then sure, by all means, you and Carlos take some time together," Ava told her. She'd have to revisit her ideas about getting her sister to look after her business while she and Nico were away on honeymoon. It didn't seem fair to ask Rona to work and it was definitely not fair for Carlos, since he'd made the effort to come over for the wedding a few weeks earlier than planned.

It must have taken some heavy convincing to take so much time away from the busy family run restaurants he worked in with his father and brothers.

"Have you tried on your bridesmaid's dress? Does it need any adjustments?" Ava asked.

"I tried it on a couple of weeks ago—sure it fits. It was fine then, it'll be fine now. Remember, I'm not the one who's growing by the hour."

"And that kind of comment isn't going to get you any half days around here," said Ava, wanting to wipe that smug smile off her sister's face. At times she still had to remind her sister that she was the boss.

Rona's face turned somber. "I'm almost done with filing all the most recent orders and I updated the website this morning. If I finish what you gave me, could I take the afternoon off?" Rona never changed. But if it meant Carlos got to have some downtime, then who was Ava to stand in the way? "If you've done everything you needed to for today then you're free to go."

"How about *you* finishing *now*?" Nico asked her.

And do what? She still had more emails to go through, a call with Kim to schedule, and some statistics she wanted to check.

"How about you at least stop for lunch with me?" Nico suggested. "We can make a list of the things we need to do between now and Friday. That's our wedding day, in case you forgot."

"I haven't forgotten," she said quickly, not wanting this wonderful man to think that she was treating their wedding day as a normal day of the week.

"Lunch would be a good thing for the baby," Elsa reminded her.

"Shouldn't you be resting, Mom? I don't want to hear about any more dizziness or falls from you."

"Your doctor has given me different medication and this one suits me better. I haven't felt dizzy in days."

"No more hospital visits or being taken out on a gurney, okay, Mom?" Rona insisted.

Elsa gave her daughters a haughty look and made a move

towards the door. "I'll leave this to you, Nico," she said, nodding at him. "I'm going to check on that new gardener of yours and to make sure that he hasn't hacked my lemon trees." She addressed the girls. "Your Uncle Hugo and Aunty Camile arrive tomorrow, and I've been telling them about the gardens. I hope that man hasn't ruined them," she said before slipping out of the office.

"Since when did they become *her* lemon trees?" Ava wondered out aloud.

"Mom seems to think she has dominion over the gardens. Poor Salvatore," said Rona. She flitted back and forth between her desk and the filing cabinet, and put away a pile of recent order sheets. Ava watched her, not having seen Rona move so fast before.

Her sister's early arrival, almost a month and a half before the wedding, had been a gamble. Rona had helped and over time she had become more diligent and conscientious about her work. But, goodness, she took her sweet time doing it. Not for nothing did Kim have good reason to complain about her. Ava considered Kim to be a valuable addition to her business for it was Kim who held the fort over in Denver, dealing with customer queries and sending out orders. Together with Rona, the women worked out of Ava's old apartment but they seemed to clash more than they got on.

"I'm done," exclaimed, Rona, standing up and getting ready to leave.

"That was fast," Ava commented, drily. "Did you—"

"Yes, I've filed the recent orders, double-checked the new order for Andrea, and I've updated the product descriptions for the new high-chairs. You said I could go now. May I? Please, Miss?"

Ava tut-tutted with her mouth. "Go on," she said. "Be nice to Carlos." With only her and Nico left in her office, Ava sat back in her chair, resting her arm on the armrest. Nico smiled at her. "I swear, each day you get bigger and rounder —" He stopped abruptly as the scowl settled on her face. "You're going to look lovely," he told her. But she knew he liked her this way; softer, more curvy. Just as well there was no need for birth control anymore because Nico couldn't keep his hands off her. As her pregnancy had progressed, her sexual drive had shot through the roof and each night ended well. Happily.

"Rona and Carlos might have reached a truce," Ava commented, then shrugged away the tension that was beginning to build up in her shoulders.

"I agree," said Nico. "Maybe coming that close to losing Tori—"

"*Thinking* they lost her." Ava corrected him.

"Same thing. They didn't know she was safe with Lizzi. All the same, it must have been scary for them both. I think it brought them together—and it's a good thing. It's one less thing to worry about on the wedding day." He held out his hand to her.

"Are you worried about the wedding day?" she asked him. Because she wasn't. Her only concern was how she would look in her dress, and it wasn't the image of the svelte bride that she'd had in mind. She got up slowly and took his hand.

"I'm not worried, especially now that I've given the priest a sweetener to turn a blind eye to the fact that we've obviously gone beyond the kissing stage in our courtship." He ran his fingers over her belly.

"Don't say that." Sometimes she wasn't sure whether to believe him or not.

"You know I didn't. Thank goodness my father was held in such high esteem in Montagnano," he said, referring to the village he grew up in and the place where they would be married.

"I can't wait to marry you, Ava Ramirez."

"I can't wait to marry you, Mr. Cazale."

"You don't have to change your name, you know."

"So you keep telling me." Many women in Italy didn't take their husband's surname. "But I want to have the same name as our baby. And I don't like double-barreled names."

"No?" asked Nico, considering it. "Cazale-Ramirez doesn't hold much appeal?"

"*Ramirez-Cazale*," she insisted, changing the order, "is too much of a mouthful. It's the sort of thing Connor would have done."

"Must you mention him?"

"I store my products in his garage. Be nice to him." She wanted to tell him before the wedding.

Nico raised an eyebrow. "You haven't secretly invited him to the wedding have you?"

"No," she said slowly. She would never have. But his recent request for her to loan him some money had put her in an awkward position. She didn't want to hide this from Nico.

"Good. I'd rather you didn't mention his name to me, and I'm going to get your space issues resolved so you'll never have to feel obligated towards him." He kissed her lightly on the lips. "Lunch, and lists, and freedom. I've booked lunch in Verona, at that restaurant with a balcony view."

"How thoughtful of you." It would be better to leave news of Connor to the side, for now. As they walked out of the double glass doors and she carefully walked down the steps, she asked, "When do you plan to tell me where we're going on our honeymoon?"

"Not yet." He was obviously still sticking to his guns.

"I need to know so I know what to pack," she protested.

"Dresses and skirts for the day, nothing for the night." He slipped his hand around her bulging waist. "I can't wait to get away from here and to spend all day and night in bed with you."

HONEYMOON BLISS is available everywhere

BOOKLIST

Honeymoon Series: Take a roller-coaster journey of emotional highs and lows in this story of love and loss, family and relationships. When Ava is dumped six weeks before her Valentine's Day wedding, she has no idea of the life that awaits her in Italy.

Honeymoon for One
Honeymoon for Three
Honeymoon Blues
Honeymoon Bliss
Baby Steps
Honeymoon Series (Books 1-3)

Italian Summer Series: This is a spin-off from the Honeymoon Series. These books tell the stories of the secondary characters who first appeared in the Honeymoon Series. Nico and Ava also appear in these books.

It Takes Two
All That Glitters

Fool's Gold
Roman Encounter
November Sun
New Beginnings
Italian Summer Series (Books 1-4)

The Billionaire's Love Story: This is a Cinderella story with a touch of Jerry Maguire. What happens when the billionaire with too much money meets the single mom with too much heart?

The Promise (FREE)
The Gift, Book 1
The Gift, Book 2
The Gift, Book 3
The Gift, Boxed Set (Books 1, 2 & 3)
The Offer, Book 1
The Offer, Book 2
The Offer, Book 3
The Offer, Boxed Set (Books 1, 2 & 3)
The Vow, Book 1
The Vow, Book 2
The Vow, Book 3
The Vow, Boxed Set (Books 1, 2 & 3)

Indecent Intentions: This is a spin-off from The Billionaire's Love story. This 2-book set consists of 2 standalone stories about the billionaire's playboy brother. The 2nd story is about a wealthy nightclub owner who shuns relationships.

The Bet
The Hookup

Indecent Intentions 2-Book Set

The Seven Sins: A series of seven standalone romances based on the seven sins. Emotional, and angsty romances which are loosely connected.

Underdog (FREE prequel)
The Wrath of Eli
The Problem with Lust
The Lies of Pride
The Price of Inertia
The Other Side of Greed
The Seven Sins Books 1-3

A Perfect Match Series: This is a seven book series in which the first four books feature the same couple. High-flying corporate executive Nadine has no time for romance but her life takes a turn for the better when she meets Ethan, a sexy and struggling metal sculptor five years younger. He works as an escort in order to make the rent. Books 4-6 are standalone romances based on characters from the earlier books. The main couple, Ethan and Nadine, appear in all books:

Lost in Solo (prequel)
The Proposal
Heart Sync
A Leap of Faith
A Perfect Match Series Books 1-3
Misplaced Love
Reclaiming Love
Embracing Love
A Perfect Match Series (Books 4-6)

Standalone Books:

Tomorrow Belongs to Us
Love Among the Ruins
Love Inc
An Unexpected Gift

ABOUT THE AUTHOR

Lily Zante lives with her husband and three children somewhere near London, UK.

Connect with Me

I love hearing from you – so please don't be shy! Email me (lily@lilyzante.com), message me on Facebook or connect with me through these different platforms:

Instagram | Facebook | Twitter | Website

Follow me on Bookbub
Follow me on Goodreads
Follow me on TikTok
Join my FB Reader Group